BELOW
THE
THUNDER

ROBIN DUVAL

Matador
9 Priory Business Park
Kibworth Beauchamp
Leicestershire LE8 0RX, UK
Tel: (+44) 116 279 2299
Fax: (+44) 116 279 2277
Email: books@troubador.co.uk
Web: www.troubador.co.uk/matador

ISBN 978 1780883 830

British Library Cataloguing in Publication Data.
A catalogue record for this book is available from the British Library.

Typeset in 11.5pt Sabon MT by Troubador Publishing Ltd, Leicester, UK

Matador is an imprint of Troubador Publishing Ltd

Printed and bound in the UK by TJ International, Padstow, Cornwall

For my wife

Old men are dangerous: it doesn't matter to them what is going to happen to the world.

GBShaw

Chapter 1

If you really needed to flaunt your wealth and influence and cultural superiority – all at the same time – then this had to be the place.

Bayreuth.

The most exclusive music festival *in the world.*

And here he was. In a borrowed dinner jacket, with a vinyl carrier bag dangling from his hand, standing on the terrace in front of Wagner's opera house. Watching the audience promenade, and waiting for his girlfriend.

High summer in Franconia.

A hazy, sunless sky, as creamy as porcelain. Hot, humid, thundery…

He still could not believe his luck.

Naturally there were music lovers here too. It's just that exclusivity was the festival's defining characteristic. His own two seats had come with fierce imprecations about the penalty for selling them on the black market – the *nicht autorisierte Schwarzmarkthandel.* So much more threatening in German. There were tickets for sale on the internet for thousands of dollars a pair. But if they caught you at it, you could be turned away at the door. With contumely.

Only a week ago in Salt Lake City, he had kissed his wife goodbye, and flown home for a round of catching-up visits. An aunt in Shropshire, a married daughter in Essex, old friend Dieter in Ealing.

Which is where it all started.

To cut a long story short, friend Dieter had a rare, inherited right – as a member of the *Gesellschaft der Freunde* – to attend the festival. Always with his partner, Graeme. But Graeme had died a year ago, and Dieter's heart no longer lay in Franconia. Bryn found the two tickets for *The Mastersingers* propped behind a candlestick on the mantelpiece, and Dieter had impulsively stuck them into his top pocket. And made him promise to use them.

The *festspielhaus*...

The composer's own do-it-yourself wooden theatre on its green hill, commanding the town like a citadel. The audience streaming out in a babel of languages and nations. East European, South American, Asian. A glittering parade to make all those English festivals – those lonely couples wandering damp lawns – seem like garden parties for the Third Age.

He held his iPhone up to record the occasion for posterity. The party of Japanese posing below the balcony, each dropping out in turn to photograph the rest. Russians strolling through the multitude, fanning themselves like characters from Chekhov. A spectacular pair from the Middle East – he in flowing Arab robes and she in a sprayed on, backless, strapless gown, with the gauziest shawl to protect her modesty. From Beirut to Bayreuth.

The Americans though. Where on earth were the Americans?

He spotted an elderly couple standing alone at the edge of the terrace, sipping champagne. The wife had the huge and unfeasibly raven hair of an east coast matriarch. The husband was small and stooped, with an air of ancient authority. In his lapel was the blue and white Star of David of the American Friends of Israel.

Bryn wondered what was going through their minds. Did the history of the place worry them? How did they feel about this evening? In a few hours the leading character would be urging his countrymen to beware of evil, non-German influences corrupting their country from within. And bring proceedings to a triumphant close by proclaiming the cleansing rise of a great '*deutsches Volk und Reich*'.

No surprise that *The Mastersingers of Nuremberg* was Adolf Hitler's favourite opera and that he came regularly to Bayreuth to see it. Until the end of his life, that is. Then he began to prefer the final Act of *The Ring of the Nibelungs*, in which the main protagonist destroys the old order in an all-engulfing, terminal cataclysm.

Bryn's companion emerged from the theatre – at last – smoothing down her tiny cocktail dress and skipping through the promenaders to make up for lost time.

My God, she looked gorgeous.

He had been staying in a *Klassik Moderne* industrial hotel on the north side of Bayreuth ('convenient for the A9 motorway') and the only establishment left with rooms at short notice. Its most attractive feature was breakfast. For four hours each morning in a hall as large as a ballroom, across a dozen serving stations, there was more food on display than in an average-size supermarket.

'Breakfast' barely hinted at it. German *sekt* and Italian *prosecco*, exotic teas, juices and mineral waters. A dozen different kinds of bread, ranks of preserved fruits, sausages, cereals and cakes. Forty minutes in this comestible cornucopia could keep a person going for the whole of the day.

Mostly it was self-service and nobody minded a guest returning again and again to the *gravad lax* or the American muffins or the chariots of cheese and cold meats. The professionals only intervened if they were required to make scrambled eggs, omelettes, porridge or – for the Americans – waffles and syrup.

Or to provide coffee. Then the procedure was for you to sit down with your laden plate at a vacant table, until a waitress arrived to pour the first cup and place a fresh pot beside you.

Which is how he had met her.

The conversation ran roughly on these lines:

'*Kaffe oder tee?*'

'*Ein Kaffe, bitte. Grüss Gott, schönes mädchen.*'

'Oh you're English, are you? Are you here for the festival?'

'Yes. And you've got a very good accent for a German.'

'Thanks. I'm Danish.'

'Why are you in Bayreuth?'

'The same reason as you?'

'You're going to the opera?'

'Actually... no.'

'Why?'

'I have not been able to get hold of a ticket.'

She was standing over him, filling his cup. Her white-yellow hair was roughly tied in a bun on the crown of her head. Some stray fronds tumbled across her face and, every five seconds or so, her left hand would attempt to push one aside. He had never seen such eyes. They were palest blue to the point of achromic, fired by some inner light; and her gaze – when it locked briefly on his – was as penetrating as a laser.

'I've got a spare ticket,' he said suddenly. 'Would you like to come with me tomorrow?'

She pulled a face.

'No, seriously.'

The blue eyes flared.

Time stood still.

'All right then,' she said at last.

And so it was decided. Within a minute, at the most, they had agreed to meet before the performance, return to the hotel for a late meal, have a few cocktails and...

But she was already on her way with another blue coffee pot to another table. He would just have to wait and see how things fell out.

At least by the second interval of *The Mastersingers* he had learnt her name. Agnete. *Ow-nay-tuh*. And told her something about himself. His interests: history, music, America. His teaching job

6

at the Western University of Utah. She was, however, less responsive than he had hoped. And gave very little information in return.

At her suggestion, they left the theatre concourse and walked back up the road away from the town, past the car parks, until they arrived at a gate recessed within a long, high hedge. Beyond was a stretch of neatly mown grass and some tables, chairs and parasols.

This was where the *cognoscenti* went to cool off during the sweltering hour-long intervals. Agnete knew all about it. She led him across the lawn towards a hidden, hedged-round enclave into which dinner-jacketed gentlemen were disappearing one by one, like honey bees into a hive. The object of their interest was a marble-clad, kidney-shaped pool, a foot deep in limpidly clear water fed by a bubbling stream. Wooden handrails lined the steps down into the pool, and handrails circled its centre.

Agnete settled down on a bench below a sign listing the restorative benefits of the waters – indispensable for the production of bile, the soothing of nerves, the reduction of cholesterol – while Bryn joined the queue of paddlers. Shoes round necks, dress suit trousers hoist to knees, legs as white as milk. All calf deep in a cooling paradise.

Through a gap in the hedge, he could see some more bashful patrons sitting under their enormous parasols, sipping flutes of *sekt* or – like one perspiring onlooker in sunglasses and open shirt – nursing a solitary *weissbier*. Nothing to match the heavenly chill now radiating through his body: this air-conditioning programmed (so Agnete assured him) to last to the end of the evening.

It was while he was thus luxuriating – eyes closed in a kind of ecstasy – that Bryn encountered the American. Or – to be more precise – bumped into him.

Agnete had become bored with her wooden bench. It was also possible – in spite of the subatomic economy of her clothing – that she too had begun to find the heat oppressive. At all events, she joined the line of shuffling males, and jumped in behind Bryn. She'd not bothered to remove her pretty little kitten-heel shoes.

7

So she slipped on the marble floor of the pool, grabbed at Bryn's arm, missed it, lurched again and finally knocked him into the older gentleman in front. A sharp wave of the icy waters shot over both of them.

The American was most understanding. Agnete was abject – or affected to be – even offering to sponge down his satin sheen dress trousers with the hem of her dress.

'That's really not necessary, young lady,' he said, not very discouragingly.

He was a distinguished looking gentleman, with an immaculate helmet of steel grey hair and large, rimless glasses. He turned his attention to Bryn.

'But are *you* alright, sir? You appear to have shipped more of the creek than I.'

And so they fell into conversation.

Americans abroad, in Bryn's experience, loved the British. They were someone to talk to whose first language was their own; and a useful bridge to all those – other – foreigners. He suspected at the root of this was a belief that the British, being Europeans, were accustomed to mixing with people with peculiar languages; and, as the last great Empire builders, had a bred-in-the-bone understanding of alien races. One should never underestimate how far the old imperial role still coloured American perception.

'You're British, right?' said the new friend, in the lazy, gravelly tones of a thousand Westerns.

'I didn't realise I was so obvious.'

'Heard your wonderful accent. Lon*don*?'

He pronounced the last word with such heavy stress on the second syllable that for a moment Bryn barely recognised it. But, before he could answer –

'He's a professor in America. In Utah,' said Agnete.

'Now is that a fact?' said the American.

Bryn did not disguise his irritation at this unrequested revelation. Agnete responded with a quick laser stare and a shrug of her exquisite shoulders; and climbed out of the wading pool and sauntered away.

'I teach history to American students.'

'To Mormons? So you're a Mormon?'

'No, no. Church of England.'

'What's that? British for no religion, right?'

An American being ironic? But he seemed interested enough and began to ask about Bryn's background, what he did. Bryn mentioned a monograph he'd recently published about the American Civil War, and the American made him write the details down on the back of a card. He had a way of asking for things to be repeated and Bryn noticed he was wearing a tiny, probably extremely expensive, hearing aid. He guessed he'd be in his mid seventies, and gym-fit and diet-driven.

They were back now on the main lawn and two of the *sekt*-sippers, both Frenchmen, were trying to engage Agnete in conversation. Nothing penetrated her enveloping boredom. She wrinkled her nose contemptuously and joined the queue for ice-creams.

'I left Martha behind,' continued the American. 'She hates travelling. Anything over water. And I guess she's not as young as she was.'

'My own wife prefers to stay at home. And I could never get her to come on a jaunt like this.'

'Are you sure you'd want her to?'

He sat down at a table and shook out his trousers. They rippled down to his feet like a theatrical curtain. There was the faintest hiss of silk.

'Good job,' he added, nodding almost imperceptibly in Agnete's direction.

'Oh. She's just a friend. I hardly know her,' said Bryn, with a forced laugh.

'Always the best way, buddy.'

They sat together, slipping on their socks and shoes: the American's old-fashioned, gleaming, box-fresh patent leather; and Bryn's... he wished he'd at least polished them.

'What do you make of the show?'

'Bayreuth in general? The Mastersingers?'

'You call it, buddy. The whole deal though. What do you think of it? I bet you know all about this stuff.'

Bryn found himself in a familiar conundrum. It would be uncharitable to describe him as one who tries to be all things to all men. Perhaps he simply put too high a premium on social courtesy. But he was torn between a sense that the American might be a complete beginner on Bayreuth and Wagner. And the opposing fear – the worst sin – that he might end up patronising him.

So, as he usually did when at a loss as to how to proceed, he shot off at a tangent.

'Did you know Henry Kissinger came from here?'

'Nixon's Kissinger? You're kidding.'

A promising start.

'No truly. What you need to know is that long before the Wagner family and their bosom pal Hitler – '

'*Aye-dolf* Hitler was a friend of the Wagner family?'

'Oh yes. He used to come here every year.'

'Waddya know.'

Time perhaps for a short lecture after all.

'Well, you see, centuries ago, Bayreuth was a prosperous market town in the then independent state of Franconia. They were proud Protestants, with a famously incomprehensible dialect, and they never reconciled themselves to being annexed by Napoleon and handed over – in 1803 that would be – to the royal family of *Catholic* Bavaria. They will still not thank you for confusing them with Bavarians. So don't... Well anyway, there was also a large Jewish population here and Henry Kissinger was born down the road. Another Franconian who never lost his weird local accent as long as he lived.'

'I'll be damned. Where did you find this out?'

'It's what I do. I'm a historian.'

'Right. So did Kissinger ever come back here?'

'Absolutely. They made a film about it once.'

'Kissinger was here? With a broad, I'll bet.'

'I really wouldn't know.'

10

But of course Kissinger was here. With a glamorous new blonde on his arm. In a sprayed-on, strapless, backless gown…

'I never liked the little schmuck,' growled the other suddenly. 'Or his goddamn brother.'

For a moment, the conversation appeared to be over. Then –

'What are you doing after the show?'

'I'll be returning to my hotel.'

'How d'ya feel 'bout supper?'

He clapped Bryn on the shoulder. Declining the invitation was *not* an option.

'It's my 75th birthday. Tomorrow. You can help me celebrate a day early. Bring your new girlfriend.'

On the way back to the *festspielhaus*, he revealed a little more about himself. Including – to Bryn's surprise – that he was not quite the neophyte he appeared. He even had a seat on the Board of San Francisco Opera.

'Oh you know. Social obligation and business. That's all. You don't have to be a friggin' opera buff. Don't get me wrong. I love opera but, oh dear me, a little Wagner goes a long way, wouldn't'tya say.'

'So, if you don't mind me asking, what exactly are you doing here?'

The American gave the question some thought.

'Well, the truth is,' he said at last, 'I happened to be here on business and the opportunity arose and I thought why the hell not.'

'You were lucky to get a ticket, then.'

'Sure. Yeah, I guess so.'

But the beat between the two phrases gave him away. It was clear that he fell into that special category of people for whom a ticket was never going to entail a ten year waiting list.

'Yeah. I did what I generally do. I wrote a big cheque and, yeah, seats were not a problem.'

'Ah,' said Bryn. 'You're a sponsor.'

'Right. And now, to tell you the truth, I'm surprised how much I'm enjoying this baby. Would you believe I booked a restaurant

11

table for nine o'clock this evening, on the assumption I could take at best two Acts. I guess I'm in for the duration now.'

'Don't forget to tell the restaurant, will you.'

He gazed at Bryn with an expression of mixed disbelief and bewilderment. Then shrugged his shoulders and made a curious gurgling sound, as if he was clearing gravel out of his throat.

'So how about your wife, my friend? How much do you really miss her?'

'A lot!'

What a bizarre question.

'You reckon she's OK back there in Utah, all on her own-some?'

'Well, yes, naturally.'

'Fine,' he said. 'Fine. While the cat's away.'

It was Bryn's turn to look surprised. But the American was watching Agnete. She had gone on ahead and was flicking through some racks of postcards across the road from the *festspielhaus*.

'The doll's certainly a looker,' he grinned. 'Goddamn it, I wish I were your age.'

He was about to turn away when he stopped, and fished a card from an inside pocket.

'Udell Strange,' he said briefly.

As he strode off into the theatre, a red-faced man in sunglasses and an open-necked white shirt walked out of the shadows and followed him in. Bryn wondered if it could be the same individual he had seen under a parasol earlier, sipping a *weissbier*.

He looked at the card. It had Strange's name on one side and a cell phone number on the other. Nothing else. And he had never asked for Bryn's name. Nor left any arrangement for meeting later. Was he serious; or was this the way the rich and powerful normally behaved? Perhaps all would become clear in the fullness of time.

Meantime, Agnete had disappeared too. He hung around as long as he dared, until well after the little brass band on the balcony had made the last of its three summonses to the audience. Fortunately, he'd given her a ticket. She should be able to make her own way back.

But when he returned to his seat near the rear of the stalls, Agnete was nowhere to be seen. Perhaps, after all, the final lap had turned out one too many. The auditorium doors had begun to close and he looked around the audience for the American. There he was, settling down in the small private box slightly left of centre at the back of the theatre. The box normally reserved for the Wagner family and their friends.

Strange acknowledged someone in the darkness and rose to his feet and shook hands with a tall man in flowing robes – one of the rich Arabs Bryn had seen parading earlier. The new arrival eased into a second armchair. A shadowed third person was just discernible, standing behind them but apparently part of the conversation.

And still no sign of Agnete. Bryn settled onto one of the ill-padded bench seats that Bayreuth provided for ordinary mortals, grateful for the two inflatable cushions he had brought from London. He flicked through to the English language section of the festival programme which, as with most things Wagnerian, flowed onward at epic length. Thirty or forty double-columned pages at least.

The lights dimmed.

The music for the beginning of the third Act stole in – almost inaudibly – on the lowest strings of the orchestra.

Chapter 2

He had been waiting on the steps for some time.

He'd not anticipated that it would be the last night of this particular production. Or that it was the custom of Bayreuth audiences to celebrate the close of a run with an orgy of curtain calls. Thirty, forty minutes of them. The Bismarck-moustached Munich businessman in the next seat told him he should have been there in the sixties, when Knappertsbusch was conducting. Then the final curtain calls went on for an hour or more.

There were no aisles at Bayreuth. Between his central position and the side doors, thirty celebrants had been on their feet in each direction, frenziedly applauding, blocking any prospect of an early exit. He'd looked back once for the American but the Wagner box was empty. By the time the ovation had peaked, and a few plucky souls (with him squeezing along in their wake) forced their way out of the theatre, it was a sound assumption that Strange was long gone. He did not seem the kind of person who hung around for groundlings.

Nevertheless, Bryn took up a post at the top of the steps where he hoped he'd be obvious to anyone looking out for him. It was the least he could do. But the American was nowhere to be seen. Nor, for that matter, and as regrettably, was Agnete.

He remembered Strange's calling card and rang the number on his iPhone...

An elderly English couple passed by. The man was elated by the performance and asking his wife what she thought of her first Wagner opera. 'Oh I suppose it was all right, darling,' she said languidly. 'If you like that sort of thing...'

No reply. The American's phone had been turned off. It was possible that he had not left the theatre. Or that he might still be talking to his Arab friends in some private room.

Bryn went back indoors and – a little apprehensively – worked his way round to a small, balustraded, internal stairway which he guessed might lead to the Wagner box; and climbed the stone steps.

The stairway ended in a pink sitting room with French doors to the right and vivid nineteenth century paintings of scenes from the great composer's works on the walls. The room was empty and the two doors opposite the windows were locked. Off to one side was a chamber so small that he took it at first glance to be a cloakroom. But a door at its other end was still ajar, and he slipped through it.

Bingo! The family box. The sanctum where the Wagners had entertained Hitler on all those private visits. It looked like a bunch of students had passed through. A drinks trolley had been overturned, a bottle of champagne was dribbling wine on the fitted carpet, and an armchair lay on its side.

Of Udell Strange, however, there was no sign.

He went back to the pink sitting room and, more or less on a whim but with an odd sense of foreboding, pushed through one of the French doors to the balcony beyond. He recognised at once where he was: he was standing on Hitler's saluting balcony.

Memories of the 1930s. The familiar photographs of the Bayreuth audience massed below on the terrace – right arms raised towards a distant figure in white tie and tails. Acknowledging his worshippers with a small, effeminate, broken-wristed flap of the hand, like a waiter supporting a cocktail tray.

15

Bryn stood precisely where he had stood. Looking down on the multitude, the little town twinkling in the distance, Wagner's massive bust in the woods below. Searching the crowd for faces he might recognise.

He put down his battered orange Harrods carrier bag, stuffed now with the cushions and programme, and took a picture or two. The *glitterati* lining up for their chauffeured cars. Evening-dressed businessmen chatting together in pools of lamp-light. His seat neighbour from Munich standing alone, tall frame hunched into a mobile phone.

There was a sudden, sharp, throat-clearing noise behind him and he had to stop himself wheeling round in a reflex of guilt.

'Splendid view isn't it?' he murmured nonchalantly.

He turned back towards the new arrival.

A uniformed man in a black peaked cap was standing in the frame of the balcony door. For a second, Bryn would not have been surprised if it had been an officer from the *Waffen-SS*. He had the look for it. The man was wearing a short, belted leather jacket with immoderately tight trousers, and he had close-cropped Aryan hair the colour of sun-bleached wheat.

The temptation was too great. In these circumstances and that uniform. He took a quick photograph.

'You are Professor?' said the man in a thick, stage German accent. '*Kommen Sie mit mir.* Please.'

Bryn followed him down the stairs, past the stone memorial to the first Bayreuth production back in 1876, round the side of the theatre where the red *Feuerwehr* engines were still parked nose to tail, to a wide, arc-lit alleyway along the rear of the building. The man waved him towards a silver Mercedes, gleaming as if fresh that day from the factory. The car had a personalised Californian licence plate, picked out in small white stars against a blue background which read, quite simply: US PATRIOT. Bryn wondered if the vehicle had been bought in America and transported back to Germany in air freight. It was the kind of thing an excessively rich person might do.

16

Udell Strange was standing by the Press Bureau door, talking to another tall, fine-looking, north European blonde. She was dressed casually and entirely in black – sweatshirt, floppy *gilet*, baggy trousers, dark glasses – and sucking on a long, 120mm cigarette. Her only possible concessions to a festival dress code were a huge pair of *diamanté* hoop ear-rings flashing in the arc lights and long, aggressive, glittery nails.

The chauffeur opened one of the car's rear doors and invited Bryn towards it with a cool, almost distracted gesture, as if his mind were on something else. As he climbed in, Bryn felt the man's assisting hand on his back, held in place for just a fraction longer than necessary.

Something the American had said amused his statuesque friend and she broke into a deep smoker's cackle. They were well settled in each other's company, so Bryn passed the time admiring the car's white leather and walnut interior, and checking emails on his iPhone. One was from his wife Marion, briefly promising 'a much longer letter very soon'. He sent her back a similarly economical reply, and – for her amusement – attached two or three of the pictures he had taken.

Meantime, Strange was exchanging cheek kisses with the blonde. She strode back into the theatre, tossing her long yellow hair behind her, and the American settled into the front passenger seat of the car.

'Katharina Wagner,' he said. 'I should have called you over. You'd know her, I guess.'

If only. The composer's great grand-daughter and hereditary director of the festival. If he'd not been concentrating so hard on getting out of the theatre he might have recognised her from the curtain calls and joined in the conversation. A once in a lifetime opportunity. Missed.

The Mercedes accelerated out of the alleyway and turned left – not right, as he'd expected. Right would have taken them towards the exclusive establishments north of town favoured by the higher-class *festspiel* clientele. But maybe Strange intended instead to patronise the restaurant of the *Goldener Anker,* the most expensive hotel in Bayreuth…

Wrong again. They swept down *Siegfried-Wagner-Allee*, past three or four side streets named after celebrated German writers, and past the railway station. A wind was beginning to whip up and the car's wipers switched to double-speed to clear away the clouds of tiny brown lime blossom seeds scudding through the air. They drew up outside the *Nibelungenlied* restaurant, a busy establishment on the main street.

Bryn had eaten at the place before. It was popular partly because it was cheap, but mainly because members of the festival cast and crew often congregated there after a show. He wondered if Strange knew this and hoped to do some star-spotting of his own. Or was anticipating the company of Katharina Wagner or some guest of similar luminosity.

A waiter in a long white apron was standing at the door, expecting them. He exchanged remarks with Strange, too quietly for Bryn to hear distinctly, though he thought for a moment they might be speaking in German. Then the waiter led the way through to a table at the far end of the restaurant, threading past a noisy crowd of German diners, some elderly Americans from the Wagner Society of New York cheerfully slumming it, a quartet of silent businessmen – one of them his tall, moustached, seat neighbour – nursing pottery *steins* at a side table, and a solitary Japanese taking photographs of his food.

Bryn hovered awhile, not quite sure where to sit, and Strange settled down on a banquette against the wall, so that Bryn had no choice but to take a chair facing him, with his back to the restaurant. Waiters cleared away the spare place settings.

There were only the two of them.

'I hope you don't mind the music,' said Strange.

At least that's what Bryn assumed he said. There was a folk dance band on the tannoy – he supposed it was traditional Franconian music but it was all Bavarian to him – extremely loud and getting louder.

'It's very difficult to hear you,' he bawled.

18

'We may have to lean together a tad. You don't mind shouting, do ya?' said the American amiably, adjusting his earpiece.

'Mr Strange – '

'It's OK, I got ya now,' he said, making no effort to raise his own voice. 'And call me Udell.'

'Udell. I don't think you know *my* name.'

'Do I not?'

'It's Bryn. Bryn Williams.'

'*Doctor* Bryn Williams. Right?'

'That's right… '

'Very good. Glad we got that sorted.'

It was not to be one of Bryn's happiest suppers. Strange had no evident difficulty with the acoustic, perhaps as a consequence of the technology at his disposal. But Bryn had to strain to hear the American, and the effort exhausted him and began to give him a headache.

They ate *wurst* and *pfifferling* and drank bacon-flavoured *rauchbier*. Bryn had half-hoped his host would be offered more ambitious fare – though he did have the impression the service was more attentive and rapid than on his previous visit.

'The guys told me this joint would be schmuck-free,' mumbled Strange through a mouthful of the mushroom. 'It does not appear to be so.'

Bryn twisted round and followed his eye-line to the Japanese diner, now focussing his top-of-the-range Canon upon a copy of the hand-written menu.

He laughed. Strange was not amused.

'Oh surely. As long as he's happy.'

'That's not what I came here for,' said Strange, with some vehemence. 'The photographer should be removed. *Removed*,' he repeated, in case he hadn't been heard clearly the first time.

He pushed the fungi irritably around his plate.

But he was a good host. He interrogated Bryn – about his work, children, interests – with almost female sensitivity. When Bryn made a comment – for example, about his relief that his wife was enjoying her new life in America – Strange did not move unresponsively to the next question but quizzed him as to why she'd originally not wanted to leave London, and the particular reasons now for her happiness in Utah.

Then, when Bryn – rambling on about his holiday plans with Marion that summer – confessed they intended to visit Yosemite National Park in California for the first time, Strange advised him energetically to avoid it. A Disneyland for picnickers, he growled, lousy with tourists. Not for a bright couple like you. Move northwards. Twenty Lakes Basin, up the Cascades, Lassen Peak, the Lava Beds. *No one* goes there. Except young guys with boots.

He chuckled.

' 'Course you may wonder why the US government preserves them as National Parks at all. That would be a good question.'

He froze into silence. He was looking at Bryn so intently it seemed like he was trying to burrow into his brain. And the moment was held for so long that Bryn even began to worry that Strange might have been taken ill.

But then the American – just as abruptly – took a deep breath and redirected his attention to his meal. He forked a portion up to his mouth.

'Tell me more 'bout what you think of the great Wagner,' he said, cheerfully mispronouncing it with a soft English "w" and short "a". 'The guy was anti-Jewish, am I right?'

'Well, yes,' said Bryn. 'And no.'

Strange choked over his plate, scattering bits of mushroom. He lifted the trailing edge of the tablecloth from his lap and wiped his mouth with it.

'What kind of an answer is that? Was the guy against the Jews or not?'

Once again, Bryn was unsure how to proceed. He held forth as instructively as he could about Wagner's many inconsistencies – from his well-known anti-Semitic writings to his self-description as a Wandering Jew and pragmatic decision to entrust the first performance of *Parsifal* – his crowning achievement – to a Jewish conductor. The son of a rabbi.

Strange brooded on all this.

20

'Like Nixon and Kissinger,' he nodded. 'You're right. Good boy. Nobody ever said Jews couldn't be useful.'

Bryn did not know what to say. He had meant to be fair to the great composer – a difficult enough task in itself – but now he felt as if he was being congratulated for taking the nasty side of the argument. Maybe he had misunderstood.

An unrequested second tankard of *rauchbier* arrived at his right hand.

'Gee, it's neat to have a conversation with a real professor,' said Strange and raised his own tankard in an ambivalent salute. 'I hope you're enjoying this as much as I am, sir.'

And then he set off on a monologue of his own.

He talked about a recent visit to London, when a taxi driver had told him the English were so disillusioned with the failure of successive administrations to control immigration that voters were going over to 'your National Party' in droves. Could Bryn confirm this to be true? And he'd noticed also that the present government had returned to the traditional English public schools for its leaders; leaving the Jewish faces to (what he called) the Socialist Party.

'Americans have always looked to the British to set standards' he said, with a confiding smile.

He'd read a book recently, which he commended. It was a new one on Bryn, notwithstanding that the author – according to Strange – was a world-renowned British history professor.

'You gotta read it,' he exclaimed. '*The Rise of Zion* by this man Godwin. It's a damn fine book and everybody ought to buy it. The guy says Western foreign policy has been captured by Israel. Even our intelligence services – the CIA, your people – they've all been co-opted. We're the Zionist enforcers now. But Godwin says, it's not too late. It's up to *us* – America and the British because we are the natural leaders of the West – to set things in the right direction again. If we don't, we're all gonna be dragged down into a goddamn Armageddon. A final conflict triggered by the Israelis. Just like in the Bible.'

It was strong stuff. Stronger than Bryn could handle. What made it even more tricky was the mismatch between Strange's disturbing remarks and the civilised urbanity with which he expressed them; and his obvious assumption that Bryn agreed with him. How was he going to find a way of disabusing Strange without seeming rude? It was a too familiar predicament.

'You gotta understand Israel,' said Strange. 'It's a country where the people are accustomed to realising their ambitions through violence. They have no tradition of persuasion or legality.' He grinned. 'I guess it takes an American to understand that.'

He looked across at Bryn and delivered again that half throat-clearing, half-laughing rattle.

The *rauchbier* had worked its way through. Bryn cursed his habitual lack of bladder stamina, excused himself and went off in search of the toilets. They were not easy to find. After a couple of false journeys down corridors at the back of the restaurant, a kindly waiter set him in the right direction.

Afterwards, as he was working his way back through the building, the first thing that struck him was that the all-pervasive tannoy had actually been turned off.

Then, when he opened the door into the restaurant, people were standing at their tables and shouting and milling about. The place was building to uproar. Two *landpolizei* had just come in from the street and another two were hauling someone away in handcuffs.

It was the little photographer. As he passed, he looked directly at Bryn as if he knew him. He had a sallow complexion, like a Japanese by all means, but – now that Bryn saw him more closely – much more obviously Middle Eastern in appearance.

Udell Strange was deep in conversation with two men, one of them the chauffeur. The other – a shorter character in wrap-around dark glasses, the same (Bryn was convinced) whom he'd seen stealing in behind Strange at the end of the opera interval – was holding the miscreant's camera in his hand, swinging it idly by its strap.

It looked very much as if the evening was at an end. The elderly Americans were beginning to settle their bills, and the businessmen had already left. Waiters were clearing tables. A group of young people passed by and made for the door. Bryn caught a glimpse of one, blonde and unseasonally muffled. Surely that wasn't Agnete stealing away with them?

While he stood, marooned in the confusion, Strange marched briskly towards the exit. He called out to each of his two acolytes to follow and they left without a further word. There was a short, rasping growl from the Mercedes as it pulled away from the kerb.

Bryn went back to his seat to collect his belongings. A waiter presented him with the bill. In other circumstances he would have tried to refer it to his absent host, but his German was not now up to a complicated argument, so he bit his lip and paid. It was a modest enough sum.

And then he discovered that his Harrods carrier with its cushions and programme had disappeared. He was certain he had put it under his seat. Worse than that, he had absent-mindedly slipped his new iPhone into it. And all was gone. Nowhere to be seen. With a mixture of mime and a few phrases that fell serendipitously from his brain, he tried to explain his plight to the waiter. The waiter looked around half-heartedly and shrugged his shoulders. Another waiter came over but he must have misunderstood the situation because he took Bryn to the cloakroom, where unsurprisingly there was no sign of the bag. One of the policemen came back into the restaurant and had the situation explained to him and he – to his national credit – responded in perfect English, and wrote down the details. His firm advice, though, was to return to it again in the morning.

There was nothing left for Bryn to do.

He walked back through the wind and rain and the flying lime seeds, empty-handed, to the hotel.

He did not see Agnete again that evening, though he hung around in the hotel lobby, hoping she might turn up. Nor did he see her at breakfast next morning. He asked at the desk about her but, after some conversations among the desk clerks, the nett response was a pantomime of shrugged incomprehension. It was the day of his departure and he had clearly missed his chance. It was all very depressing. He hoped he had not lost his touch.

There was one excellent piece of news, however. The head clerk went back into the hotel office and re-emerged with the missing bag. 'I believe you left this at your restaurant, sir,' she said. More astonishing yet, programme and cushions and – most especially – iPhone were still stuffed and intact within.

A ringing phone on the reception desk prevented further explanation.

He had a little time before he was due to catch the train for the first leg of his return journey to Salt Lake City. He sat down at the hotel's computer to copy off Marion's promised email. After so long away, what he needed now was a good, old-style, sentimental letter, three pages or more. And here it was. It looked as if Marion was of a similar mind:

'*Dear Bryn*

'*Years ago when we first met we used to write long letters to each other and I've kept all yours. They'll always be treasured memories. So I thought it would be appropriate since I have so much to say to you now if I wrote a letter just like in the old days...* '

A little stiff maybe. But it needed to be enjoyed at leisure. He pressed the print button and surrendered the computer to the next hotel guest.

Later, when he brought his bags down from his room, two things struck – and disturbed – him. The first was some breaking news on the television set in the lobby. The sound had been turned down but there was a digest of what was happening on a crawler across the bottom of the screen. A group of Israeli agents had been operating illegally in Germany, using false German passports. Amongst the footage of them being expelled, one face caught his eye. It looked remarkably like the little photographer in the restaurant.

And then he noticed a policeman standing outside the main entrance to the hotel. He had never known this before in Germany: it was more the kind of thing you might expect in a third world country. Of course there were any number of reasons why an officer might be on duty. Perhaps an important German politician was staying at the hotel for the festival. Or maybe the policeman was there to discourage rogue taxi drivers. Who could say?

He did wonder whether – after the previous evening's restaurant experience – he was becoming just a little bit over-sensitive.

The train from Bayreuth to Nuremberg was packed with festival visitors going home. Bryn sat by a window watching, for probably the last time in his life, the unchanging Franconian countryside reeling past; and felt an unexpected affection for it. It was so far away from that other much less pleasant world of international news, violence and politics.

Broad fields of ungathered maize, birch woods, brown horses and brown sheep, the summer's dust rising in a cloud around a tractor, a little red and white Franconian flag fluttering gently in the middle of a field. Then a cluster of houses with the high-peaked gables of the region, a tiny church and onion-shaped tower, buzzards circling in the sky. And – as if to remind him of the present century – a small aeroplane above the horizon, flying parallel with the railway track.

When the train ducked down into a cutting and all he could see were trees and undergrowth, he pulled out Marion's email. She had said she was intending to send a 'proper letter' when they had last spoken on the phone, but he had not expected quite such an extended missive. He settled himself comfortably to read it.

'Dear Bryn

'Years ago when we first met we used to write long letters to each other and I've kept all yours. They'll always be treasured memories. So I thought it would be appropriate since I have so much to say to you now if I wrote a letter just like in the old days.

'We have been together for nearly 25 years, since we were students, and I think for most of that time we have been happy more or less. I never regretted marrying so young or having to give up so much to have our family. So I will always be grateful for that part of my life.

'You know how I fought to avoid going to America. I always told you I didn't want to move because I had my own life in London – and I didn't want to travel because I didn't like flying

– and all of that was true. And then when finally I agreed to come to Utah with you last year, you were surprised at how well I settled in. You said how contented I seemed to be. And you were right. But there was a reason for that which you have never guessed. Sometimes – I'm sorry to say this, Bryn – I think you're the one person in the world it would not have been obvious to.

'*The truth is – I love Dan and Dan loves me. I first fell in love with him ten years ago when he came over that summer and stayed with us. Do you remember? Yes, we slept together – but only once. And then decided the situation was impossible. He went back to his wife in Salt Lake City and I went back to you. Because neither of us wanted to hurt either of you.*

'*I had hoped that the passage of years would erase my feelings for him and in the end I foolishly persuaded myself they had. That's why last year I agreed to come with you to Utah – even though you would be working alongside Dan – because I really believed it was over between him and me. I'm really sorry. I couldn't have been more wrong...* '

He stopped reading. The letter ran on for a couple of pages more but he could guess what it contained. Proposals for an amicable divorce. Two divorces, in point of fact. Something about Dan's plans for their new life together. More regrets. Assurances of enduring friendship. Concern about his feelings. How and when they should announce all this to the children. Other sensible considerations.

The train emerged from the cutting and he gazed through the windows at the medieval landscape beyond. The little plane was still there on the horizon, as if fixed to the same position, like a blemish on the glass.

Chapter 3

You move on. That's the time-honoured response to calamity; or the collapse of a relationship.

For a time, though, Bryn had clung to the pain. So long as it remained, he found it preserved some outline of his loss. He had resisted sharing his misery with friends who might have tried to alleviate it; and certainly the last thing on his mind was any sort of therapeutic advice. What he felt was an enduring, living thing and it belonged to him.

And that was why he was now in the Yosemite Valley: by himself. Added to which, it would have been an awful waste of a reservation so over-subscribed that he'd had to book it the previous autumn...

But – inexorably – time had begun to lend distance and bind the wounds. He had even become a little ashamed of those earlier feelings – raw, furious and natural as they surely were. After a couple of weeks, they were becoming a burden. There was little enough temptation now to pour them out to sympathetic friends. He had decided that he did not do public grief.

By the same token, the memories of the last twenty-five years were beginning to take on a quite different colour and shape. The past may not be another country but the married couple he and

Marion had been seemed well on their way to becoming other people. He did not begrudge himself his self-indulgence and nostalgia. But he was inclined to regard it now more as a necessary rite of passage before getting on with the rest of his life.

He had already been amusing himself with a whole host of bright new options. A change of life. Jacking in academia and returning to England. Or trying something even more radical. Transplanting to a distant warm country – like Australia – and bar tending or patrolling beaches for a year or two. Setting up an eco-community and raising vegetables. Writing a novel. Joining an amateur drama society and getting laid.

There was a singular flaw in every one of these – apart from their general and obvious impracticality. All had to do with flight. And it did not, after all, make a huge deal of sense to run away from a relationship that had already fled from him.

So if not precisely moving on, then carrying on.

At least he had made one decision. He was determined that the bad news from Utah would not disrupt this part of his holiday. He was damned if he was not going to enjoy it.

He was sitting at a table in the Food Court of Yosemite Lodge, in the shadow of the Yosemite waterfall, and had given himself till the end of breakfast to write a reply to Marion. He had not, to be honest, made much progress. He had hoped that something in manuscript this time, and running – of course – a few pages, might strike a helpfully heartfelt chord.

The difficulty lay in reconciling his objective, if he could identify it, with what might be achievable. For a start, was he even certain – after everything she had told him – that he wanted her back? He had spent two weeks exploring the proposition and still did not know the answer. The nearest he had come to a conclusion was that – if he came to no conclusion – there were at least two other people who would reach one for him. So maybe – and without prejudice to some greater clarity in the future – he should do whatever he could to preserve the status quo. And that meant, for the time being, making whatever arguments he could to keep the marriage alive.

There it was. A decision.

Best to move on before he was tempted to revisit it.

The next question was whether a direct appeal would be effective. Probably not. If he knew anything about Marion, her mind was already made up and any pressure from him, rational *or* emotional, would merely make her more determined. Should he simply aim instead to keep open the lines of communication? Employ a strategy of general availability? Be ready to respond helpfully to whatever twists and developments and unpredicted difficulties lay ahead?

That was good. Very promising.

On the other hand…

There was always the other hand. The running thread throughout their relationship – and even in Marion's most recent email – was his supposed lack of purpose, ambition, resolve. What he reasonably took to be sensible consideration, she would perceive as feeble indecision. What he saw as contingency planning, she characterised – in a favourite phrase – as displacement behaviour.

Was it not Cocteau, though, who said: 'What others criticise you for, cultivate. It is you'?

On the other hand… a letter from him which carried on as if no gulf had opened between them would serve only to reinforce her prejudices.

'Dear Marion,

You were right: I never guessed it.'

That was as far as he had got.

The nine hand-written words floated in front of him. And the more he brooded on them, the more unreasonable Marion's action appeared. So sudden and arbitrary. So disloyal. And unfair. Something bilious and disruptive began to well up and he shoved the sheet of paper away.

Maybe, after all, he was not quite ready to move on.

It was mid morning but he had still not finished his breakfast. He sipped his weak coffee in its pale brown Yosemite mug speckled like a hen's egg, and gazed through the windows at the Douglas firs, the plummeting backdrop of the mountain, and – along its topmost edge – a ribbon of brilliantly blue sky. At this time of the year in California it was always hot; but in Yosemite it was a fresh, burning heat, as unlike the adhesive humidity of Bayreuth as could be imagined.

He wished he had made more of an effort with Agnete. If he had not been flattered and distracted by the American, she and he might now – who knows – be in the midst of a splendid affair.

And so little to remember. Wisps of silver blonde hair drifting across those electric blue eyes. That unblinkingly frank, challenging, alarming, opaque gaze. The cocktail dress and defiant – contemptuous – stride. Had he seen her smile? Perhaps a fleeting glimpse, unless he'd imagined it, of just the tips of her teeth, as secret and white as icebergs. Would their paths ever cross again? Was it the baggage of a married man that had held him back... ?

A tanned young hiker in shorts and boots was sitting opposite him, alone at a table with her eggs over-easy and crispy bacon. Her hair was a light ash brown, shining and curly, flecked with product-induced highlights – not by the sun, as Marion's used to be. She had the fresh, child-like glow of a woman who had recently stepped from the shower.

Her thoughts seemed also to be on other things than Yosemite. A Park Guide was spread beside her speckled mug but her gaze was fixed on something deep in outer space. Her vivid prettiness made Bryn smile – and he tried to catch her eye. She immediately beamed back, a radiant, uncomplicated response that took his breath away.

'Hi,' he began. 'I don't suppose you're – '

A strapping young man swept past his table and embraced her. The moment may not have lasted more than a second or two. It felt longer. Then the young man dragged round a chair and the pair chatted away in West Coast American, while he helped himself to the remains of her meal.

It was less than a year ago – Bryn reflected – that he had left a safe academic job in London and moved to Utah. In pursuit, like many before him, of a mid-life fantasy of freedom and opportunity on the sunnier side of the Ocean. How trite it sounded. The elusive, illusory 'Yes We Can'. He would hardly be the first immigrant to discover an America as problematic as the country so recently left behind.

Not that he'd lacked fair warning.

He had an older, cleverer, oppressively successful cousin called Marcus. Early the previous September, Marcus had taken him to lunch at the Travellers' Club in London for the grand purpose of advising him against taking up the associate professorship he'd been offered at the Western University of Utah.

'You are not a natural expatriate, Bryn,' he said. 'You're not cut out for it. You are too British.'

Marcus had – since Cambridge – worked for the Foreign Office so naturally he knew about these things. He was in fact, not to put too fine a point on it, a spy. Or, as he might designate it: a senior intelligence executive. This he had revealed in strictest confidence only the previous year – probably because he needed to explain to Bryn why, contrary to expectations, he had not risen to an ambassadorship. His employer was the Foreign Office's Secret Intelligence Service, or MI6 as it was more colloquially known; or 'Six' as Marcus called it. Marcus was the brother Bryn had never had, who had known him since birth, and who had successfully patronised him for nearly forty years.

'What on earth do you mean, Marcus?' he retorted.

'Well, I've had postings all over the world. Moscow, Pretoria, Washington, Geneva,' he drawled, between intervals for sipping his club port. 'And I've seen enough to know which colleagues are likely to assimilate and which not. You indubitably fall into the latter category. You'll always prefer soccer to baseball, your dreadful Guardian newspaper to the Salt Lake City Tribune, our weather to Utah's eternal sunshine, draught Bass to Budweiser and – above all – conversations about the things that matter to British people to all that up-country Republican stuff you will surely get in Mormonland. It won't work, Bryn and you'll be back in a year.'

'You're half cut, Marcus. And I won't.'

But of course he was right. He was always right.

That was the last time he'd seen him. He wondered what Marcus was doing now. Curing the world's problems, drip-feeding his unimpeachable British model into less enlightened societies – the Middle East, for example, various post-Soviet republics – or the USA. He probably had his email address. Perhaps he should get in touch. Not to allow him the satisfaction of saying I told you so; merely to... pick up again. For the first time in a year, Bryn felt homesick for old friends and relations. Even for Marcus.

And now the young couple at the table opposite were having an argument. A lovers' spat. The man had pushed his chair away and was glaring at the map of Yosemite while the young woman gazed sullenly out of the window. With an expression Bryn had seen on Marion's face. Many times.

He wondered if women had mid-life crises, like men. Had Marion reached an age where what she needed was some sort of 're-affirmation'? In which case, if she'd achieved that with Dan, should he expect the crisis to pass? Or – a more sober alternative – was this the culmination of all the dissatisfactions of their life together, gathered up and brought to sharp focus by her affair?

If the latter, then their relationship really was over. The genie out of the box. Nothing left but the dry legal rehearsal of his deficiencies and the end of any prospect of reconciliation. Damn.

He was, he concluded, demoralised. Like a dog worrying a dry bone, he had even fallen to analysing what depressed him. Was it the loss of that trusty old comfort blanket, marriage? Was it the shock of realising that Marion might actually prefer someone else? Both were perfectly good reasons to be gloomy. But no: there was a better cause. He was demoralised because he had made a fool of himself. Over Dan.

Dan, about whom he'd never had any doubts. The pillar of the Utah establishment, his mentor and friend since his twenties, Dan who for years had been pressing him to take his chances in America. And all that while with a private agenda. Dan's was a betrayal more undermining than anything of Marion's. He could not (he supposed) blame him for falling in love. But he could/should blame him for his manipulation, his persistence, his pantomime of bemusement at Marion's unwifely reluctance to join her husband in America and at her feisty, un-Mormon-like, attractive, independence of spirit.

Enough.

So here he was enjoying the crowd-packed splendours of Yosemite National Park by himself – Marion having exchanged their planned holiday in California for a rafting trip with a girlfriend in one of Utah's own National Parks, while Dan sorted things out with his ever complaisant wife. Bigamy not being allowed these days by the mainstream Mormon church.

What next? That question again. The job had not worked out. He had missed the sparky scepticism of his students in London. The earnest attentiveness of his Mormon students had flattered him at first but over time he'd begun to long for something a bit more challenging. He had not been prepared for their incuriosity about the world outside America and their lack of political engagement – beyond an easy-going acceptance of the conservatism of their parents. He had been frustrated by their reluctance to debate, argue and embrace less conventional positions. Perhaps, after all, the clean-cut Utah model was not for him.

But the main problem was that the job had not been what he'd expected. He realised now how much Dan had managed to finesse its substantial downside in his eagerness to lure Marion across the Atlantic. Although the post was nominally a senior professorship, there was no chance of tenure for years, and meanwhile Bryn remained effectively on probation. The curriculum was rigid and insensitive to modern historiography; even such matters as reading lists and lecture topics were determined by an elderly head of department.

It was not surprising that relations with his superiors had deteriorated. His somewhat revisionist, not to say hypercritical, approach to the origins of Mormonism – as mythological as the Old Testament's version of Jewish history – had raised influential hackles. Even without the marriage crisis, it was unlikely he could have survived for long.

'Sir? Will you have finished here yet?'

A green uniformed Hispanic lady had been pushing a trolley from table to table and tidying away the customers' leavings, and was now hovering over him. In the background some anxious European tourists had passed through the pay points and were scanning the room for a spare table. He shook his head apologetically and gestured towards his coffee mug.

He recalled all too well Udell Strange's warning about how overcrowded Yosemite was in season. He had several days to use up before the next part of the holiday. Perhaps he should take the advice he'd been given in Bayreuth and travel on up north. He could drive through the less visited National Parks along the Sierra Nevada and the Cascade Mountains and still have time to get back to San Francisco for his second dose of Wagner this year, at the War Memorial Opera House.

Chapter 4

A man sat down at his table. A short, stocky type, wearing an old-fashioned black San Francisco baseball cap with 'Giants' scribbled across a red ball on the front of it. The deep, curved peak jutted out over his face like an awning.

There was no 'Do you mind?' or 'Is this free?'. Bryn wondered if he had even registered that he was sitting there.

There was a brief flicker of the man's eyes before they disappeared within the shadow of the cap peak.

'OK, dawg?' he said.

He took several plates, a coffee mug and cutlery from his tray and began to arrange them in front of him. With the flat palms of his hands, he moved the maple syrup dispenser and the glass container of the 'no calorie sweetener' packs of Splenda and Equal, over to an empty corner of the table.

He was so engrossed that Bryn was able at leisure to study the unsheltered part of his face. The man had puffy jowls, as if he was on steroids. Or maybe he'd had plastic surgery. Bryn guessed his age at no more than forty, too early, one might have thought, for improvements – he wondered if he had suffered a facial injury. He might be an old soldier, recently retired with a Purple Heart for his wounds.

When the man had ordered the *placement* to his satisfaction, he folded his hands together and raised his head slightly so that the cap peak aimed directly at Bryn's chest.

'You Brits must be pissin' yourselves laughin' at us,' he said.

Bryn suppressed an impulse to ask how he knew he was British. Perhaps he'd heard him speaking earlier, or picked on some characteristic element of his clothing or demeanour or haircut. Or it could have been the old Harrods carrier bag hanging from the back of his chair.

'Three weeks before Election Day and the guy turns out to be a friggin' closet gay. Hot damn! Waddya think of that?'

Bryn knew exactly what he meant. Everyone on the globe would have known. Around autumn the previous year, the Presidential front runner – with the polls predicting a landslide – was revealed to have had a homosexual affair. He'd reacted with a categorical and self-righteous denial. Then a thirty year old photograph had emerged of his youthful self, naked and *in flagrante delicto*. He challenged the authenticity of the photograph. And the man who took the photograph was wheeled out to contradict him. The general view was that his enemies had orchestrated the process to perfection, and stitched up the would-be President as neatly as a triple by-pass.

By now, the November 4th ballot was days away. The candidate stubbornly refused to stand down. To be fair, it was unclear under the American Constitution whether he could legally do so at such a late stage. At all events, the expected landslide completely reversed direction. The conservative evangelical constituency which had built up the candidate recoiled in horror; and his no-hoper liberal rival, a black woman senator, swept in on the lowest popular turn-out in nearly a hundred years.

'Could that ever happen in Ing-e-land, man?'

'Not under our system. No,' said Bryn, trying not to get drawn into an extended conversation.

But at that point, regrettably, the inner pedant took over.

'You see in Britain, technically,' he said, 'we vote for a party not a leader. So in principle it should be easier to unload the candidate even at a late stage.

'Though I suppose,' he added, more reflectively, 'the nett effect might be much the same. But maybe we wouldn't worry quite so much about what a man did when he was twenty.'

The most remarkable effect of the debacle was that the new President – once unelectable because of an agenda closer to socialism than any in American history – now had a two-thirds majority in both Houses of Congress and a genuine if brief opportunity to change the whole direction of American policy at home and abroad.

'Waddya think of that?' said the man again, waving a hand towards the neatly folded tabloid newspaper he had placed beside his breakfast setting. All Bryn could see was a screaming headline attacking the latest government policy.

'It'll be the end of freedom, I tell ya,' he exclaimed vehemently. 'Freedom of speech for a start. You can wave goodbye to all that, dawg!'

In fact Bryn had rather enjoyed the humiliation the Election had wrought upon the American media. Its partisan identification with the disgraced candidate had – in particular – made a bonfire of the credibility of the television and radio channels. To such an extent that there was now a Bill before Congress to renew the old 1950s 'Fairness Doctrine' abolished in 1987 by President Reagan. Significantly toughened up to enforce political balance across all news and comment programmes.

'You're right,' he said. 'It could be the end of Glenn Beck and Fox News.'

'It's like goddamn Soviet Russia!' said the man, even more passionately.

He had a peculiar voice, reedy, thin, almost falsetto. Bryn reckoned himself pretty good at identifying accents, but failed to pin this one down at all. Not from California anyway.

'I wouldn't worry,' Bryn replied. 'You can't legislate for texting and twitter and the blog networks. I'd say the people are now finding their voice and the views of the mainstream channels will become irrelevant. The problem for the ruling classes is that it'll get more and more difficult for them to spend their way to power.'

But he was on a roll and could not resist a little gratuitous provocation.

'Who knows,' he added, 'you could get real American democracy at last.'

The man lowered his cap towards Bryn's middle shirt button and lapsed into silence. For a moment Bryn thought that his professorial authority might have cowed him into submission. But no. For the second time in a month, he found himself marvelling at the capacity of people with fixed political views to assume that he must agree with everything they said.

'The American people won't stick for it. Right. If you ask me,' the man added, confidingly, 'the real problem is the guy she's got as Vice President. Flaxman. East Coast Jew. He never thought he'd be anything – you know, like Harry S Truman. Now he's runnin' Congress and it's gone to his head. No way is she ever goin' to get re-elected. But *him*. Hell, she's a friggin' woman, for Christ's sake. How would she deal with a war? Commander-in-chief? Don't make me laugh. Flaxman would take over. He needs to be stopped hard, know what I mean? You're an expert on history, aren'tcha? What's the odds on a VP takin' over before the friggin' President completes her first term?'

You're an expert on history?

Where did that come from?

The cap peak continued to target Bryn's shirt as if awaiting its reply.

'Why would I know?' he murmured.

There was a long pause.

'I thought you knew about these things,' the man replied. 'From what you said earlier.'

And that seemed to be it, at least for the time being.

The young man at the table opposite was writing something on the back of the Yosemite map. He pushed it across to the young woman. She continued to study the landscape through the window. He pushed it again, like a dog nudging his mistress's ankle. Eventually she consented to look down, and picked the document up. Her features began to crumple. She grabbed his hand. And kissed him full on the lips.

Bryn had to look away.

Somewhere in the background, his new companion had changed topics and was now developing a private theory about the malign intentions of objects.

'Have y'ever noticed,' he said, in his high, thin alto, 'how stuff works against ya? Sure you've noticed. But have y'ever wondered why friggin' computers always crash before you've saved the friggin' work? Why stuff falls out of the highest part of the cupboard? Hey, have y'ever thought there might be some kind of mind behind all this? Somethin' messin' with us. Like I'm walking through woods and a poison ivy vine... '

He paused to check Bryn was following him, and continued –

'... falls across your face the goddamn second I pass below it. How many times has your car run low when you're miles from anywhere? It never happens in town, does it? Always when you're out there on the turnpike, two hours from the next gas station. Don't nobody tell me it's coincidence, dawg.'

Time, Bryn felt, to make his excuses and leave. He put his coffee mug down.

'Have you done here, sir?'

It was the trolley lady again. As she reached out for Bryn's empty mug, his companion pushed a plateful of untouched hash browns and eggy French toast towards her.

'You can take that,' he said.

She stared at it as if non-plussed.

The man produced a wallet from the back of his jeans and laid it open on the table and teased out a dollar bill and thrust it at her. She backed away in embarrassment.

'Why you give me that?' she said, her voice rising up the scale. 'I not waiter. I just do my job.'

And with that, she swept his plate onto a tray with a pile of other dirty crockery and scuttled away to her trolley.

The interruption gave Bryn his opportunity and he rose to his feet. The man's California State 'Driver License' was in a transparent window in the open wallet. He could see a San Francisco address and a name. Jack Wilson. A name he felt sure he'd heard somewhere before.

'Nice knowing you,' said the man, as Bryn prepared to leave.

But something seemed to have disturbed him and he started looking around anxiously.

'Do you have the salt?' he said. 'Do I have to get it from somewhere else?'

He began to get up too, as if he intended to raid the next table or pursue the departing trolley lady.

'No no,' said Bryn. 'I think you'll find it's behind the napkin box.'

'No way, buddy.'

'Behind the paper napkins. Really.' He picked up his carrier bag and backed away.

'There's no salt on this fuckin' table, you fuckin' idiot!'

Or that's what Bryn thought he heard him say.

It stopped him in his tracks. He returned to the table and quickly moved aside the napkin container – not a particularly substantial item – to reveal the salt and pepper shakers. The man stared at them perplexedly.

As Bryn left him, he was still sitting deep in his private contemplation – and was in the exact same position when Bryn reached the self-service counter at the far end of the room and took a last look back.

It was then that he realised the man was wearing short, expensively tooled, cowboy boots, one of which, like a child, he'd kicked off. They had the highest and slimmest Cuban heels he had ever seen; and though Mr Wilson's torso was that of an average-sized man, his legs were so short that the boot-less foot did not quite reach the floor.

The room began to clear. It was the mid-morning exodus when the tourist parties rose as a single person, as if a starting gun had been fired, to catch their coach tours. One of them must have bumped into the trolley lady because there was an almighty crash as her pile of crockery cascaded to the floor. She burst into tears and colleagues scrambled across the restaurant to comfort her. Every head turned to gaze at her humiliation.

Except for one. Jack Wilson remained absorbed in the mystery of his salt shaker.

Bryn returned to his room.

He needed a breath of fresh mountain air. He rummaged in his travelling bag for the iPhone. He'd not used it since Bayreuth – it had been a present from Marion and its facilities had rather lost their charm. But he was beginning to feel more relaxed. Sufficient to memorialise his magnificent surroundings with a few snaps.

He walked down to Yosemite village, bought a large-scale map in the serious hiker shop, two bottles of water and some milk chocolate Hershey bars, and set off for the less populated eastern end of the valley.

He wanted to get away from a multitude that was as dense now as the summer crowds in Oxford Street. To somewhere remote from the hundreds of cars parked nose to tail or drifting round the one-way system endlessly looking for that precious space. Away from the listless columns of day trippers shuffling towards the next photographic opportunity.

There was some thinning out as he left the central valley. At Mirror Lake a bus load of foreign tourists decanted onto the approach path. He decided to carry on up the narrowing canyon towards the relative solitude of the forest.

He continued past a notice warning of a recent rockfall and earth tremor, up a rough path overlooking the thundering torrent of the Merced River, until he arrived at a kind of crossroads. The main route curved away to the right, while a narrow left-hand track pointed straight up the face of the mountain.

There was not a tourist to be seen. This would sort the sheep from the goats.

The track did not take long to reveal why it was so deserted. At first it wound its way steeply through forest, over rocks and under fallen trees. By the time it emerged into the sunlight, it had become a sequence of hair-pin chicanes tighter than the terraces of a paddy field. After an hour or so of hard labour, he calculated that he had covered a mile by foot and barely a hundred yards by elevation.

He sat on a boulder in the shade of a stunted pine tree, sipped his water and sucked at one of the melted Hershey bars. Two young people with bedrolls and backpacks passed on their way down, eyes fixed on the path ahead of them. 'Halfway there,' gasped Bryn, as much in hope as encouragement. The girl saluted him with a cheerful flourish of her fist.

Only stubbornness and the fear of failure kept him going. Whenever he passed a waterfall, he bathed his head to cool the blood surging at his temples. Every fifteen minutes, then ten and five, then every time he found a shaded corner, he crumpled back on a rock to recharge his drained batteries. His knees and lungs and head ached…

He was at his lowest ebb when two tanned young men in hardcore hiking uniform (boots and ankle socks, shorts, check shirts, huge backpacks, hatless) came up the track from below, chatting to each other. They passed Bryn's sanctuary without breaking stride. 'How's it going?' asked one, in a Middle-Eastern accent. As they disappeared into the trees above him, he could hear them both laughing.

But he made it. He reached the top.

And there was nothing to be seen.

Though the summit was as flat as he'd expected, it was all pine forest. Cooler and sweeter smelling, even muddy underfoot from little streams carrying away the last of the snow melt. But the trees that had blanketed the upper slopes of the precipice were now so densely packed that there was no view of the valley to be had at all.

He wandered on despondently in search of the vista that might – just might – vindicate the whole mad exercise.

And, two or three miles further on, he found it. A break in the trees and a breathtaking, bird's eye view of the valley below.

Clear and brilliant in the sunshine, and so distant that he could imagine it empty of tourists, cars, hotels, any trace of humankind. The moment needed to be celebrated and he pulled out his iPhone. But when he attempted to take a photograph there was no response. The iPhone's battery, for no reason that he could understand, was – like its owner – quite exhausted.

He settled down under the Douglas firs and slept a while.

He awoke to the sound of a voice talking in a language he did not understand. Two hikers – perhaps the young men he'd seen earlier – were standing together among the trees with their backs towards him. One was talking into a cellphone. He was lucky to get a signal in such a remote area.

It was time to move on.

After the agonies of the ascent, the way back was a carpet ride. He passed two or three upward toiling couples, gasping and red-faced, and made it his duty to encourage them all. 'Not far to go' he piped, regardless of distance. But as he neared the bottom, his energy began to flag again. An overweight Texan in stetson and embroidered jeans asked him if it was far to the top. 'Hours to go,' he said bleakly. 'It's a brutal climb.'

When he got back to Mirror Lake, flat and featureless as polished glass, the occupying army had grown to hundreds. He settled behind a family group at the water's edge for a rest. On the other side of the water, down on his haunches photographing the reflected Douglas firs and mountains, was his breakfast acquaintance, Jack Wilson. Bryn edged back into the shadow of the trees and watched him.

Though Wilson clearly possessed a top of the range camera, he did not appear to be a skilled photographer. He spent as much time fiddling with the settings and peering into the lens, as he did composing an image. Clouds passed across the sun while he puzzled at some baffling detail of functionality. Even the process of taking a picture was a pantomime of uncertainty: he shuffled up and down the edge of the lake, still on his haunches, searching for an angle; or experimented with lying flat on his stomach, zooming in and out, twiddling the focussing ring.

In the end, his infinitely complex task seemed to defeat him and he stood up, and put his camera to his eye like a telescope, and started scanning the scenic backdrop to the lake. It was time for Bryn to leave. A crowd of hikers were coming down the valley trail; he slipped in amongst them and strolled back to the Village.

That evening, as he trimmed his rather straggly academic beard and gazed at his tired reflection in the bathroom mirror, a plan settled in his mind. He would retrieve his hire car first thing in the morning and drive east out of Yosemite through the Tioga Pass. A few miles beyond the Park exit, his map showed a track which would take him to the unvisited wilderness of Twenty Lakes Basin. After he had explored that, he would travel on north into the deep solitude of the Cascades. It was pretty well in every detail what Udell Strange had advised at their dinner a month ago.

Braced by a resolution well made, he settled down in front of the bedroom television with a can of huckleberry-flavoured beer. It would have been two or three cans had not the cleaner – he assumed it was her – removed them from his fridge and – insult upon injury – deposited the drained, squashed cans in the waste bin.

When he turned on the set it came up with the last channel he would have chosen: he was just in time for 'America's Newsroom – your Fox News on the hour'. He lingered long enough to get the gist. The first item was about a shocking government plan to fund a new health service for the poor from a 'robber' tax on all forms of bank trading.

The coverage majored on Wall Street's reaction. Goldman Sachs, Morgan Stanley and Bank of America representatives queued up to voice their outrage. Bryn remembered a line from an Edward Albee play: 'We're not a communal nation. Giving but not sharing, outgoing but not friendly.' No spokesman was invited to give the other side of the argument.

He went off in search of something, anything, more balanced than Fox; and landed on CNN. More millionaires' television, but at least reporters were allowed a view of their own. Mad-eyed veteran anchor Richard Quest had been released from his London base for a special report on alarming developments in the Middle East. Something about a regime change in one of the Gulf states, with serious implications for the peace of the region. A ninety year old westward-leaning Sheikh overthrown by his Wahhabist, al-Qaida supporting son. Sabre rattling by the Israelis and an emergency session of the Knesset. A special United Nations envoy on her way to mediate between the alarmed parties.

A bit *too* depressing.

He flicked back to Fox and a story about yet another baseball player on the verge of beating Babe Ruth's iconic home run record.

This was followed by an item reporting an attempt by a group of senators to tack a wrecking amendment onto what the newscaster described as 'another of the White House's controversial liberal initiatives'. It was Bryn's old friend: the Bill to renew the Fairness Doctrine for news and current affairs. The wrecking amendment characteristically had nothing to do with the Bill's main business and sought to deregulate some National Parks so that their mineral rights could be exploited. A spokeswoman appeared for a new grassroots movement calling itself 'The Friends of the Right', supporting the proposal and inveighing against the President.

This was cut short by an outburst of excitement as a new headline-busting story came in. A Hollywood starlet had been arrested for drunk-driving.

His attention wandered. As he drained the last of his beer, he noticed with some irritation that the clock-radio by his bed was out by several hours. He knew it had been correct when it awoke him that morning. He leaned over to reset it. As he did so, it occurred to him that, bizarrely, it had been showing British Summer Time.

Chapter 5

The track, alternately tarmac and rutted dirt, ran north up a valley creek, with the dark shadow of Tioga Peak lying across its eastern side. After two or three miles it swerved abruptly right into a small parking lot which was where he left the car. Saddlebag Lake stretched away below, flat and silent. It was so early in the morning the mountain air still carried a sharp bite.

He crossed a small dam and headed up the lake shoreline. The path led to the northern end of the lake and through a meadow of daisies and goldenrod, and upwards into a scrubby landscape of brown earth, scattered rocks and stunted pine trees. There were smaller lakes on the right hand side, their shorelines shrunk back by the summer drought. He passed a tinkling stream, and noticed for the first time a whiff of sulphur in the air. The same kind of smell, though less offensive, as he remembered from a visit to Yellowstone many years before.

The going became harder. Falls of small stones and rocks littered the path and threatened his footing. Then the way turned downhill towards another silent lake, flatter and even more mirror-like than Saddleback. He crabbed his way towards it, sometimes on hands and feet with stones and small boulders tumbling away in little landslides of scree, until he reached the security of a rocky promontory overlooking the water. He sat down and unzipped a bag of chocolate bars and bananas and composed himself to enjoy the beauty of his surroundings.

On the other side of the lake, a canyon wall rose towards the sky. Its rock face shone in the morning light like blue steel, a burnished memory of some mighty eruption millions of years ago. The landscape had the brilliant precision of a newly finished oil painting. The lake was so translucent he could see small fish feeding on the bottom twenty feet below. The silence was absolute and he revelled in it.

Then from somewhere far away – or deep underground – there came a faint rumbling sound, like a distant motorway or an aircraft. It lasted for perhaps two minutes before the silence returned. A tiny ripple spread in concentric circles from the centre of the lake, until it lapped at the water's edge, and died. A jumble of rocks and stones rolled down the far mountainside into the valley.

He followed the path round the head of the water and crossed a stream by a pine log bridge. The way curved south past a series of ravishingly china blue lakes. Mountains began to crowd in from the north, with patches of snow still on their highest slopes. The granite rock face changed from blue through red to an almost porcelain white.

Apart from a couple of backpackers far away on the skyline behind him, he saw no one else that morning. But around mid-day he reached a campsite where a group of young men had not yet begun to fold up their tents. He settled on a bench for a water break; and a friendly Australian offered him a can of beer, which he did not refuse. He asked them if anyone else had heard the strange rumble earlier in the morning. No one had.

'It's probably what you thought it was,' said a hiker with a West Coast accent. 'This is still earthquake country after all. I've been in Yosemite when the windows rattled. It's no big deal. The last real quake was in '89 but you still get micros around 2.4 Richter. Nothing to worry about.'

The Australian chortled into his beer.

'No big deal, matey? Isn't that what you guys said before Mount St Helens?'

'Yeah. Well,' said the Californian, 'you can always be wrong once. But I ain't gonna panic till the frogs start migrating.'

'The poor bastard lives in San Francisco,' said the Australian, derisively.

'It's what you call a sense of perspective, kangaroo boy,' retorted his mate.

He left them happily breaking open a second six-pack, evidently settled in for a period. Not a bad way to see the wilderness. But Bryn was already beginning to feel tired – he wondered if he'd quite recovered from the previous day's exertions – so he made his way back to the head of Saddlebag Lake where a water taxi was now ferrying less robust hikers to and from the parking lot. At five dollars it was a snip.

At first he could not find his car. The once empty lot had completely filled up with vehicles and he supposed that was what had disoriented him. When he located it, it was away to the side, badly parked and facing the entrance. He checked the keys: they were still there, safe in his pocket. But when he went to open the driver's door, it was unlocked. He sat behind the wheel, trying to puzzle it out. He poked around the back seat and in the boot: everything was normal enough. He tried to recall his behaviour earlier that morning. Was he so absent-minded that he'd done this himself and simply forgotten? That way surely madness lay...

He drove east out of the Pass and took the highway north towards the Cascades.

The journey was more fatiguing than he had anticipated. Not for the first time he was reminded that distances in the American West, which on the map might look like a taxi ride, can roll on for hours. The steep mountain highways were as packed with switchbacks as an Olympic grand slalom. He had intended to keep going until he reached Lassen National Park. But late in the afternoon, after Lake Tahoe had drifted by on the right, he decided instead to look for somewhere to eat and spend the night.

By now he was passing through the little town of Truckee. Too hungry to bother about refinement, he pulled up at a roadside takeaway and ordered the 'pint-sized' version of the Mountain High Big Hoss Meathouse Pie with gluten-free crust (gluten not being an option); and took a bottle of Arrowhead water from the walk-in cooler. But when it arrived, the pint-sized portion – as he should perhaps have anticipated – looked sufficient to feed a troop of ravenous boy scouts.

He sat in the car with the open carton beside him. Even one slice (one of six) was a challenge. He took a diversionary slurp from the water bottle.

Truckee. He had assumed this to be a typical quaintly-named small American town that nobody ever hears of and no stranger visits. But the word had triggered some inaccessible memory that troubled him. He had that same prickling sense of foreboding that had assailed him when he'd stepped out on the balcony in Bayreuth. He pushed the pie box across to the passenger seat and drove on.

A street sign gave him the answer. He was on the Donner Pass Road; and travelling through the site of the most terrible event in the history of nineteenth century American migration. He recalled a wagon train of pioneers, trekking thousands of miles from the east, arriving exhausted and out of supplies in these same mountains, after a disastrous short cut which had added weeks to their schedule. Here they were stranded through a terrible winter, succumbing progressively to starvation, exposure, sickness and – most notoriously – cannibalism.

Something he might explore tomorrow, if time permitted...

He continued on across a motorway and followed the shoreline of a lake until he found a motel. A ski-lodge in the winter season, it was now making the best it could out of the local boating and fishing. There was no difficulty getting a room and he settled down in front of the television with his Brobdingnagian feast on the table beside him.

He was in a low mood and the news channels were a vision of dystopia. Politics and yet more politics. Corporate fury at the government's plan to fund its health service directly from a tax on Wall Street. Two major banks threatening to move their centres of operation to a country more amenable to unregulated independence. Not Switzerland or Liechtenstein or any of the usual suspects, but – and hardly astonishing any more – post-Soviet Russia.

It was an open secret that the old Cold War enemy, looking to become more capitalist than Wall Street, had its ambitions set on a global financial role. Excellent terms were on offer to any enterprise that might wish to relocate to Moscow. A spokesman for the American Bankers Association signally failed to deny that an overseas move was an option for its members. The channel's political pundit predicted a new Russian hegemony by stealth, gathering more international influence than was ever achieved by Stalin. But was it 'merely bluff and bluster' to force the President to abandon her plans? Would she be able to hold out against the mounting pressures?

He put down the unsubdued slice of pizza pie and reached for his glass of water. The surface of the liquid was vibrating. Not radiating in a concentric pattern as on the Yosemite lake – more a faint all-over shivering of the meniscus. And just for a few seconds. It had faded away before his fingers reached the glass.

The guestbook lay on the table, open on the first page: the usual instructions about what to do in case of fire. Bryn flipped to the second page.

'EARTHQUAKE

Most earthquakes last only a few seconds, doing little, if any damage. In the event of an earthquake please remain calm. Avoid all glass such as windows and mirrors. Get to your knees, bend down and cover the back of your neck and ride the quake out. After the quake has stopped, safely exit your room, walk to the nearest accessible exit and leave the building. Go to the Central Checkpoint in the back parking lot (see map on back of this page)… '

In the background the news agenda moved on to the unfortunate starlet picked up for drunk driving, who had now also been charged with racist abuse of the arresting officer.

The vibration did not return.

In the morning, when he went to the welcome desk to pay the bill, a single distracted young woman was on duty. While he waited for her to come off the phone, he browsed through the Visitors' Book. The entries were relentlessly cheerful, as frequently from children as adults. He flicked back a week or two in case anyone had been bold enough to slip in a criticism, until he came across one heavily underlined comment ('Preevius persons pizza still in bin') by a guest signing himself – with a gothic flourish – as 'Richard Wagner'.

'That'd be one of your older guests then,' he quipped to the receptionist as she came back to the desk.

She revolved the book one hundred and eighty degrees to look at it.

'No, that's not the Hollywood guy,' she said, after studying the entry for several seconds. 'We don't get the stars here.'

She took Bryn's credit card and ran it across her machine.

'Yeah,' she continued, 'I remember him though. He was no way good-lookin'. Short and kinda heavy built with a baseball hat – San Francisco Giants. Always paid cash. Weird. Not my type, sir.'

What were the chances?

'I don't suppose he was wearing high heeled cowboy boots?'

'I think so,' said the woman. 'Yeah. Right.'

'High voice, perhaps?'

'Sure. Friend of yours?'

'Sort of. Did he do anything here?'

'Gee, sir, I wouldn't know. He went into the bait store across the road. And then I guess he drove north. You should have said you knew him.'

What she had called the bait store was more like a general hunting and fishing shop. There was a small section at the back devoted to wildlife books, with the names and pictures of the fish and game locally available for slaughter. Bryn found a cheap guide to American birds and took it to the counter.

As he waited for his change, he asked the shop-keeper if he had much passing trade.

'Not much,' the man replied. 'Local people and hunting parties staying at the motel. Business is lousy these days. Not much money around any more. The feds are taxing everyone to death. The sooner we get rid of this black dame the better. You're not from the East Coast?'

'No. British,' Bryn said hastily, with a self-deprecatory little laugh.

The man seemed pacified.

'You were recommended by a friend of mine,' Bryn said. 'I don't suppose you'll remember him. Short, stocky, likes to wear high heel boots and why not. Though I can't defend the baseball hat. Let's Go Giants!'

The shopkeeper cheered up.

'I know your friend. He comes here regular.'

He stuffed the book into a brown paper bag.

'Talks a lot, your friend, would you say?' he added, after a pause.

'I'm afraid he does.'

'He sure does.'

'Yes, he likes to chat, my friend.'

'Sure as hell he does.'

Nothing like common ground to break the ice.

'And I suppose he still insists on paying cash?'

'Always does,' said the shopkeeper.

'He would do.'

'Do you know,' said the man, warming to his topic, 'your guy only buys one thing? Phones me up a week before to make sure I've got it. Not much call for it otherwise. Can you believe that?'

'And what would that be?'

'Well I shouldn't tell ya. But since I guess you're his friend. It's a special arrangement, see. Would you believe lead free thirty-eight handgun ammo. Who wants that?'

'Not much used?'

'What for? He's the only guy ever asks me for it. And when I get the stuff, he wants to check it matches his hand-piece.'

'That sounds like him.'

'Sure. And what a piece of business that is. S and W Bodyguard double action with laser sight. And customised. Special hand grip. Barrel down to an inch. You gotta have a lot of big ones for that. More than folks round here could ever run to.'

An elderly man came into the shop and picked up a two kilogram bag of ground-bait.

'I reckon you could still catch up with him if you get a move on,' said the shopkeeper.

It took a moment for this to sink in.

'I thought he was here last week,' Bryn said.

'Sure. And again this morning. Not more than an hour past. Are you guys not together?'

'No. Not so far as I'm aware.'

The man shrugged his shoulders and turned away to the other customer.

Bryn went outside and stood for a while, gazing at the lake.

A V-shaped formation of geese came in from the north and settled noisily on the water. He pulled the bird guide out of its paper bag and flicked through until he reached a picture and a description he recognised. Cackling Geese: birds that summered in Canada and migrated south on the so-called Pacific Flyway, down the line of the Cascade Mountains – in late autumn. If his identification was right, then this flock was way ahead of its schedule.

Donner Memorial State Park lay a couple of miles east of the motel, within a forest of pines. On a high concrete plinth, like a socialist-realist monument raised to the workers of Soviet Russia, stood a bronze family group, the husband peering heroically into the distance. In a low nearby building was a museum full of sad mementos of that terrible winter of 1847: children's toys, letters from survivors ('Never take no cut-off and hurry along as fast as you can'), contemporary photographs, candle moulds, shaving kit, salt cellars. Beyond the museum, nature trails looped through the forest and alongside the lake.

It seemed ironic that most visitors came to this dreadful site in the high summer, with temperatures in the seventies and fat-bellied wildlife – deer, squirrels, chipmunks, racoons, porcupines – scampering through the Park's sparkling meadows. Not for tourists the privations of that winter: snow more than twenty feet deep, supplies exhausted, the survivors reduced to gnawing on leather and – finally – each other's corpses. By the time the snows melted and the rescue parties arrived, many that were not dead were stark mad. The women survived best, preserved by their slower metabolism and body fat.

The families had built cabins amongst the trees. The position of the Murphy residence was the most precisely known: widow Murphy and her adolescent children raised it against a monolith of polished rock that had bubbled from the earth in some primeval upheaval of molten granite. The three other sides of their dwelling had no window or door, merely a hole to crawl through. Pine logs formed the walls and the flat roof was ox hide – until the starving family dragged it off to chew on or boil down to a glue-like, barely digestible jelly.

Bryn was glad to leave it all behind and drive on again to the north. Through more mountains and national forests, past Sierraville, Clio and Quincy. Towards the small town of Chester and beyond that to his current objective: Lassen Volcanic Park.

There was only one lodging place in this wilderness – at least only one that had revealed itself to an internet trawl. He'd rung up a Sacramento management office and made a booking. Even scribbled down some helpful how-to-get-there instructions; and mislaid them.

And now he was lost.

He pulled up on a highway west of Chester. The hire car had come with a (very small scale) 'vacation guide' to the (very large) state of California. But he reckoned he might compute his position by comparing the mountains on the northern horizon with the pattern of tiny elevation triangles helpfully provided on the map. He could remember that he was supposed to take a turn-off that ran directly towards Lassen Peak itself. Identifying Lassen Peak, then, would be a start.

He left the car by the road and climbed up through the forest to get a better view. A mountain rose before him, not twenty miles away. It had the classic pyramid shape of an old volcano, with a depression at its peak scooped out by more recent eruptions. It was smooth-sided and shone in the sun, like a pailful of wet sand poured out on the beach. Even at this time of the summer, there were ribbons of melting snow on its highest flanks.

He stretched out on a rock. An eagle was soaring against the sun, a tiny silhouette of splayed wing tips and fanned-out tail. A skein of familiar geese passed down the eastern horizon. A white dirt track glinted between the pines to his right, running directly towards the peak. And again, as on the Tioga Pass, there was a faint rumbling sound, like a giant snoring in his sleep in some distant valley.

As he climbed back to his feet, a puff of fine grey ash arose with him. There was more of it in his hair and on the palms of his hands. He walked back, kicking at the ground, and a gossamer mist of the stuff swirled up in the sunlight, and as quickly vanished. When he reached the road, a fine film of powder had settled upon the car.

Chapter 6

He drove away from the sun towards the north-east until he picked up directions to Chester, the only settlement thereabouts of any size. It was a typical sleepy, one street, one-storey town with one turn off to the north – identified by a signpost as the route to his overnight lodging. He followed the track as it ran like an arrow towards the mountain, through the overhanging forest, on and on till it arrived at a group of pine cabins scattered among the trees at the edge of a flat, open meadow.

Outside the first of the cabins hung a wooden sign with the word OFFICE roughly branded on it. A yellow-bellied marmot, as fat as a stuffed toy, watched him mistrustfully before scuttling away under the raised lodge floor. Some horses stirred in a corral. It could have been the sun, or the long day, or simply a random rush of nostalgia, but he was reminded of the imaginary landscape of his own childhood. Perhaps a little of the Hundred Acre Wood; and a good portion of the Ponderosa.

Then when he climbed the steps into the office, he was met by an elderly gentleman with a north European accent who introduced himself as the owner and invited him to write his name in the guest book. A bedquilt hung on the wall. There was even a rocking chair in the corner of the room.

He had entered the Hollywood version of pioneer history. A forest clearing in a hostile wilderness. Wood cabins. A corral and horses. To cap it all, a strange old man who – whatever his actual name – was clearly Jorgensen from *The Searchers* or Ericson from *The Man Who Shot Liberty Valance*; or whatever emblematic Scandinavian immigrant the script required. A mythic world away from the version he had glimpsed by the lakeside near Truckee.

'Vild turkey for dinner,' said the old man. 'Mash. Salat. Cheesecake dessert. You happy vid dat?'

The old man's wife, many years younger than him – the Vera Miles role of course – took Bryn to his 'bungalow', which was a smaller cabin raised well above the spring snow melts, with a single room inside. All the walls, the ceiling, the floor, even the bed and the cupboarding, were pine-planked.

'No key,' she said, with the same taciturn economy as her husband. 'Folks don't lock up here. No electricity neether. Kerosene lamp and early shut-eye.'

When she had gone, he lay down on the bed, on a 'homespun' quilt probably fashioned by the owner's wife herself, and composed himself for sleep. A small bird was chirping in a pine tree nearby, monotonously, like a ticking clock. As his eyes closed, he was vaguely aware of a faint odour of sulphur in the air.

He awoke to the noise of hikers coming through the meadow, shouting to each other in unfamiliar languages. Someone – most likely the elderly owner – was remonstrating with a group of teenagers for feeding the horses. There was a smell of smoke now from a campfire that had been lit below the dining lodge and men and women were gathering around it with cans of beer. He splashed water over his face and shoulders, put on a fresh shirt, and went out to join them.

It was already dinner time. A mix of different-sized tables were set out in the lodge, and the owner directed the guests one by one to their pre-selected places. Bryn found himself with four tanned young Israelis in big hiking boots, shorts and check shirts; and a couple of fit-looking all-American women of around his own age. As promised, the no-choice meal was roast turkey (in family-sized helpings), mashed potatoes and salad. The Israelis stuck with beer; the ladies fancied a Californian 'blush' Zinfandel and, since they were coyly uncertain of how much wine they could manage, Bryn gallantly agreed to share a bottle with them.

In the event, one bottle became two and the evening blossomed.

The Israelis, it emerged, were walking the Pacific Crest Trail from Canada to Mexico, and already more than halfway down it.

'We are a hiking nation,' said one man. 'In Israel we have one six hundred mile national trail but there is nothing like walking a fine distance with nature surrounding you. We have nothing like that in Israel.'

'And you're walking too, are you?' asked another.

'No. But I might go up Lassen Peak tomorrow,' Bryn said.

'Why so?'

'I really don't know. Because it's there?'

The absence of a more structured plan puzzled the hiking nation and they tried hard to understand the reasons for his holiday. Their attention only wandered when he began to enlarge on local pioneer history and the special significance of their present location. As he had discovered in his internet trawl, the meadow had for thousands of years been a sacred summer site for native American tribes, principally the Maidu and the Atsugewi.

'That is so interesting,' offered the (to Bryn) less obviously attractive of the two ladies. 'Thousands of years. Don't you think we should give it back to them?'

'Why?' replied the oldest of the Israelis, vigorously returning to the conversation. 'Because a bit of land has some totemic significance from way back, doesn't mean it has to be theirs for ever.'

'Interesting principle,' said Bryn.

'It's tough on the tribes though,' said the lady.

Over the meal, the dynamic of the group began to settle out. The younger Israelis concentrated upon the second American lady who was doing a skilled job of flirting simultaneously with all three. Bryn guessed she might be old enough for any of them to have been her son, and he admired the coolness with which she strung them along. This was a woman who had been manipulating boys and men since she was a toddler; and was not about to put aside all that accumulated expertise for the sake of some notional age difference. He wondered if the energy the young men were investing in a quite complicated relationship might end tonight in tears, for someone.

Her companion's manner, by contrast, was self-effacing and unsure. To dismiss her, as he had a moment previously, as the *less obviously* attractive was unkind, probably to both of them. She had a figure that a much younger woman would have been proud of, and looked as if she could hike thirty miles a day with ease. Unlike the other, she wore no makeup, and her angular features had a healthy – and attractive – honey-coloured, Californian glow. It was not that she lacked conventional looks: rather that she seemed to have surrendered her sexual confidence to her man-eating friend.

He made some attempt to strike up an acquaintance; but the going was hard. It was difficult to break through her diffidence and discover a viewpoint that did not merely echo his own. He was not helped by the continued presence of the fourth Israeli – whom he took to be inexperienced with the ladies – frequently bursting in on their conversation. After a while, however, these interventions – usually expressing some opinion too forthright even for her – began to have a more useful effect. To escape the young man's attentions, she became markedly warmer towards Bryn. And he, naturally, responded in kind.

'Are you both single ladies?' he asked.

'I am,' she said. 'Nadine is never single.'

'I meant, unmarried.'

'That too.'

She looked deep into her wine glass as though even this tiny *aperçu* had been an intimacy too far.

'Do you ever worry about hiking alone, just two women?'

'We can look after ourselves,' she said, with a faint flash of contention.

'We'll look after you,' said the Israeli. 'Why don't you come with us? We can take you on to Truckee.'

'We're going further than that,' she replied. It was a quiet response, but firm enough to close off discussion.

The rest of the table started to get to their feet. Bryn caught one of them gazing at him and had a momentary sense that they had perhaps met before. But the man turned away and called to his friend.

'Are you coming with us, Eyal?'

'No,' said the unwelcome companion. Then 'Yes'. And, without a goodbye, he joined the little crowd, all jostling excitedly around the departing Nadine, like carp at feeding time.

'Looks like they're going to enjoy themselves,' Bryn said.

'They're going back to our bungalow, I expect,' she replied, and pursed her lips.

'Not your scene?'

'No.'

She toyed with the remains of her cheesecake dessert.

'This is what I don't like about Nadine. She's a very good friend, the only one who walks with me. But we don't have the same attitude at all.'

'She's a free spirit.'

'She's not a Christian.'

It took a moment or two for this to sink in.

'Do you think she's immoral?' he asked.

'Do *you* think she is?'

'I... I... think she's having a good time.'

'Well, I wish she wouldn't.'

And as if she had already gone too far: 'I guess you think I'm some kind of old maid.'

He didn't know how to respond. He should have come back immediately with a tension-dispelling quip, but nothing offered itself. Her humility unmanned him. And he wished he had the wisdom to understand what was going on. If she was so trapped by her principles, why did she choose the scandalous Nadine as her companion? Not, so far as he could tell, in order to convert her.

Somehow they had worked their way into a third bottle of the blush. The other hikers were beginning to disperse to their cabins and a small group, clustered around the campfire outside, were singing boy scout songs. Vera Miles was already setting for breakfast and their table would soon be the last one to be cleared. He was at a loss as to what to do next.

'Shall I take you back to your cabin?'

She shook her head.

It was clear that their jointly shared lodging would be busy for some while yet. And she did not seem in the mood for campfire anthems.

The solution when it came took him by surprise.

'Do you mind if we finish the wine in *your* cabin?' she asked. There was a tiny edge of coolness, even severity, in case he might have misunderstood her.

They took the bottle and two tumblers across the clearing, past the bungalow where the party was in full swing, and along a narrow linking boardwalk to Bryn's own little lodge. He had no easy chairs for them to sit on, so they perched sideways on opposite flanks of the bed.

They managed conversation well enough. He asked her what part of California she came from; Sacramento, she said – not so far away. She enquired if he was a church-goer and he said that, mostly, he was not. He asked if she had ever been to Europe and she said she had been on honeymoon to Paris, which she had not liked very much. No, she was not still married: it had been a student mistake. No children, fortunately. And many years ago.

All this while boisterous outbursts of enjoyment were spilling from the nearby bungalow. It was difficult not to be distracted. Even when the party subsided into silence it was all Bryn could do to rein his imagination back to the four walls of his cabin and prevent it rambling away down the boardwalk. It was a close run thing.

Then... he was never clear how it happened, the wine of course, the usual reasons, but – as he leant across to refill her tumbler – he kissed her cheek. Her face was next to his and it was the natural thing to do. And, to his surprise, she responded immediately and took his mouth to her lips.

61

He juggled one-handedly with the bottle and the glasses, until – without breaking the embrace – he was able to settle them somewhere on the floor below. As they stretched out on the bed he was moved to try what in most languages in the world is called a French kiss though not, as it happens, in France.

And she did not refuse.

The blood and the alcohol began to surge and his hand slipped towards her breast where he was startled to discover that, notwithstanding its firmness, the only supporting fabric was a light cotton blouse; which, almost by reflex, he began to unbutton.

And that was as far as he got.

'No,' she said firmly. 'Not now. We must not do this.'

So they both sat up on the bed and tidied themselves down.

Somewhere in the outer darkness, the silence was broken by a single joyful female cry.

Time passed.

'Oh God,' groaned his companion.

'I'm sorry,' said Bryn reflexively.

She caught him trying to check his watch.

'I can't go back yet.'

'I know,' he said at last. 'But I need to sleep. Why don't you stay here till you're ready to leave.'

He got off the bed and went to get a blanket from the pine cupboard.

Quite without warning she dropped her head into her hands and started, soundlessly, to rock to and fro.

'I've had enough,' she whispered through her fingers. 'I'm done.'

'Look,' he said, half-surprised at the words that emerged. 'If you like, you can kip down on my bed for the night. I'll be somewhere else.'

'Kip?'

'Sleep. And I'll take the floor.'

'Oh,' she said, a picture of uncertainty.

'It's not a problem. Would you mind if I had the hand-sewn quilt though?'

'Homespun,' she corrected, and handed it over.

He left her fully clad and dozing on the bed, and retreated into the tiny enclosed cell tucked away in the corner of the room, for whatever discreet toilet duties he could perform. When he emerged, she was asleep under a couple of blankets.

He turned the kerosene lamp down to a gentle glimmer and settled for the night.

'Are you comfortable there?'

He had pretty well dozed off. It took him a little time to get his bearings.

'Are you comfortable?'

'No,' he replied. Perhaps a little grumpily.

'Why don't you come in here?' she said. '*If* you promise to behave. It's too cold without the quilt.'

Still confused, he dragged the quilt off the floor and flipped it over the blankets. He climbed in on the empty side of the bed, with his eyes already closed.

'Sleep tight,' he said and leant over automatically to kiss her. As if he had been in bed with Marion.

He stopped himself just in time.

He was looking down on her face from a few inches above and she was gazing up at him. In the dim kerosene light, it was impossible to tell what emotions lay in her wide unblinking eyes. No anger or shock at least. He had a fleeting, inconvenient, image of the last time he had shared a bed with Marion, when she had turned aside with some comment about how tired she was; away to that foreign country of hers. But this woman stayed unmoving and awake, watching him. So he kissed her, again.

She did not respond as before; but neither did she resist. He was careful after the previous experience not to presume too far but somehow, in the natural order of things, his right hand found itself on the back of her thigh and – even as their equivocal, guarded, uncertain, enigmatic kiss continued – eased upwards to her hip.

And there, in the absence of any better encouragement, the story might have ended: with another reminder of that eternal truth that a kiss may be all you will get and all you should hope for; followed perhaps, if you are lucky and not too greatly disturbed, by a good night's sleep.

What changed the terms of engagement entirely was the discovery that, while she was still wearing the cotton blouse from which he had earlier been so decisively repelled, there was no other garment now beneath his hand. Nothing whatever.

To a female the signals described here may be perfectly comprehensible. But for Bryn the moment was one of perfect confusion. Here he was, dressed in Levi walking trousers and a sturdy tartan shirt, lying under two blankets and a quilt, with a woman who had earlier made it as clear as it could possibly be that intimacy was unwelcome. But in whose bed he seemed now, in more than one sense, to be an invited guest.

It was not a situation from which he was ever likely to emerge with credit. His partner's unresponsiveness should perhaps have unmanned him. But he had arrived at a tipping point, that onrushing moment when some other power takes over the controls leaving the rider in as little command of his trajectory as, well, a boy on a Coney Island roller coaster. A clear signal could have stopped him in his tracks. But, after what had passed before, that she was acquiescing at all was a brain-spinning revelation. Only once did she say anything. As he began to unzip and unbutton his own garments –

'Be careful,' she said softly. 'You must be careful.'

'I *will*,' he replied.

For a while she lay quietly beneath him; then as the minutes passed – for he was more tired than he had realised – her legs began to tighten around his and her breathing to quicken. Her body lifted upwards and he came to a climax more quickly than he had intended. As he subsided, she took his face in her hands again; and again kissed him.

He fell asleep almost at once.

He awoke once in the middle of the night. They were facing away from each other at opposite extremes of the bed.

And he still did not know her name.

Chapter 7

The community was already stirring when Bryn awoke in the morning. Muted clangs and clatters and lowered voices. Sunrise hikers setting off down the trail to walk in the coolest part of the day. The owners and their little team of vacationing students organising breakfast.

His night-time companion did not move. He guessed by the unevenness of her breathing that she was feigning sleep. She was still turned away on her own far side of the bed, legs drawn up. Probably with eyes wide open. He moved a hand interrogatively towards her and she shrank back like an anemone, and gathered her legs tighter.

He might have hoped for a warmer awakening. He was sorry if she wanted to avoid a difficult start to the day. Though... perhaps... he welcomed it. He eased out of the bed and dressed as quietly as he could.

The sun was low on the horizon and a mist hung in the forest undergrowth. He walked past the cabins towards the meadow. A couple of startled marmots scuttled away. Tubular black lumps of bear scat lay on the ground outside the dining lodge. At the edge of the forest a family of deer drifted along in the shadows, nibbling sporadically at the grass. The meadow was vibrant with birds: American robins, killdeer plovers, black-headed juncos.

The air was blissfully sharp and clear. Lassen Peak filled the horizon and the faintest thread of steam was rising from its summit. There was a flash of light in the dirty sky above, like sun reflected on a passing aircraft. Bryn stayed for fifteen minutes or so waiting and watching. No sound, no company. Himself and the shades of the past. Walls of forest on either side, the nave-like shape of the meadow, the living mountain rising in the east like an altar.

At breakfast he was directed to the same table as before. There was no sign of the Israelis or of Nadine. He filled up a bowl with cornflakes and – since he was on holiday – toasted himself a Strawberry Sensation pop tart. He was still trying to figure out a tidy and grown-up way to eat it when his night companion arrived.

She must have calculated that Bryn had already taken breakfast and that it was now safe for her to come out. She hovered unhappily at the dining room entrance until Vera Miles pointed inexorably towards Bryn's table and she came over, slowly. Bryn offered to get her some cereal. She nodded; and he went off and found her something sugarless, healthy and Californian.

The hikers, in the meantime, were gathering at the other tables. A hubbub of anticipated morning pleasures filled the room. At any moment Nadine might burst in upon them – with delighted questions about how her puritan companion had spent the night. There was nothing Bryn could say to ease the situation. He began to collect up his crockery.

'Where were you this morning?'

Her head was still bowed over her bowl.

A couple of the Israelis settled at the other end of the table.

'I went out to look at the mountain.'

'Why would you want to do that?'

'It's very beautiful first thing.'

'Oh really?'

'And I was wondering how anyone would know if it was about to erupt.'

'It's not about to erupt.'

Her eyes were fixed on the bran flakes and chopped banana. As he contemplated her obscuring veil of uncombed hair, he felt immediately ashamed. He had sleep-walked into a relationship begotten of confusion, pity and opportunity. Oh and lust. He was in a *bad* place.

'Have you heard of Mount St Helens?' she said.

He had heard of Mount St Helens. In 1980 its summit had sheered off in the most serious eruption of modern American history. It was in the same range of mountains as Lassen Peak, three or four hundred miles northwards.

'Oh and by the way,' she said. 'My name's Margaret. I'm a teacher.'

She looked up at him, their first eye contact. Her gaze was sad and hostile and puzzled.

'People knew for months that Mount St Helens was going to erupt. They just couldn't say when. All kinds of signs. Earth tremors. Steam explosions. It doesn't happen out of the blue, you know.'

And that was it. She gathered up her bowl and cutlery and rose from the table.

'My name's Bryn,' he offered to her departing shoulder blades.

He watched her cross the room and tip her detritus into a black plastic container. She was a truly fine looking woman.

A little later, as he was settling his bill, Max the owner asked what he was planning for the day.

'I was thinking of walking up the mountain. Do you think that would be dangerous?'

'Vy should it be dangerous? Great valk.'

'There does seem to be a lot of volcanic activity.'

'Vot the hell d'ya expect? Vy d'ya think it's called a Volcanic Park?'

'Well... you know... tremors, steam, that kind of stuff.'

Max planted the flats of both hands on the table and stared Bryn full in the face. He spoke very carefully and slowly and clearly.

'Ve do not have a problem here. The mountain is a plug volcano. Know vot that means? It means it's *plugged*. With granite. So it can't blow no more. Ve do not need another boy like you putting it around that the place is dangerous. All you monkeys ever achieve is a goddamn threat to our business. Vidout any reason. Do I make myself clear?'

Bryn nodded. The old man seemed satisfied.

'The problem round here is the snows and the spring melts knocking our buildings down. But it's summer now. OK?'

'OK.'

'You best take your sack lunch,' he said, passing over a well stuffed brown bag. 'You'll need it. Enjoy your valk, von't you.'

Bryn drove out and round to the main entrance to the Park. It was the usual dappled mountain highway, intermittently overcrowded by pines, so that the car plunged alternately through dense gloom and blinding sunshine. He approached as near to Lassen Peak as the regulations permitted. It was still early enough to be mostly free of tourists. He reckoned he could see the Pacific Crest Trail, white in the sunshine, gleaming to the east; and a few tiny figures passing up and down it. The mountain was now a few miles ahead, with that wispy plume of steam still rising from its apex. The smell of sulphur was stronger than ever.

He was in a deep despond. Somehow the disaster with Margaret the teacher had stirred up afresh his depression over the break-up with Marion. He felt contrary and irresponsible and possessed by a mighty desire for solitude, and with a mass of pent-up energy to expend. Walking into the mouth of an officially inactive volcano would be the least of his concerns.

He became rapidly bored with the safe main tourist path and diverged to investigate a pool of furiously bubbling mud circled by a fragile white crust and with a sign warning visitors to keep away. A hundred yards further on was a small hole in the ground through which steam was gently venting. This was already

69

becoming a serious climb. He was in an unvegetated no-man's land of sand-coloured rock, way off the official route. The mountain peak, however, was plain enough ahead. It should not be too difficult to reach it.

A mile and perhaps an hour or so later, he was working round a swollen outcrop of granite already warm in the morning sun when he came up behind a vehicle barring the way. It had been neatly parked in the shadow of the rock, and – to all appearances – abandoned.

It was a black Dodge Pickup, new and unblemished. One of its two doors hung open and there was a map spread out on the bench seat inside. The flat back of the truck was covered over with a tarpaulin sheet loosely tied down at the edges.

He made a note of the Oregon number plate – in case it would be useful to the authorities. He laid his hand on the bonnet for any evidence of recent use but – with no sun falling on it – it was as cool as the morning air. He thought he might look under the tarpaulin. There was a small electricity generator there, a rifle – broken open and empty – and a couple of pneumatic drills. In the corner were some items wrapped in a canvas sheet, which gave off an unpleasant, rather chemical smell. He did not investigate further.

There could of course be a perfectly reasonable explanation for the vehicle's presence. The Dodge might after all be an official vehicle, left there while a couple of park employees went off on a morning recce. So, half-expecting to find company on the higher slopes, he continued up the mountain.

Some small, furry creatures, rabbit-shaped but with rat-like ears, scurried away as he climbed. It was harder work now and he began to regret that he had left the tourist-friendlier main track. The rivulets of snow visible from across the valley were building up, deeper and more extensive than he'd expected. On the edge of one of them lay a blacktail deer, quite dead. In the sky above, an eagle – perhaps the same one he'd seen the previous day – was slowly circling.

Some way further on he looked up again to see if the bird was still there. It was in the air, but ahead of him, in fact almost directly over the summit. Then a few hundred yards short of the lip of the crater, he became aware of a second dark brown shape in the snow, as clearly dead as the first one. He had almost passed it, with his attention fixed on the way ahead, when the disturbing thought occurred that the huddled creature this time could not be a deer; nor any other four-footed animal. He turned aside to take a closer look.

It was the body of a middle-aged man.

He was lying on his side with eyes open, unblinkingly fixed on the valley below. Sparely dressed in jeans, scuffed boots and a well-worn sweatshirt, as if ready for a hard day's labour. But he did not look like a labourer. He was lightly built and narrow-shouldered and the domed bald crown of his head rose out of a curtain of long, fine, very white hair.

Bryn debated what he should do.

First, look in the trouser pockets for some form of identification.

Coins, and some small stones. And a handkerchief with the letter S embroidered in a corner.

Now close the man's eyes.

The skin was still warm... perhaps he should check the pulse in the neck – just in case.

As he pushed the hair aside, a small round hole materialised between his two fingers. It was neat and clean, with no blood or discolouration. Precisely at the base of the man's skull.

It took Bryn less than an hour to get back to his car. He intended to report his find to the Visitor Centre near the park entrance but before he had even started the engine, a ranger in a Chrysler Jeep came up the road and drew alongside him. Bryn explained the situation as succinctly as he could and they travelled back in convoy to the small cabin that served as the ranger's office.

As he learned later, there were few homicides in this part of America. The average number of murders in the entire county was less than two a year. The annual report of the Sheriff's Office revealed a far greater concern with boating accidents, livestock crimes and mountain rescues.

So the shocking news threw the young ranger into a spin of confusion. After checking a number of documents for guidance, he called the Park Superintendent. When she shortly arrived, the pair withdrew to the other side of her Jeep and held a lengthy conference call on their handheld radios. After that they climbed into the Superintendent's vehicle and sat together silently for twenty minutes, while Bryn passed the time in the ranger's office pecking unhungrily at his sack lunch and reading brochures about Park wildlife. He discovered that the furry creatures high on the mountain were American Pikas. And was still reading an article about their significance to climate scientists – Pikas, he noted, were unusually sensitive to heat and withdrew to higher elevations as the temperature rose, providing a most useful indicator of global warming trends – when the police turned up in force.

The first arrival was a helicopter, which swept overhead and sped away towards the mountain. Two four-wheel drive SUVs shot straight up the track after it. A third vehicle, a white sedan with gold go-faster stripes down its sides, came to a sliding halt by the Superintendent's truck. Two officers from the Sheriff's Department emerged.

They were both large individuals, with large square moustaches like Thomson and Thompson; dressed in identical smart brown uniforms with dark brown tie, *über-cool* aviator shades, aluminium star on the breast, and a black leather belt laden with guns, ammunition pouches, handcuffs and – by the look of them – lunch. They huddled either side of the Jeep, heads through the side windows in close discussion with the Superintendent and the ranger sitting inside. For quite some time.

Eventually they withdrew their heads from the truck and studied him awhile, like a pair of prairie bison interrupted in mid-graze.

Finally they began to advance upon him, rather slowly and cautiously.

'Good morning, sir,' said the one with the shaven head.

'Hi,' said the grey-haired one.

'I'm Sergeant Whitney Crockett,' said the first.

The other said nothing.

'And this is Officer Shawn Mouser,' said the first. 'I understand you've reported a homicide. Is that correct, sir?'

'Yes,' said Bryn. 'I'd been hiking on the mountain and I came across a body near the peak. It's up near the top beyond the snow line.'

'There's been folks hiking up the trail since daybreak,' the shaven-headed one responded. 'How come no one reported it afore you?'

'Oh well. I didn't go up the trail. I went round the side of the mountain.'

'Why would you want to do that, sir?'

'I was looking at the Pikas.'

'Looking at the what?'

'The fat little rabbits that live at the top.'

'You a naturist or something?'

'I'm a historian. A professor. And,' irresistibly correcting him, 'I think you mean naturalist.'

'Is that a fact.'

The grey-haired one was walking round him in a wide circle, his right hand resting on the bulky automatic weapon strapped to his belt. Bryn at first thought it sensible to hold his own hands away from his body. Then it occurred to him that such a posture might suggest too great a familiarity with police routine, so he slipped them more negligently into his jeans pockets; and prayed that his pockets looked small enough to be above suspicion. He had had a few run-ins over the years with traffic policemen. But never with a lawman with fingers wound round the grip of a pistol.

'OK,' said the shaven-headed one. 'See if I understand this. Whilst everyone else is going up the main track, you and this other guy go some completely different route that nobody uses. And it's the same route for both of you. Why do you think that would be?'

'I've no idea.'

His voice had acquired an almost operatic vibrato.

Pull yourself together.

'I'm a tourist,' said Bryn. 'I'm English, out for a stroll, and I came upon a body. Still warm, by the way. I mean, there was obviously some other person up there as well as me.'

'What did he look like, this other guy?'

'I've no idea. I never saw him.'

'You're both on the same piece of mountain at the same time and you never saw the guy?'

'Maybe he hid.'

The grey-haired one completed his ambulation and took up a position alongside his colleague. He spoke at last in a nasty, lazy, menacing whisper.

'Have you ever tried hiding on that mountain? Sir?'

'Look. I can see where you're going – '

'Is that right?' said the first.

'Can I point out… '

It should be possible to pull *some* thread of rationality from this rapidly unravelling situation.

'… point out that I was the one who reported the crime and that I would hardly have done so were I the perpetrator.'

'As I understand it, sir,' said the first, 'you were intercepted by Ranger Rothmuller as you were leaving the park. In something of a hurry? Do I recall correctly?'

'To report it. In a hurry to report it.'

He struggled to collect his thoughts.

'You're very welcome to check me out. You can search my car. I do not have a weapon. You won't find anything suspicious. I am a responsible citizen reporting a crime.'

'We're checking the mountain, sir. Let's hope there's nothing there neether.'

Of course there'd be plenty. His own footprints in the snow. He had seen no others. And a rifle lying in the back of the black Dodge Pickup. Had he been foolish enough to pick it up? He no longer felt certain of anything. Nor had he any idea what to expect from two country policemen with guns unhitched and – quite clearly – dreams of crime-busting glory buzzing in their heads.

The shaven-headed one pulled a radio phone from his belt and took a call. A long call. A very serious call. Then he buttoned the phone back into his belt, and pulled a folded sheet of paper from a breast pocket and started to read its contents out, carefully and slowly.

'I am going now to read you your rights, sir,' he said. 'You have the right to remain silent. Anything you say can and will be used against you in a court of law. You have the right to speak to an attorney. If you cannot afford an attorney, one will be appointed to you. Do you understand these rights as they have been read to you?'

'Absolutely not,' said Bryn, shrilly.

'I can read you them again if you wish, sir.'

'No.'

The grey-haired one snapped open one of his belt pouches and produced a pair of handcuffs. He invited Bryn to offer his wrists in the time-honoured fashion. That accomplished, Bryn was ducked into the back seat of the sedan, a hand easing his head under the door ceiling. The car gunned and spun and wobbled on the gravel road, till the tyres gripped and it shot away.

After an hour's rapid drive to the west, they arrived at a small town. They drew up outside a stone building embossed with the words *County Jail* and, in smaller letters below, *Sheriff's Department*. A group of townsfolk had gathered on the pavement. Bryn was led through to a desk where his handcuffs were removed and he was required to empty his pockets, remove his belt and jacket, and sign a form listing all his possessions.

A man he took to be the desk sergeant came out of a rest room with a paper cup of coffee.

'Whitney, you son of a gun!' he exclaimed. 'How you doin'?'

'Bright-eyed an' bushy-tailed an' jus' 'bout ready to kick ass,' said Bryn's escort.

With which he was guided, amiably enough, through a door to a corridor of white painted iron-barred gates. One of the gates slid back and he was ushered into the small room beyond it. A bed, a chair, the usual accoutrements, all perfectly clean and tidy. The hum of air conditioning. Dry and cool. And the ambient smell of pee and ammonia.

He was too enervated to brood on his condition. He lay down, pulled a blanket over his body, closed his eyes, and composed himself for sleep.

It was late evening when he woke up.

Someone was talking in Spanish in a nearby cell. A metal tray with a mug and a covered dinner plate lay on the floor beneath him. On the blank corridor wall opposite was a poster with the strap line: 'Serving our Community with P.R.I.D.E.' And under that the words 'Professional Respect Integrity Dedication Equality'. High standards indeed.

He did not at first register the man watching him through the bars. The newcomer was tall and slimly built and wearing a shiny dark suit; but his features were difficult to make out against the strip light on the ceiling behind him.

'You've had a good sleep,' said the man.

It was an urban accent, Los Angeles perhaps or San Francisco.

'I'd like a chat,' he continued. 'Not here though. You wanna eat first?'

He gave the metal gate a gentle push and it rumbled back on its tracking rail.

Bryn studied his tray. Under the plate cover was a taco folded round some congealed mince. But there was also a stack of French fries in a paper cup, which he picked up along with the mug of cold coffee; and followed the man out of the corridor to the sheriff's office. The man waved Bryn towards a comfortable couch, settled himself in an armchair and pulled a small notebook from an inside pocket.

'You are Professor Brynmor Jonathan Williams of the Western University of Utah. From England originally, I see. British passport.'

The in-tray on the sheriff's desk was piled high with Bryn's belongings.

'That's right.'

'Well, Professor, I'm sorry you got mixed up in all this. I'm Detective Henry Slocumb of the SFPD, San Francisco's finest. I'd like to ask you a few questions.'

And he did. About what Bryn was doing in north-eastern California. Whether he had been with friends. What he planned to do next. What he had seen on the mountainside. As the man went along, a number of interesting new features began to emerge.

The police had found evidence of a third party on Lassen Peak that morning. Whoever it was had been at some pains to avoid leaving a trace, but a CSI unit officer had discovered a single footprint in a patch of snow near the abandoned truck. It was possible to judge from the speed of melt and the depth of the print that the individual who had left it was present around the same time as the victim was killed. There were curious characteristics to the footprint also which tended to rule out Bryn. That and one or two other specifics relating to the killing itself meant that he was free to go; but Detective Slocumb would like him to keep in regular touch.

Bryn gave him the name of the motel he intended to use in San Francisco. Slocumb handed over a card with the address of the SFPD station where he was based. He explained, almost apologetically, that he would be keeping Bryn's passport and return e-ticket to Salt Lake City for the time being; but that he expected to be able to release them before Bryn had finished his stay in California.

'That means I'm still under suspicion.'

'No, sir. It means we need to be sure we can get in touch with you. If you hi-tailed it out of 'Frisco without telling us, that would be suspicious. So please don't do that, sir.'

There was one other question.

'Do you know who the victim was?' Bryn asked.

'Sure. A scientist guy. With some business on the mountain. You saw the rock drills and the generator?'

'But why should anyone kill him?'

'Now, that's the sixty four thousand dollar question, isn't it sir?'

And that was all he was prepared to divulge.

Bryn collected his belongings and left. His hire car was parked outside the main entrance, with the keys on the dashboard. He was not due to make his first San Francisco rendezvous with Detective Slocumb for a few days, so he decided to continue with his holiday plans and drive on up to Medford, Oregon. He would complete his tour of the Cascades with a leisurely visit to Crater Lake. The deepest and bluest in the entire Western Hemisphere.

At Medford, he booked into a chain motel by the motorway and went online. Some of what Slocumb had said had begun to prey on his mind. What did he mean by 'curious characteristics to the footprint' and 'other specifics relating to the killing itself'? Was the footprint perhaps an unusually high and thin Cuban heel? Had those specifics anything to do with an unusual bullet? And had not the motel receptionist in Truckee seen his Yosemite breakfast companion driving off to the north, towards Lassen?

He put the name Jack Wilson into the search engine. A fruitless waste of time. It came up with a string of hits about a famous baseball player, several young men on Facebook, a rising Hollywood actor – one and a half million entries altogether. He tried to narrow it down with added-in references to San Francisco, gun clubs, purple hearts, other social network websites, driving offences, anything. As a final act of desperation, he put in all the details he could remember of the man's gun and the ammunition he had purchased in Truckee.

And at last something came up. A local newspaper report about a court case in Nevada where a very similar combination of weapon and bullet had been employed. An Israeli tourist had got into an argument in a casino in Reno. Weapons were drawn and the Israeli killed. The accused, a professional security guard, had made a successful argument of self-defence and was acquitted.

His name was not Jack Wilson, though.

It was Richard Wagner.

Chapter 8

Two days had passed.

Crater Lake, disappointingly smaller than expected, and as uncomplicated as a reservoir, was behind him. A straight fast drive down the Sacramento Valley had taken him back to San Francisco, where he'd found a motel in the low-rent barrio area east of Van Ness Avenue, within easy distance of the opera. Late in the afternoon, he strolled up to the box office to return Marion's tickets for *The Ring of the Nibelungs*.

Lettering at the edges of the frontage identified the building as the 'War Memorial Opera House' and its heavy, Greek colonnaded structure had every appearance of a mausoleum to music. It had been built, in that spirit, to commemorate those who had died in the Great War. The flags of America and the State of California hung limply above in the breathless summer air. Touts stood about on the steps, offering *Ring* tickets at inflated prices. A bearded beggar squatted in the shade and another was rooting through the rubbish in a street bin.

The box office was in a shallow ante-chamber fronting the street. Bryn turned his spare tickets in successfully, with the promise of a tidy sum of money when they had been resold. He was on his way out when he noticed that one of the doors to the gold-coffered main lobby was open. So he slipped through.

A party of British tourists was being shown around by a woman in her early thirties – one of those English public school alumnae who are obligatory for cultural parties travelling abroad. Her group were twenty or thirty years older and probably more than capable in this internet age of organising a simple trip like this for themselves. The point of course was that they did not need to.

Bryn attached himself to them.

He thought the lady good value. She was enthusiastic about Wagner and his *Ring* Cycle, and was animatedly describing aspects of the production her party was shortly to see; though he noticed that not all her clients, notwithstanding the financial investment involved, were more than loosely familiar with the operas. One woman standing beside him even appeared to be expecting Gandalf instead of Wotan and a chorus of Hobbits rather than Nibelungs.

The guide was half-way through a persuasive feminist analysis of Wagner's work (demonstrating that it was always the male characters who got it wrong and the women who had to save the situation) when she stopped speaking and asked Bryn if she knew him.

'No,' he said. 'I do not believe I have had that privilege.'

'I see you are from England,' she said, 'but not, I think, a part of this tour.'

He explained that, while that was true, they were attending the same performances and he'd been unable to resist listening in on her erudite comments. She was better informed – forgive him, but he was bound to say this – than most people he had met at Bayreuth at the *festspiel* a few weeks past.

After that, unsurprisingly, he became a welcome addition to the group. They would shortly be going to dinner at a nearby restaurant and would he care to come along? He'd be delighted. One member, a clerical-looking gentleman in his fifties, balding with grey-blonde collar-length hair, was impressed by Bryn's track record and anxious to learn more about Wagner. Bryn was happy to oblige, and they sat together at table.

David Burton – and it took Bryn a while to realise this – was not what his manner suggested. He was one of those quite dangerous men who like to conceal their intelligence beneath a cloak of diffidence. It was easy to overlook the subtle counter-indicators – the quiet watchfulness, for example – and Bryn, that evening, was not in the mood for analysis. The other man's interest drew him forward all too willingly on the warm tide of his own self-indulgence. The name of the game was charm. Burton was engaging, uncritical, and attentive; and irresistible. It was only when Bryn got back to his motel that night that a perception of the other's shrewdness, and of his own absurdity, began to gather in his mind, like bitter lees settling in a bottle of wine.

In particular, he realised that once again he had talked far too much about himself and his life, acquaintances and interests; and learned almost nothing in return. This was chiefly because, while Burton had asked many questions about him, he – somehow – had never got round to any kind of reciprocal interrogation.

For example, he did not know what Burton did for a living or how he spent most of his leisure time. Burton knew what Bryn did. He had told him about Bayreuth – boasted would be more accurate – and been indulged with a string of questions about the people he had met, the restaurants he had been to. And he had not even asked Burton if he'd been to Glyndebourne.

Drink as usual may have had something to do with it. At one point, with glass in hand, Bryn had expatiated to the table at large about modern cinema. One of his new friends sitting opposite challenged his view that film was the great twentieth century art form. How could it possibly compare with opera?

'Well now,' Bryn said. 'There could be no more apt comparison. It is no coincidence that, as opera began to lose its mass appeal early in the last century – in Italy as in other countries – so cinema was rising. Because cinema was, and remains, the new opera. It was always, from the beginning – *like* opera – theatre set to music. Even in the silent days they had orchestras accompanying the action. As sound came in, composers – opera people like Korngold or Max Steiner – filled the soundtrack with their music. And the stories were always operatic. Melodramas, dying heroines, murders, heroes. Then there's the way films were constructed. Think of those swooping arias – Bette Davis, Marlon Brando, Meryl Streep. The more operatic the role, the more likely the star to be acclaimed as a diva and win the Oscars. Wagner's Leitmotifs? Films are full of them. Lara's theme, Tara's theme. And so on. And so on. Don't tell me you can't compare cinema with opera.'

The memory of that particular *coloratura aria* still lingered mortifyingly next morning. That and a vaguer sense of all-round hubristic arrogance. A late-night exchange with Burton returned to haunt him even as he was having breakfast.

'All art aspires to the condition of music,' he had opined.

'Is that original?' asked one of the older ladies.

'Sadly not,' he said. 'Walter Pater.'

'And does that gentleman record what all music aspires to?' asked Burton mildly. 'Perhaps you have an aphorism for us of your own?'

'I do,' Bryn had said, with relish. 'All music aspires to the condition of love. Sometimes gentle, sometimes furious. And very often, to the act of sexual love itself. The climax – that explosive moment of resolution and physical release – is after all fundamental to music.'

'How fortunate in that case it is so rarely achieved,' observed Burton, after a lengthy pause.

It was around this juncture that the party broke up, leaving Bryn to make his way back alone to his motel room. Though – even now – he was inclined to think it quite an apt maxim...

He'd had rather a disturbed night. Rackety air conditioning is endemic in cheap American hotels and this was no exception. Had he not been overwhelmed by alcohol and exhaustion, he might not have slept much at all. Before he left in the morning, he made a polite, ritual complaint about the noise. He did not expect anything to be done but felt at least a duty to guests yet to come to register some form of protest.

Today was the first opera of the Great Cycle: *The Rhinegold*. In which a swarthy dwarf called Alberich steals the eponymous mineral and transforms it into a ring which gives its possessor universal power; loses it to his enemy; and embarks upon a quest to retrieve it which will end in terminal destruction. Bryn was familiar with the more elevated expositions, involving gods and goddesses, brave heroes and the rise of mankind. But that seemed to him the essence of it.

His tickets for the four operas – *The Rhinegold*, *The Valkyrie*, *Siegfried* and *The Twilight of the Gods* – were in the rear balcony, the second cheapest available (though still a serious investment). His new friends from England were in the orchestra stalls at an eye-watering four-figure expenditure for the seats alone – and not counting the cost of their flights, hotels, dinners and lady guide. He could just see them from his eyrie.

The audience divided into two parts, not entirely based on ticket price. One part – much the smaller – sought to emulate the standards of Bayreuth, with dinner jackets and gowns. Many of these sat in the stalls. But most were in the phenomenally expensive boxes ranged in eighteenth century fashion round the three sides of the auditorium, from which they emerged like rabbits from their gilded hutches, to take padded armchair seats at the circle rail; and to which they scuttled back for their interval champagne, soft shell crabs and socialising. A few similarly well-dressed souls filtered up as high as Bryn's humble balcony. He admired their determination to make such an event of their visit.

And then there were the others: the majority. Some were in suits but many wore jeans or chinos, even – in this hot weather – shorts, with the women correspondingly equipped. Nor was their habitat by any means confined to the cheaper seats. A number of very casually dressed patrons could be seen wandering around at stalls level. Casually dressed, that is to say, by Chanel and Jimmy Choo. Though some distance short, he felt, of the elegance of the *festspielhaus*. Or, for that matter, Glyndebourne.

But you could hardly fail to be impressed by the auditorium. Gold had always been the default pigment of opera houses, albeit mediated generally by less strident colours. In San Francisco, however, it was gold and nothing but gold: gold walls, curtains, proscenium, statues and bas-reliefs, pillars, balconies and ceiling. As a statement of municipal self-confidence it could not have been clearer; and wholly befitting a city created by the '49 Gold Rush. So appropriate also for this evening's performance.

The Rhinegold was the shortest of the four operas of *The Ring*. The production was an example of what Germans call *Regietheater,* in which the subtext of the work is mined by the director to produce an original piece of art not necessarily comprehensible to its audience. The inspiration on this occasion – or so Bryn concluded – was the history of America itself, with the thieving dwarf a Gold Rush forty-niner (Black Al Berwick) who stumbles upon the mother lode of his career and makes off with it to a life of limitless riches and power. The Gods – his competitors – refugees from the pages of F Scott Fitzgerald – were a troupe of effete, blazered, champagne-swilling party-goers led by a ruthless tycoon in riding boots and duster coat with a tame politician in tow – otherwise Wotan, and his scheming advisor, Loge.

Two and a half hours later, after the triumphant Gods had finally climbed their rainbow to Valhalla, the audience began to leave the theatre. Van Ness Avenue was as full of waiting limousines as Los Angeles on Academy Awards night. Bryn hung around in case the English tour, with its attractive girl guide leader, had not already departed.

He heard a familiar, gravelly voice behind him and an elderly male with steel grey hair and large, rimless glasses passed through the crowd and eased into a waiting black stretch limousine. The man looked up and caught his eye.

'Mr Strange! What a coincidence!' he began.

The expression on the other's face was as dead as stone. Even as Bryn advanced, he was closing the rear door and the car pulling away. A different model from last time but with the same number plate: US PATRIOT.

The traffic was beginning to clear. Across the road a small sedan with tinted windows was parked half on the pavement, half on the roadway. A short man in a baseball cap was watching them from beyond it. Bryn tried to return his gaze but immediately he ducked into the car, did a noisy U-turn in the middle of the highway and shot off after Strange's limousine.

David Burton was standing beside him.

'I think you could do with a drink,' he said, with a smile.

Bryn wondered if Burton had been a witness to his embarrassment. But he was glad at least to have a chance to redeem himself from the previous night's excesses. They found a bar nearby – they had to step over some sleeping pavement derelicts to get into it – and this time Bryn made a conscientious effort to induce Burton to talk about himself.

He was a bachelor, though if he was gay he gave little evidence of it – aside from a characteristic interest in grand opera, and a tendency to clutch Bryn's lapel to make a point. He explained – and Bryn had to press him quite hard for this information – that he was the chief executive of a luxury goods mail order company, run from offices in South London. Overseas travel, with some theatre on the side if he could manage it, was part of his business. He produced a card: E. David Burton, Ziggurat Exports; and a phone number, which – as they parted – he urged Bryn to call next time he was in London. Bryn promised to do so.

Back at the motel, the helpful receptionist dug out a charger which matched Bryn's battery-dead iPhone and he left it plugged in through the night. He wanted to check the photographs he'd taken a few weeks before in Bayreuth, and test a presentiment that they might offer some clue to help him understand the curious events that had happened to him since.

He waited until after breakfast.

It was a great disappointment. Every photograph, in fact all the iPhone's data, had been wiped. Even his address book had gone. He rang through on the motel telephone and talked to a troubleshooting Apple adviser who tried in vain to restore the factory settings. In the end, the helpline recommended that Bryn cut his losses and acquire a new appliance.

Instead he went on the laptop in the motel lobby. For an hour, under the tolerant eye of the receptionist, he Googled his way round the internet searching for an online fix. Twenty websites and any number of anoraks later, he had still not cracked it.

And then it came to him with perfect simplicity. All he had to do was hack into Marion's emails.

It took him a further two seconds to square his conscience. After which he went directly to her service provider's website and put in her password, knowing she would not have changed it since he'd originally set the system up for her. One effect of his irregular entry was the instant opening of her latest private message; he hoped she wouldn't conclude from this – correctly – that he was the one who had hacked it into it. The message was a brief one-liner from one of Marion's girlfriends: a man's name, Harlan J Hackett. He moved on quickly. It meant nothing to him.

He scoured back through her in-tray for emails he had sent to her. Nothing again. At which point he remembered that Marion never emptied her Delete file.

And there it sat: her promise of 'a much longer letter very soon' with his brief reply. And three attached photographs.

He opened them up. The first was of two beautifully dressed Arabs passing through the *festspielhaus* crowds. Followed by the view from Hitler's balcony. The third was the last picture Bryn had taken – of the SS chauffeur confronting him from the balcony door.

He posted it to a greetings card website so that he could manipulate the image until the background to the chauffeur filled the frame. He wound up the brightness and the contrast to their maximum.

And there the man was. Blurred and a little pixillated. But unmistakable.

In the shadows of the pink sitting room behind the balcony stood a short, stocky individual in an open neck shirt and sunglasses. Impossible to tell whether he was wearing high heeled

Cuban boots or not. But that it was the same person was beyond doubt. Jack Wilson, or whatever he called himself. And enough evidence, surely, to take to the police. Detective Slocumb's card was still in Bryn's pocket. A quick search on mapquest.com revealed that his station was a short drive away.

Slocumb came out to see him at the reception desk.

'Professor Williams! Didn't expect to see you so soon. Should have told you a phone call would do.'

Bryn explained how anxious he was to catch up on further developments. Was he – for instance – off the suspects list yet?

Slocumb laughed.

'Sure thing. Come on through to the interview room. And have a cup of coffee. Happy to tell you 'bout it.'

And he had some interesting news. The dead man on Lassen Peak was a scientist called Sidney Stratton. A nuclear scientist no less. They had done an autopsy on his body and discovered that he was desperately ill. He had some time recently suffered a critical – indeed terminal – irradiation and would probably have known that he had a couple of weeks to live. Investigations were under way at his government laboratory to find out whether he might have irradiated himself by accident or even intentionally. What was especially interesting was that he had never reported it.

'Have his employers shed any light on what he was doing on the mountain?' Bryn asked.

'None at all,' said Detective Slocumb. 'But we're talking about the federal government here. Whatever they know I don't think they're gonna share it. They clammed up as soon as they heard he was up there with mining equipment.'

'Are you sure that's what it was?'

Slocumb made no reply. Bryn sensed some discontent with the way his investigation had developed. He might welcome an opportunity to talk it through.

'And the murderer? I take it it's still a homicide even if the murderer only shortened the poor man's life by a week or so.'

'We're gathering information,' said Slocumb. 'It could be the other guy was known to Stratton. Or that, if he wasn't, Stratton had good reason to fear him. He may even have taken precautions.'

'The rifle in Stratton's truck?'

'That's right.'

'So how exactly was he killed?'

'Oh, very professionally, Professor. The killer intercepted him – most likely tracked him up the mountain – and came up behind and shot him at point-blank range. Stratton may never have seen him. Like dying in your sleep.'

'How do you know this?'

'Well, sir. Because of the burn marks – not visible to the naked eye but they showed up in forensic. That means a silencer barrel was held right up against Stratton's head.'

'No lead residue?'

Slocumb looked at him narrowly.

'No, Professor, there was no lead residue.'

'So it was a lead-free bullet.'

'That is obvious.'

Bryn could feel the adrenalin rising.

'Does that mean forensics know the gun too?' he asked, eagerly. 'Let me guess. Was it a Smith and Wesson Bodyguard?'

Slocumb stood up and gazed out of the window. When he turned back, his expression was noticeably harder and less friendly than before. It was evident that Bryn had overplayed his hand.

'What exactly are you trying to tell me, sir?'

'I think I know the man you want.'

'Do you really? How 'bout that.'

The hostility was now palpable.

With some diffidence, Bryn explained about Jack Wilson, about his conversation with the bait shop owner and about the cowboy boots with their peculiar high heels.

He waited for a reaction but Slocumb just stared at him.

'Didn't you say there was a footprint in the snow?' Bryn reminded him.

The other nodded.

He explained about his acquaintance with Udell Strange and the connection with Wilson; and how Strange and Wilson might both be in San Francisco at this moment.

'It should be easy to locate Mr Strange,' he said. 'He could lead you to Wilson or whatever the killer's real name is. Probably an alias.'

'Do you know what I think, Professor?' said Slocumb at last. 'I think you've done 'bout enough for us. I think from here on you might like to leave the rest of the policing to the SFPD.'

'San Francisco's finest.'

'That's right,' he said.

Bryn reflected on how very sensitive professional people could be when a layman encroached upon their area of expertise. It was a lesson well learned in his university career. Even so: he was disappointed to find such a precious streak in a policeman. He had expected something tougher.

Slocumb had made it clear that he had no further interest in whatever Bryn might have to tell him. He watched while Bryn climbed into his car and drove away. The last he saw of him, Slocumb was standing outside the entrance to his station, taking a call on a mobile phone.

He drove back to the motel, complained ineffectually again about the air-conditioning, and sat in his noisy room to review the draft letter he had finally managed to write out in longhand to Marion.

It was no more likely to find favour with her than any of his previous attempts. But he had settled for a pragmatically defensive mode. He felt now that he needed to show that he was the reluctant party. That whatever she was doing was not of his choice or a consequence of his actions. He hoped also that it would not come to a legal fight. It seemed sensible to occupy whatever high ground was left.

He was pleased with what he had achieved. Reasonably and modestly expressed, hurt but not resentful, dignified and affectionate. And not too self-righteous. It might make a difference.

The friendly receptionist was on duty again so he took it to the motel computer and sent it off as an email.

'Might have a new room for you, señor,' said the receptionist encouragingly. 'A leettle bit better than the last.'

'Couldn't be worse,' said Bryn.

That evening was the second instalment of the Cycle: *Die Walküre. The Valkyrie*. The production had now moved forward in American history from *The Great Gatsby* to the 1950s. Valhalla was a General Motors' boardroom overlooking a sky-scrapered metropolis, and the King of the Gods its lounge-suited chief executive. The *Valkyrie* war-maidens had become the US marines on exercise. Meantime the fleeing human lovers, Sieglinde and Siegmund, were taking refuge in a trash-strewn automobile graveyard beneath a freeway flyover. The production had already modulated into the familiar trope of *The Ring* as a story of capitalist greed – with global warming and urban desolation thrown in for good measure. Entertaining to watch but bewildering for anyone unfamiliar with the original. Bryn was again too late for his English friends but – near midnight and after more than five hours in the Opera House – he was dog-tired and ready for bed anyway.

There was a night man on reception. When he gave Bryn his key, he realised that it was for a new room.

'Say thanks to Juan-Carlos for me,' he said.

'OK?' the night man replied, with a shrug of the shoulders.

'But has my bag been moved?'

'OK?'

An interpreter might have been an advantage.

He made his long way down two or three corridors to a door round the far back of the motel. What the room lacked in convenience, it made up for in tranquillity: the air-conditioning was a faint and sleep-inducing background hum. Bryn's bag had been helpfully placed on the Queen-sized bed; and he dropped down alongside it without bothering to undress.

He was deeply asleep when the bomb went off.

In the peculiar way of dreams, he had imagined himself on the very lip of Lassen Peak, gazing down into its volcanic bowl. A single blue flame danced above his head and the air smelled sweet and pure and not at all of sulphur. At the bottom of the bowl lay a collection of small dead animals: marmots, birds, rat-like rabbits. As he watched, he heard a distant crack, deep down within the mountain, and a mighty rushing, rumbling commotion. Pieces of rock and ice flew past him. The centre of the bowl began to rise and crack like an egg hatching. There was a terrible, thunderous roar as the whole mountain lifted upwards.

All this must have passed in a micro-second of dreaming because he awoke to the full blast of the explosion. Followed by a moment of absolute silence, and a rising tide of screams and shouting. A fire alarm burst violently into life. People started running down the corridors.

He rushed out, grateful that he was fully clad, and followed some men and women in shorts and towelling down the corridor and out to the front of the building. Flames were bursting from a shattered room near the entrance to the hotel. He recognised at once that it was his room. Or rather: the room that until a few hours previously had been his.

There was no point in hanging around. He retraced his steps and gathered up his bag and ran to find his car. Too late to pay the bill: they had his credit card details in some safely remote database anyway. Too late to retrieve his passport and tickets from the police. Too late to bother about the rest of the *Ring* Cycle. The only imperative was to get the hell out of there. It was not that he was scared. He was terrified.

As he accelerated up the alleyway from the motel's underground car park, he could hear the ear-splitting scream of incoming San Francisco City fire engines. Two police cars were already drawing up, their sirens howling like dogs in desperate misery. *Nessun dorma* indeed.

His one thought was to drive north again. Utah and the south was out of the question. That was where they – whoever they were – would expect him to go. The north was where wilderness and open spaces lay, and if necessary the safety of the border.

He feinted south towards the airport and found an ATM where he withdrew as much cash as his cards allowed. Then he turned a hundred and eighty degrees and took off up Route 101 on and on and on into the dawn. Through Manchester and Rockport, Eureka, Crescent City and Florence to Route 5 and across towards the northern Cascade mountains.

He had never claimed to be a brave person. If his reaction to the explosion was excessive, so be it. He was in too febrile a state of mind. He was in no doubt that an attempt had been made on his life, he did not know by whom or for what reason. But he had also recently witnessed a murder, been in the company of the suspected gunman, even been pursued by him to San Francisco.

In other circumstances, the wisest course might well have been to drive straight to a city police station and throw himself on the protection of the authorities. But his last meeting with Slocumb had left him disturbed and uncertain. It was – as likely as not – the purest paranoia. But he needed to gather his wits and think.

He had arrived in Washington State, beyond which lay Canada. The Canadians were reputedly less protective of their border than the Americans and he might be able to slip across and make for the British consulate in Vancouver. A story about a lost passport should do it. He could fly straight back to London. After all, there was nothing any longer to detain him here.

He had driven virtually non-stop since leaving San Francisco. Seven or eight hundred miles in eleven hours. It was mid afternoon but he needed to stretch his legs and get a night's sleep. He was not far from Mount Rainier National Park. Perhaps there was lodging there.

The Park's Paradise Inn was a long, dormered, cedar log building standing back from the road. Everything about it looked full – the car parks, the lobby, even the mountain ridges to the east were packed with hiking groups queuing down the tracks. He'd expected at best a slim chance of accommodation; but a receptionist found a just cancelled 'historic' lodge room – very rustic with no en suite shower or toilet, but cheap. Exactly what was needed. He declined the credit card machine and paid, in advance, in cash.

All he had eaten since early morning was half a bag of some huge red *rainier* cherries bought by the roadside a hundred miles earlier. He stocked up at the Inn takeaway with a beefburger and a Budweiser and set off up the mountain.

The higher he climbed the thinner the crowds became. The well marked trails at the lower levels were as busy as Piccadilly Circus – or as Yosemite – but few walkers strayed beyond them, as if there were bylaws against adventure. He struck off on his own, up paths scarcely wide enough for mountain goats, past yellow potentilla bushes and through thickets of huckleberry. The air was colder and damper than it had been in California. It felt a lot closer to home.

He passed an occasional hiker, usually a young man and woman travelling together. He could hear one couple approaching from a quarter of a mile away, shaking a necklace of bear bells every few steps – to frighten off hungry grizzlies, no doubt. He had not progressed far beyond them when he saw, away to the left and deep amongst the huckleberry bushes, not the Great Predator he'd half hoped for, but a smaller, slimmer, less dangerous Black Bear. He held his breath and stood as silently as he could, watching it gorge on the blue-black berries; until it must have heard him, and dropped to all fours and scuttled away.

He came to a natural rock bench beside the path, overlooking a glacier tucked like a curling tongue into the opposing mountainside. He could make out the tiny Lowry figures of a school of student skiers, strung out across it in Indian file, silhouetted against the dirty white ice. At so great a distance they barely seemed to move at all.

A bleached disk of sun was struggling to break through the cloud cover. It was a good moment to break open the Budweiser, the burger, and the remains of the cherries. For a while, with only the faraway matchstick figures for company, he was entirely alone. Relaxed and able to turn his thoughts to the wild events of the last few days.

And formulate some kind of plan.

So it was an irritation to spot, away to the right where the path disappeared around the northern crest of the mountain, his first pair of hikers since the bear bell shakers. He watched them work their way downwards. They were both carrying frame backpacks, both goggled against the snow, with woollen skullcaps crammed down over their heads: a middle-aged man and a slim, athletic-looking woman, noticeably more agile than her partner.

He turned away as they drew nearer, not wishing to encourage unnecessary socialisation. The woman passed behind along the path. But the man stopped. He sat rudely alongside him on the rock; and unloosed the muffler around his throat.

'So we meet again, Professor Williams,' he drawled.

Chapter 9

Marcus.

Why should he have been surprised?

As long as he had known him, periods of years without contact had been separated by unexpected encounters – on the street, in a restaurant, at the opera. Very often in some foreign country. He'd even once accused his cousin of following him around. So meeting now on a ridge high in the northern Cascade Mountains, in the lee of Mount Rainier, six thousand miles distant from their last conjunction in a gentleman's club in London should – perhaps – have been less of a shock than it was.

But at first all he could do was stare while his cousin drew a box of Japanese sushi and a tin of chocolate brownies from his backpack, and laid both fastidiously on the rock between them. He squeezed a tiny drop of soy sauce onto a California roll.

'Marcus?' said Bryn finally.

'Have one,' said his cousin, and offered the box. 'If you insist on leaving your mouth open, you might as well pop something into it.'

'This is too much, you know.'

'Of all the bars, in all the towns, in all the world… which reminds me.'

Without bothering to turn around, he held out his hand and his female companion placed a bottle in it. Thirty Year Old Douglas Laing, already a third empty. Not a distillation frequently found in duty free.

'A couple of tumblers, Agnete. Three if you're joining us.'

And then Bryn's brain really began to swim – queasy and light-headed as if it was filling with air. He could never have prepared himself for this. The blonde hair buried within a red and white beanie, a muffler covering the lower half of her face. The cool mist-blue eyes exactly as he remembered. She handed him a glass – typical of Marcus not to bring plastic – with the same appraising basilisk gaze that had so riveted him in Bayreuth. He made an uncoordinated attempt to scramble to his feet, slipped on the rock, and sat down again.

'You know each other?' he enquired fatuously.

'*Ja*,' she replied.

'Have you been working together for a long time?'

'*Nej*.'

She settled down on the other side of the rock. Tumblers, scotch, sushi and soy passed to and fro across him.

The sushi was fishing-boat fresh, a bouquet of disparate flavours. He could not guess how his cousin had come by it or what new wonder he might next produce from his travel pack. With Marcus, the original jack-in-a-box, the unpredictable was only to be expected. The one thing he knew for sure was that this entire visitation had been contrived for maximum theatrical effect, and for *his* benefit.

Agnete leaned across and gathered in a couple of crab sticks. She braced herself for a second against his body and his nostrils caught a whisper of some Asian perfume. He was now closer to her on this silent Pacific peak than he had ever been in Bayreuth.

Marcus was watching him.

'Agnete's my assistant,' he said. 'You'll find she's very able.'

She rose to her feet and took herself and two handfuls of sashimi away to an adjacent rock.

Marcus slopped some whisky into Bryn's glass.

'Sorry about the surprise,' he murmured, between pieces of eel. 'I needed to talk to you, old boy. You are such a difficult chap to keep up with. Oh, but do try the Ikura. Salmon Caviar. Delicious. Or the Saba,' he said, pointing at a morsel of shiny, caramel-coloured meat wrapped in a strip of mackerel skin. 'First things first.'

There was no point in pressing him. And Bryn was beginning to find his presence, especially after the events of the last twenty-four hours, vaguely comforting. There would be a rational explanation for this bizarre meeting eventually; in Marcus's own good time.

And so they sat and ate and drank. Bryn's mind was less preoccupied by anything Marcus might be about to reveal, than by Agnete's tangible proximity. The memory of that tiny hint of perfume persisted like a sea mist, precluding other thought – until the shape of something less welcome began to form: a certainty that there could be no good explanation for her presence here with Marcus.

When Marcus started to talk, it was in a conciliatory – even anxious – tone of voice, one with which Bryn was unfamiliar. He'd always tried, as a general rule, not to take his cousin too seriously. What Marcus did for a living hardly bothered him. It would not have occurred to him, for example, that Marcus – whose role in MI6 he had neither understood nor attempted to understand – might ever wish to involve him in his affairs. So the further Marcus's narrative progressed, the more alarmed Bryn became.

First, he apologised. Bryn was unaccustomed to apologies from Marcus. It was not the kind of thing he did. What was even more disquieting was the evident genuineness of his regret.

'I have to be honest with you, old boy. Certain things have happened which should not have happened. You have become involved and I am extremely sorry. My excuse is that I do not think we could have anticipated how things would escalate. I'm afraid we're going to need your help to resolve a quite serious situation.'

He paused – no doubt, to let his words sink in. It gave Bryn a chance to gather his wits. He was not sure he understood much of Marcus's characteristically opaque pronouncement. Except perhaps for one thing –

'I do not think so, Marcus. Whatever this is, it is not for me,' he said. Firmly, he thought.

'Of course. That's understandable,' his cousin replied.

'You should also know that the reason I am here,' continued Bryn, 'and not in San Francisco or Salt Lake City, is because I am getting out of this country and going home. Tomorrow.'

Agnete was standing on her rock watching the track to the north. She swivelled left to check southwards.

'Let me tell you a story,' said Marcus.

If Bryn had had any sense he would have stopped him there. But this was not the brash, confident Marcus he thought he knew. He was intrigued. And the sushi was excellent, Agnete Valkyrie-like on guard, the setting spell-binding.

'This,' said Marcus, waving a hand towards the rugged panorama of mountains, valleys and glaciers, 'this is America. In reality nothing changes here. Not the landscape, nor its government. In the rest of the world, new countries form, regimes move on, old politics are overthrown by the new. But in America the only template is an ancient constitution unaltered since the eighteenth century. Politically this was always the most conservative nation on the globe. Its presidents have never moved more than a few degrees from the centre, a few slightly to the left, a few more to the right, but never, ever, into political territory that a European might recognise as radical. Until now.'

'Is it so radical?' said Bryn.

'It is radical from the perspective of the people who matter. The people who really run this country, always have done, always will.'

'You make them sound like feudal barons.'

Marcus shrugged his shoulders.

'We have a Madame President now who plans to raise taxes from the rich to fund social adventures. I ask you: a Universal Health Service. She even proposes to impose political balance on the media. The next project will be to emasculate the banks by prohibiting them from using people's private accounts to play the markets. It will not do.'

'I don't see why not.'

'I'll tell you why not, cousin. Because your feudal barons will do anything to destroy her. I believe we are entering the most dangerous period I have known since I took on responsibility for American affairs.'

'And that's why you've come to see me?'

He laughed out loud. He could not prevent himself.

He and his cousin lived in two different worlds. Marcus and his heady sphere of global politics, *Times* leaders and absence of self-doubt. Bryn a little closer to the earth – in his view at least. Where decisions were made by normal ground-dwelling people. Two parallel realities, with quite distinct ways of dealing with problems and making decisions. A person could no more inhabit both than coexist with anti-matter.

Marcus forced a thin smile.

'Let me tell you a story,' he said, for the second time.

And that, after one further brief preamble, was what he did. It was worse than anything Bryn had feared.

'Normally we leave the Americans to sort out their problems for themselves,' said Marcus. 'A watching brief. At most a recalibration on the margins, to ensure they make the right choices. That's what I do. Only if the problem threatens to get out of control, would we intervene unilaterally. We've never done that in my time. Until, as I say, now.'

He took a slug of the Laing and passed it over.

'At the epicentre of this problem is someone you know: a man called Udell Strange. He is an easy person to overlook. He keeps a low public profile and tends not to appear in the Forbes magazine wealthy lists. But Udell Strange nonetheless is one of the half dozen or so richest men in America. With interests in many things but chiefly banking and currency speculation. And arms dealing.

'Mr Strange is now beyond wealth. Though not a politician himself, he controls politicians. Power is what energises him. For example, he is currently bank-rolling the campaign to destabilise the Madame President. Stirring up trouble in Congress. Creating a run on the dollar. Even though the President's party has a majority in both Houses, money still buys support and Strange has plenty of both.'

'Wouldn't scaring up a financial crisis undermine his own position?'

'Not Strange, nor his allies. Their main fortunes have long since been expatriated into other currencies and holdings, property in Hong Kong, rare metals, first growth French wines. High-end commodities whose value rises as fast as everything else goes down – because their availability cannot be increased and our new-rich Chinese and Indian friends need *something* to spend their disposable gazillions on.

'But you should be very concerned about Strange,' he added. 'He and his like-minded friends are what I believe you would call neo-conservatives.'

Bryn relished the irony. How unbearable for Marcus to discover himself on the same side of the political divide as his cousin. And what a culture shock, given MI6's well-known conservative perspective, if the organisation was now finding Strange's activities actually disagreeable.

'The problem,' Marcus continued, as if reading Bryn's thoughts, 'is that we believe – in order to achieve destabilisation of the President – Strange is looking to engineer international as well as domestic crises. And that affects our interests directly. Specifically, we believe he and his friends are promoting a new war in the Middle East. The usual combatants but more dangerously armed than before. This is a threat to the current President of the USA because, of all the areas in which she lacks credibility, it is in the role of commander-in-chief in a global crisis that – as a woman – she is most vulnerable. It is no accident that, of the last twelve Presidents, two alone did not do military service.'

The cloud cover had begun to disperse. On the slope beyond the glacier, a few pockets of water and ice twinkled in the emerging sunlight. Bryn was happy for Marcus to continue with his dissertation. In time, though, he would come to the point where he would ask him to do something. And would be disappointed. His mind was set.

'And now I expect you want to know what really happened in Bayreuth,' Marcus continued.

'It's the reason I'm still here.'

Agnete had taken off her cap and shaken out her hair. She raised her face to the sky to enjoy the warming rays. Her eyes were closed.

Marcus was still talking.

'The Service had been tracking Strange's arms dealing and – when I saw your name on the audience list for a Bayreuth performance he was due to attend – it was too good an opportunity to miss. We put Agnete in place. Remarkable how little difficulty she had making contact with you.'

Bryn could almost hear his lip curl. But if Marcus had intended some tasteless follow-up, he evidently thought better of it.

'It was her job,' he continued seamlessly, 'to effect a meeting between you and Strange and, if necessary, oil the wheels till you were both as chummy as could be. In the event, she did not have to do a great deal: I would say you and Strange got on like a house on fire. What a lot you must have in common.'

'He was interested in what I had to say.'

'I'm sure. At first, some basic level of acquaintance was all I dared expect. Sufficient for you to be able to recognise him should the need arise in the future. The restaurant invitation therefore was a complete bonus.'

Tolerant bemusement had finally given way to indignation. This was *in*tolerable.

'Marcus,' Bryn interrupted. 'Stop right there. You know what I do. I teach. I am not an employee of MI6, or some kind of, God knows, gun for hire. Being able to recognise one of your targets has absolutely *less* than nothing to do with me.'

'Right. Quite right,' said Marcus.

He paused.

And carried on pretty well as if Bryn had said nothing at all.

'You see, this is what we call serendipity. In my business, you are always looking out for an opportunity. You invest a fair amount of energy in things that may or may not be useful later. We were frankly struggling to find a way of getting alongside Strange. And you were a Godsend.'

'No, Marcus. No.'

Marcus swilled the whisky around his mouth.

'Now try and look at it from my point of view, Bryn,' he drawled silkily. 'I know you to be a resilient and self-reliant individual. One who, well, currently has time on his hands. And, crucially, who is what we call a "cleanskin". In my business, everyone knows everybody else. But not you. So, given such an opportunity in Bayreuth, why should I not take advantage? Naturally, there is no way I could know whether – if asked – you would agree to assist us further. That's the way it is in our business. You put up a lot of kites and see which will fly.'

'No. No, Marcus. The only flying I propose is out of Canada, if possible tomorrow.'

Agnete came down from her rock and picked at Bryn's bag of cherries. He slid his wilting burger and the Budweiser out of sight.

Marcus was already pressing on.

'When Agnete heard Strange inviting you to dinner, she got on to me and we arranged a stake-out. A surveillance.'

'You were in Bayreuth?'

'No. Not me. I was in Munich with the BND. The German Secret Service to you. Agnete was looking after things in Bayreuth. We wired her up and got her into the restaurant with some BND people. We patched her into Strange's frequency and she was able to listen in.'

'To our conversation?'

'Oh yes. Agnete's wire allowed her to monitor everything that passed through Strange's earpiece. I suppose you thought he was wearing a hearing aid. In fact it was quite a conventional two-way device. Your conversation was relayed to his men outside; and messages were also coming *in* to him. Strange is a careful man.

He likes to watch his back. What he never realised was that Agnete was a few yards away. And neither, fortunately, did you.'

'Ah. Well now...'

'You see,' interjected Agnete, 'we have been working with the Germans tracking Mr Strange's middle-eastern arms contacts. He was rendezvousing with them in Bayreuth.'

'Indeed,' said Marcus. 'So when his people ID'd the Israeli agent in the restaurant – the little fellow who was photographing you – Agnete heard their message to Strange and alerted me. We got the *landpolizei* in just in time or else, I think, there might have been bloodshed.'

Bryn could work out the rest for himself. Strange must have come to Bayreuth to meet his Arab partners in the privacy of the Wagner box. He doubted he'd have seen very much of *The Mastersingers* at all. And of course, the Israelis – or their secret service – would have been tracking Strange every bit as energetically as the Germans and MI6 and God knows who else. Espionage was beginning to seem a crowded business.

'So the photographer was from Mossad?'

'Oh certainly,' said Marcus. 'And now quite compromised. Strange's man took his camera with everything he had shot in Bayreuth. There was nothing left to do but pull him out.'

'I saw that on the news,' said Bryn. 'Mossad had been caught using fake German passports. There was a political kerfuffle. All the Israeli agents got expelled.'

Marcus looked at him pityingly.

'Wholly contrived,' he said. 'Mossad wanted them out anyway – their job was done. Meantime the Germans wanted to look good with the Arabs. It's all politics, old boy. Don't forget that the Germans have alliances with both sides in the Middle East. Like the rest of us.'

Bryn remembered the policeman at the hotel and his sense of being watched through the rest of his time in Bavaria. He wondered if his ignorance had been shared by the local Bayreuth constabulary. And how much anyone knew at levels lower than Marcus and a few high-placed international colleagues.

His cousin's words, though, had had a settling effect. At the least a degree of clarity had emerged from the confusion. It was not that Bryn felt necessarily less in danger. But he did feel better informed.

And then the truth began to dawn upon him. What had hitherto been unthinkable. That, in some way or another, everything since Bayreuth – the whole of the last two weeks – was the malign consequence of that 'serendipitous' meeting with Strange. And that Marcus – his cousin – was responsible for it all.

He drew in a large breath. Marcus was looking at him almost if he expected what was to come.

'I cannot believe what you're telling me,' Bryn said as slowly, and as icily, as he could manage.

Marcus did not reply.

'It was not his fault,' said Agnete. 'The stakes were so high.'

'Oh, please.'

'I really need your help,' said Marcus quietly.

He offered him the open cake tin, like a kid offering a trade.

Bryn shrugged his shoulders.

The chocolate brownies did look appetising.

'Events did not turn out as anticipated, it's true,' Marcus continued. 'It was unfortunate that you went holidaying to Yosemite and, of all places, Lassen.'

'Strange recommended it.'

'I know. We heard him. But nobody anticipated that Stratton would be headed that way.'

'The scientist? The dead man?'

Bryn felt as if he was in shock. He wanted to know more. On the other hand, he dared not encourage his cousin with too great a show of interest. But he was sure to tell him anyway.

Chapter 10

'Sidney Stratton is the beginning of everything,' Marcus began.

For the first time since Bryn had arrived in Rainier, the sky was clear of clouds. The ski college on the glacier was already making for home. Marcus took a pair of heavy military binoculars from his bag and watched them before continuing.

'Stratton was a nuclear scientist, working in a federal government laboratory. And an outdoors man – loved walking in country like this. One day, a few years ago, when he was hiking in Lassen, he came across a peculiar lode of rock. No one knows yet its exact location, simply that it was within a mile or so of the summit, and almost certainly thrown up in the eruptions of 1914 to 1921.

'It reminded him of some lithium bearing rocks he had seen years before in Australia. So he took a sample back to his government laboratory – didn't tell the Park authorities – and did some experiments. To cut a long story short, he managed to derive a new isotope from it. I don't suppose you know anything about tritium?'

Bryn did. There had been a story in the newspapers in the late 1990s. Revelations of a clandestine trade between South Africa and Israel involving nuclear materials and an isotope called tritium, derived from enriched lithium. It was designed to boost the explosive power of White South Africa's nuclear weapons.

'Stratton's new isotope was like tritium.' Marcus was speaking even more quietly now than before. 'But hugely more effective. It had the capacity to increase the power of a nuclear explosion at least a hundredfold.

'It was the nuclear scientist's Eldorado: an isotope which reduced the quantity of fissile material required to achieve critical mass to a fraction of what was necessary before. The downside was that he may also have generated the heaviest substance known to man. A small flask the size of a pint bottle – still enough though to fuel a sectoral conflict – would weigh in at thirty or forty pounds.

'But this is the real fear. The new isotope would allow much smaller warheads than ever before. Integrated into highly mobile systems. Capable of being deployed in suicide missions. Imagine it falling into the wrong hands. The Middle East for example – Stratton's flaskful would be sufficient to reverse the whole balance of power.'

'And make an arms trader's fortune.'

'Ah well,' said Marcus. 'You're already ahead of me.'

Agnete was back on her Valkyrie rock, monitoring the pathway. It was as if she preferred not to overhear this part of Marcus's narrative.

'Unfortunately,' he continued, 'Stratton was a complex character. At first, he was open about his experiments. But he must have realised the terrifying potential of what he was doing. And decided that he was not – or not yet at least – prepared to share it with his superiors. He began to falsify the laboratory outcomes so that it looked as though he was going nowhere. People lost interest in what he was doing.

'But, in the usual cliché, he had stumbled upon a Frankenstein's monster. He was shocked by the implications but reluctant to abandon his baby. And determined not to divulge its existence to people whom he thought might abuse it. Government, politicians, the military.

'He seems to have sat on his discovery for a while. It was easy for him to hide something so small and supposedly useless, particularly in a working laboratory with so much going on. But he must have brooded on his situation until he could stand it no more. So he shared his terrible dilemma with a trusted colleague. Or someone he thought he could trust.

'The truth is that, in any organisation dealing in assets as marketable as cutting edge arms technology, there'll always be people taking kick-backs for information. And his trusted colleague reported Stratton's discovery straight back – to Udell Strange.

'What happened next is not entirely clear. There were certainly discreet meetings between Stratton and Strange, brokered by the colleague. Stratton may naïvely have hoped Strange would ensure his product only be used for acceptable, perhaps peace-making, purposes. Perhaps he even thought that, like the atom bomb, possession by both sides would have a mutually deterrent effect. I am sure Strange tried to satisfy his fantasies. But in the end something went wrong. Perhaps Stratton rumbled the other's self-interest. Perhaps he asked for guarantees of a kind that Udell Strange was not prepared to deliver.

'At all events, we know that Strange proceeded to steal the isotope. He correctly calculated that Stratton was too far up to his neck to report the loss to his superiors. He also took the precaution of transferring a hundred thousand dollars from one of his anonymised off-shore funds into an account set up in Stratton's name; and told Stratton about it so that he would realise the extent to which he was compromised. Where the isotope is now, we do not know. Strange has spirited it away somewhere. Our job is to find it before anybody else does, or anything worse happens to it.'

Bryn felt a chill settle upon him. He was quite certain he knew what Marcus intended by this last remark; and was careful not to respond. A light aircraft passed along the line of the mountains to the west. Marcus watched it through his binoculars until it disappeared.

'Do you remember Jack C Smith?' he said.

Of course he remembered Jack C Smith.

Jack C Smith was the defeated Vice-Presidential candidate in the recent Presidential Election, the lost leader of the neo-conservatives who had gone down in flames with the disgraced front-runner.

When it had emerged within the week before Election Day that the Presidential candidate was a closet gay, with a naked photograph of him *in flagrante delicto* to prove it, the media was heavy with rumour that the information had been leaked from Jack C Smith's own office. But – disastrously – some weeks or months before he had intended it. Then, a few weeks after the Election, Jack had been accidentally and tragically shot by a political associate while out quail hunting in the Sierra Nevada. He had died without recovering consciousness.

'A terrible loss,' said Marcus.

'Why do you mention him?' Bryn asked.

'Because Strange, apparently, christened the lethal isotope in his memory. It is called *smithium*. Isn't that nice?'

'What happened to Stratton?'

'Oh. Stratton. He had some kind of breakdown. He couldn't go to his bosses. He was out of his depth with Udell Strange and his people. I wouldn't be surprised if they threatened to kill him, or even make a move on his family. A bit of a lost soul, I'm afraid.'

'And dying from radiation sickness,' Bryn said. 'The police said so.'

'I didn't know that,' said Marcus. 'It makes sense.'

He pondered a few moments before returning to his story.

'I think he decided to blow up his secret lode-bearing seam on Lassen and probably himself with it. He had the equipment. Rock drills. High explosive. At least – as a dying achievement – he might hope that no more smithium could be manufactured. I don't imagine for a moment he was good at covering his tracks. You don't buy quantities of *plastique* without being noticed. We were onto him. But so was your friend with the cowboy lifts.'

'Jack Wilson.'

'Wilson. He's an ex-CIA agent. I used to bump into him when we were working in the same theatres. He's been around a bit since, made himself unpopular in a few countries. Even had plastic surgery to make himself less recognisable. Wilson is what you'd call a hired gun. Resourceful, exceptionally private, dangerous. He works for whoever is the highest payer and we believe that, at this point in time, that happens to be Udell Strange.'

'I know it is,' Bryn said.

Marcus ignored him.

'They'd been concerned about Stratton for a while. Strange must have decided finally he was too great a risk. But unfortunately for them – fortunately for us – Wilson made a strategic error. He killed Stratton before he reached the secret lode. Maybe Wilson was disturbed. My best guess is he saw you in the distance, coming up the track behind him, put a silencer on the gun and despatched Stratton right away. But the consequence is that no more smithium can be manufactured – certainly for the time being. The prime source has been lost.

'Which leaves us of course with one very clear task. We need to find that one existing flask of the isotope. And destroy it.'

And who might Marcus have in mind to perform that labour? A 'cleanskin' no doubt. Someone with time to spare. Who could be trusted *not* to run away with a billion dollar property in his trouser pocket.

'I'm really not that interested,' said Bryn. 'Why don't you just move in and take Strange? And Wilson too.'

Marcus sighed.

'My dear cousin. We are not discussing a common criminal here. Strange is an immensely powerful and influential man. If we get it wrong now, we lose everything. It's one thing to know and even to have the evidence; quite another to be able to take open action against him. Don't forget that most of our information could never be used in court.'

'"Top secret"?'

'Yes, if you want to call it that.'

109

'I suppose you've interrogated the duplicitous colleague?'

'We might have done.'

He was curiously ill at ease, and gave another sigh.

'To be frank with you, Bryn, things got a little out of hand. We'd been monitoring Stratton and Strange discreetly for some time – well, you know that. It's important not to frighten the horses. There was always a chance that someone would lead us to the flask. And then Stratton suddenly took off before we could speak to him.'

'So if I understand this,' said Bryn, 'you've lost Stratton, and Strange has made off with the isotope, and you don't know where it is and you're in no position to do anything about it.'

For some time Marcus had been holding an uneaten brownie in his hand. He closed his fingers round it and watched the crumbs skip away down the mountainside.

'Here's the situation,' he murmured, as if talking to himself. 'Strange wants to destabilise the Middle East to put pressure on the Lady President. He's a good businessman and knows he can do that and make a packet at the same time.

'So what he's looking for is someone militant and oil rich. He's found a possible buyer in one of the Gulf States where the old sheikh has been replaced by his extreme Islamist son.

'And there's the Israelis. They've known about the isotope for some time. Longer than us, probably. I wouldn't put it past Strange to be playing them off against the Islamists. Anything that helps to ratchet up tension in that part of the world.

'I don't know how much time we have. We're still working on the flask's whereabouts. But my guess is we won't get a lead till Strange is close to a deal or needs to prove he has the isotope. At best we'll get a very brief window of opportunity.'

'To destroy it?'

'Absolutely.'

'Why?'

'Because we cannot afford to let it fall into the hands of the jihadists or the Israelis or even the Americans.'

'So the British are going to destroy it? Come off it, Marcus, you must think I'm stupid.'

Marcus was silent for so long that Bryn began to wonder if, for once, he'd actually managed to undermine that normally impenetrable self-confidence.

Agnete had returned to sit beside them.

'Bryn,' he said at last. 'No one is more loyal to Her Majesty's person than me. But, the fact is, there are a few of us who recognise that in the most extreme circumstances there may be a greater duty. So: no, my people are not proposing to risk passing the smithium on to the politicians. We, not them, will destroy it.'

'And your career, Marcus?'

He seemed so earnest and genuine that Bryn was quite moved. Phoney sentiment and sententiousness had never been part of Marcus's character. His story had the ring of truth. Bryn felt privileged to be a witness to the moment: out of such things was history made.

His cousin pulled a wry face and grinned across at him.

'Well of course,' he said, 'if all this gets out, I'm stuffed. But it will have been worth it. Don't you think?'

'I think you're doing the right thing.'

He nodded.

'I hope so.'

The light was beginning to fade. The sun was settling in the west through a bank of gathering clouds.

'Bryn,' said Marcus after a while. 'Bear with me one more time.'

The Laing passed to and fro.

'You see,' he continued, 'all the spies are now watching each other. We need someone else to get the smithium out of America. Someone below the radar to whom we'd supply a new identity and passport. Resourceful. I would never want to flatter a cousin, but you are the ideal candidate. And I trust you. A rare commodity in my trade.'

Bryn let him continue.

'The plan is for you to hand it over to me at a safe rendezvous in England. I'll arrange for a trusted scientist to destroy it. A layman might kill himself.'

Bryn pondered this a moment.

'Have I got this right? It's too dangerous to destroy but not to carry it?'

'That's right. Like HEU.'

'Like what?'

'Highly enriched uranium. It's perfectly safe to carry around so long as it's not exposed to air. The smithium flask will be shrouded in lead casing to prevent breakage – but mainly so it doesn't set off radiation detectors. If you check it through an airport it'll emit less radiation than a bunch of bananas.'

'Really?'

'Horse's mouth. Believe me.'

'Stratton's colleague?'

Marcus nodded.

'How about Strange though? How would he be intending to get it out?'

'Difficult to be certain. Probably the cocaine route. It's a connection he has used in the past when he has needed to move military matériel quickly.'

'He works with Colombian drugs smugglers?'

'Oh, Bryn. The cocaine trade and Americans like Strange have a lot in common. They both hate socialist regimes, for a start.'

'But how does the route work?'

Marcus frowned and sighed again.

'Usually up the Pacific Coast, through Canada or Alaska and Greenland, and ultimately to the west coast of Ireland or Scotland. But we need to intervene before that can happen. We really haven't much time.'

He stared at Bryn as if waiting for an answer.

He needed an iron-clad, preferably honourable, reason not to get involved.

'Marcus,' he said, and he could hear the quaver again in his voice. 'There is a flaw in all this. I am not the "clean" operator you imagine me to be. You surely can't have overlooked my acquaintance with Strange. And I know Wilson is onto me. He's been tracking me since Lassen. You should know that he, or some accomplice, tried to kill me in San Francisco. I'm damaged goods, Marcus. And that's why I'm getting out.'

The clouds were building up more heavily in the west and the sun had faded entirely from sight. Agnete was on her feet and collecting up their picnic. Bryn wondered how she could see through the silky waterfall of her hair.

'Are you referring to the motel room blast?' asked Marcus.

'You know about that?'

'Well I would do. That was actually us.'

It took Bryn a while to absorb this. He felt as if he had tuned into a radio programme whose beginning he'd missed and whose ending he would never know.

'We've kept an eye on you since Germany,' said Marcus. 'After the unfortunate Lassen business and your subsequent involvement with the San Francisco police, we decided you needed a new identity.'

'You *what?*'

This was beyond credulity.

'It's only temporary, Bryn. You wanted a different room so we... discreetly... accommodated you. As I said before, you have to take advantage of opportunities in our business.'

'Serendipity,' he said. He was exhausted.

'Yup. My men found a dead drug addict – a sad and common feature of the streets of these fine California cities – and moved him into your old room, the room in which you were still registered. The fellow was of a similar shape and age to yourself and the explosion would have made him unrecognisable anyway. Gas build up from a faulty boiler. The police will have assumed that the corpse was you. More importantly, we've made sure Wilson and Strange believe it.'

Marcus put his cold hand confidingly on Bryn's knee.

'I'm sorry we missed you. We intended to intercept you at the motel and have this conversation with you then. But you had already disappeared. Fortunately, we had taken the precaution of secreting a tracking transceiver in your hire car. Otherwise we would never have found you.'

He burrowed into his rucksack and produced a passport, slightly foxed as if already well used. It was in the name of someone called Hathrill but the photograph was of Bryn. Taken, as he vividly remembered, about two years previously by Marcus himself, when he had run into him unexpectedly (again) in the Roman amphitheatre in Arles.

'You'd shaved off your beard that summer, Bryn – too hot for you in Provence, I suppose. And you had that ridiculous short *en brosse* haircut. Made you practically unrecognisable.'

How long had Marcus been saving this up...

'And you're hoping I'll do the same now?'

'Here,' he continued, producing another document from the bag. 'This is a British driving licence in the same name. You'll have cards and access to a bank account with ten thousand sterling in it. Should be enough to get you by. You can do what you like with the residue. Oh... once you're safely back in the UK, we'll arrange for you to revert to your true identity, proper passport and so on. All your problems solved.'

'Except for one thing.'

'Really?'

'I'm not going to do it, Marcus.'

Marcus's jaw tensed and his eyes filled with something almost like fury. And as instantly he relaxed and put on a hurt little boy face, and sighed again. He began to return the documents to the rucksack.

'We've invested a quantity of work in this, Bryn.'

'And made a hell of a lot of unwarranted assumptions.'

'Trying to make it easier for you.'

'I have not changed my mind, Marcus.'

He chewed his lip; and began to hoist his backpack over his shoulders. Bryn scented success: finally Marcus's penny seemed to have dropped.

'Would it make any difference... ' he said.

He had reverted to his quiet, accommodating tone.

'Would it make any difference if I told you that Strange's coterie of war-mongering activists call themselves The Friends of the Right?'

'So?'

'And that one of their founding members is your Mormon pal, Dan? A long-term close buddy and ally of Strange and planning to benefit greatly when the President has been destroyed.'

'No, it wouldn't make any difference,' Bryn said.

But Marcus's little rapier thrust had found its target. *Touché.* No wonder Strange had been so interested that evening in Bryn's marriage. And, with hindsight now, so very well informed.

Marcus took out a small black mobile telephone.

'You don't have to say anything,' he said. 'I'm not asking for a commitment. Nothing at all. But if you ever need to get in touch with me, use this. It's a sixty second "burner". That means it's a basic cell phone with no screen or display and one number in its memory. If you call me, you must never use my name or make any reference at all to our conversation. The phone has one minute of call time. After that it's useless and you throw it away. All you need to do is give the codeword for the isotope flask.'

'Which would be?'

'"Stella Polaris".' He grinned. 'Can you remember that?'

'I should think so.'

'And if you do this job for us, the other thing I need to say – again – is that you will be safe. You know we will be tracking you. We would be watching – and from near enough to make sure we can intervene if anything threatens to go wrong.'

'You realise that what you say is completely academic.'

His cousin nodded.

'Well, well, we'll see. Agnete and I will be leaving you now. We must not be seen together. We'll meet again in London, I'm sure.'

He slipped the cellphone into Bryn's top pocket.

And with that, Marcus and Agnete set off again, like any other pair of well-kitted Pacific Crest hikers, down the single track southwards towards the Paradise Inn. Bryn stood on his rock watching them until they rounded the last granite outcrop and disappeared from sight.

But just before they did, and when they may have thought they had already passed from view, he saw Agnete throw her arm around Marcus's neck; and watched them lean into each other in a brief, and unmistakeable, gesture of mutual affection.

Chapter 11

It is possible that Marcus knew him better than he knew himself. He should have continued on his way up to the Canadian border, through the token border control, to the consulate in Vancouver, and home. That would have been the sensible thing to have done.

Instead, he put his plans on hold. He abandoned the booking at the Paradise Inn, drove the three hundred miles back to Medford and booked into the same motel he'd occupied a week previously. Again he paid cash for the room in advance. And booked a session for an hour later on the motel computer.

It was already approaching midnight but the meeting with Marcus and Agnete had driven all desire for sleep from his mind. He crossed the road to the small municipal park opposite and sat on a bench to gather his thoughts.

There *were* problems with the original scheme. Though he had taken a car into Canada without challenge a couple of times in the past, it was possible he had merely been the lucky beneficiary of a random stop and check policy. He could not be certain the Canadians would always be so relaxed; indeed there might have been some tightening up in response to the recent international tensions and American pressure.

Nor was an application at the consulate for a replacement passport without its hazards. How likely was it that the police would already have reported his death to the UK Consulate-General in San Francisco, and that this information had been fed into Vancouver's database? How might that be explained? And how concerned should he be that news of his continuing existence – and current whereabouts – might leak out to his enemies?

He was classically between a rock and a hard place.

He was flattered that Marcus thought him resourceful and courageous enough to handle his alarming assignment. Extremely flattered. But he surely knew himself better. Unlike his cousin, *his* world was lived in the mind, not on the battlefield – at least not while the battle was still in progress.

And yet. How far might he be relying on a lazy assumption gathered from books and films and television and newspapers: that espionage is invariably fraught with excitement, danger, sudden violence and death? Judging by Marcus's lifestyle, it had rather more to do with hotels, meetings, long lunches and a great deal of spare time. Probably for most of his fellow spies it was a nine-to-five world of offices, computers and canteen gossip, like any other. With perhaps a very modest portion of mayhem on the margin. And was the task Marcus had in mind for him likely to be so much more hazardous than, say, delivering the post?

He was no nearer a decision.

And there were a couple of jobs he needed to do first.

He returned to where he had parked his car outside the motel room, and opened up the boot and the bonnet. It took a fair amount of burrowing and stretching but eventually he found it: a tiny radio transceiver tucked away behind the engine block. He ripped it out and dropped it in a public trash bin.

He went online. It had been a long while since his last fix of British news, so he typed in the BBC website.

Marcus was not alone in talking about imminent war in the Middle East. The intentions of the young Gulf Sheikh who had overthrown his nonagenarian father were becoming clearer by the day. Emissaries from al-Shabaab, an Islamist movement based in

Somalia, had been seen returning from a meeting in his palace; there were well-sourced rumours of a mutual arms pact. Protests were pouring in from the pro-Western Emirates. The Israeli Knesset was in closed session. A quick check with www.foxnews.com and www.cbsnews.com revealed that even the USA-centric commentators were concerned.

His full email tray presented a conundrum. If he opened one, and particularly if he responded to it, he might immediately give his existence away. He scanned down past the academic bulletins and the unfiltered spam for any item of outstanding interest. One unusual email caught his eye. After a moment's hesitation, he opened it anyway.

It was from 'The Law Office of Harlan J Hackett' in Salt Lake City and it informed him that Mrs Marion Judith Williams had initiated proceedings for a no fault divorce, citing as grounds 'irreconcilable differences between the parties'. Mr Hackett asked to be put in touch with Bryn's lawyers.

He turned the computer off.

His well overdue night's sleep was the most troubled he'd had in years. Several times he awoke from half-dreamt tableaux of a motel in uproar, Agnete and Marcus silhouetted on a faraway ridge, dark-suited men knocking at his door.

But most frequently, images of Marion.

Marion, not as he had known her more recently, but as a younger woman. With a loud, vulgar laugh; unaffected gaze; brisk marching gait, always ahead and faster than *he* wanted to be; warm, vibrant and physical. A stream of images bubbling up uninvited through his dreams. And – increasingly – till it settled and would not be budged, an email from a lawyer's office.

He snapped the light back on.

The only available sedative was a dose of night-time television. A monochrome episode of *I Love Lucy* finally hit the spot.

When he awoke it was late morning.

As so often, a night's sleep delivered the missing clarity. He did not wait for breakfast. He pulled Marcus's cell phone from his pocket and activated the number in its memory.

'*Ja.*'

It was Agnete.

'"Stella Polaris",' he said.

It was an easy one to remember: the title of a radio adventure story from his childhood, and Marcus's.

'I have spoken to my office manager,' she replied.

She spoke rapidly and without a break, as if she was reading from a script.

'He is away on business but has told me to say that we are sorry you are not happy with your new phone. Please remove the SIM card and make a note of the number on it. My boss says you should flush it down the John. I am sorry the company cannot help you further. Goodbye.'

And with that the line went dead.

He opened the phone up and flipped out the SIM card.

On the blank part of the card, above the gold contact sphere, were two rows of neatly hand-written numbers: 41586 38332. He wrote them on the palm of his hand, wrapped the SIM card in a couple of sheets of toilet paper and flushed it away. For good measure, he stamped on the redundant mobile until it was a mess of shattered plastic, and managed to flush that away too. Then went for his free coffee and pastries.

His fellow breakfasters were all younger than him. Most of them were listening to rap music through ear phones or, between mouthfuls, tapping out text messages. He sat next to the smallest, a boy barely thirteen years of age who was fiddling with an iPhone more state of the art and loaded with apps than any he'd seen before.

'Do you ever use that to speak to anyone?' he asked him.

The boy glanced at him with that habitual teenage mixture of incomprehension and utter contempt.

There was no sign of a parent. There was probably a mutual agreement that he took breakfast on his own.

'Let me show you how to do it,' said Bryn, and deftly lifted the device from the boy's grasp and dialled in the numbers he'd inscribed on his palm. The adolescent watched open-mouthed. Bryn handed him a pink iced doughnut.

He knew enough about California to recognise that the first three of the SIM card figures matched the telephone prefix for San Francisco. A voice answered immediately.

'American Mocha Coffee House,' it said.

'What?'

'American Mocha Coffee House.'

'What's your address?'

The voice was unfazed.

'1290 Market Street. Anything else to help, sir?'

'No thanks.'

He returned the iPhone to the boy – 'It works fine, you can carry on with your game now' – picked up a cinnamon roll and left.

The journey down Route 5 was straight and fast and he was back in San Francisco by early afternoon.

The first stop was a downtown barber shop, where he asked for a crew cut. It was not evidently a term much in currency still in the twenty-first century.

'Waddya mean, Mister? Buzz cut? Ivy League?' responded the barber, an elderly Vietnamese.

The Ivy League turned out to be the less extreme alternative, so he settled for that. And, for the first time in his life – from a professional, that is – he ordered a close shave.

He knew Market Street from his last visit. It was down the road from the Opera House: a wide, busy thoroughfare striking diagonally across the San Francisco grid system. The American Mocha Coffee House was packed full of the lunchtime crowds, and not a free seat was visible.

But he spotted Agnete on a small banquette at the far end of the room, reading a copy of *The San Francisco Chronicle*. As he approached, she removed a small reticule from the seat alongside her – without looking up from her paper – and he sat down in its place.

She gave absolutely no indication that she knew him. For a while he sat in silence, taking an occasional sidelong glance at her face. She remained frowningly engrossed in some article about

121

Californian property values, even making the odd note in the margin. Bryn began to wonder if his shiny new appearance might have rendered him unrecognisable.

She lifted her pen and slowly and deliberately drew an arrow across the top of the page. It seemed intrusive to peer. The page, however, remained resolutely unturned. So he popped on his reading spectacles and discreetly leaned over. Above a headline predicting a collapse in real estate sales, she had written in capital letters the words: OPERA BOX OFFICE.

She got up, folded the paper into her bag and disappeared in the direction of the rest rooms.

It took him longer than it should to realise that Agnete was not coming back. Or that she might be expecting him to follow her. But when he got to the unisex facilities, they were vacant. At the end of the corridor an emergency fire exit stood half open. He went through and made his way circuitously to the War Memorial Opera House.

There was still one performance of the *Ring* Cycle to go and he was as anxious not to be seen by fellow audience members – including his British friends – as he was to avoid detection by whoever might be following him or Agnete. Apart from a few straggling tourists, though, the box office antechamber was empty.

He did not have to wait long. A door opened from the grand inner lobby and, White Rabbit-like, Agnete emerged and as instantly popped back in again. He hurried after her, through to the auditorium, down a side aisle to another door and along a corridor and finally into what he took to be the dressing room of the King of the Gods, furnished with a brocaded settee and armchairs, a television, ceiling-high refrigerator, fitted cupboards; and wall-width mirror and make-up shelf, wig stand, over-sized vase of fresh flowers. He wished he'd had a camera.

Agnete sat down and came briskly to the point.

'We are very close to knowing where the isotope is,' she said. 'It has definitely been hidden here in San Francisco, in an apartment or maybe someone's house. Not anywhere traceable to Mr Strange, naturally. Our information is that it will be moved very soon, probably to complete a deal.'

It was still pretty vague.

'Also we can confirm that the isotope has been sealed in a lead flask and stowed away in a safe – we think wall-mounted or under floorboards. If the safe cannot be opened, it may be possible to remove it wholesale. Tools will be needed, and a sack truck to carry it away.

'It won't be till they make their final arrangements that we will know the precise location and – providing our informant gets his intelligence out quickly enough – that's when we should have our chance to intervene. But the window of opportunity is likely to be very short indeed.'

'Or non-existent.'

'And it could be dangerous.'

She paused for a moment.

'You understand we are asking you to go in alone and find the safe and the isotope and bring it out?'

'Of course.'

'And that we cannot guarantee what you will find there?'

She looked at him intently.

'Are you quite sure this is what you want to do?'

Was she concerned? He tried to penetrate her ice blue gaze but she was as unreadable as before. Only the question itself, and maybe some hesitancy in her manner, gave him encouragement. It would have to do for the time being.

'The Service will be watching you,' she said. 'From a distance.'

Then, as if she had thought better of herself: 'But you will be fine. I am quite sure.'

She was beautiful.

He knew why he had come here. Mostly a reaction to Marion: driven along by the hubris that is the flip side of disaster. But now. Now, he had a chance to please the Dane and play the hero. Why should he not?

'Where is your car? I need your keys.'

He handed them over meekly and explained where he had left the vehicle.

'It is too dangerous for you to use it,' she said. 'If the police should stop you, it would be a disaster. I will make sure the hire company find it. It will look to them as though it had been stolen, probably from the motel where you were – as it were – killed. You will need a new car.'

And she passed him the business card of a local car hire company. Mighty Motors.

'It's already paid for in the name of Hathrill,' she said. 'They won't ask for ID, but here are your papers anyway.'

She opened the reticule, and took out a passport, driving licence and a couple of plastic cards. As she handed them over, one of the cards fell from her fingers and onto the floor.

For a second or two she appeared disconcerted. Bryn moved to help but she quickly gathered the card up and placed it firmly in his palm.

'These cards are active now,' she said, rising to her feet. 'Do not leave the Opera House through the front. Get a taxi out of town, book into a motel in the new name and have a good night's sleep. Pick up the car in the morning. Your bags and everything you need will be in it.'

He put a hand on her sleeve and drew her back down to her seat.

'And what happens next?'

'You have to wait,' she replied.

'How will I know what to do? How will you make contact?'

'We will. You do not have to worry about that.'

'And what if I don't hear from you?'

She thought for a moment.

'I think… should we not be in contact within a few days, it will all be over. You fly home to London.'

'Five days? A week?'

She shook her head.

'A week maximum,' she said at last. 'You can fly home.'

She looked up and smiled at him. The first smile he had ever seen from her. He started to respond but she rose pre-emptively to her feet. His fingers slithered away down her departing sleeve and caught her trailing hand.

'When shall I see you?'

She did not free herself immediately. Her head stayed bowed over her captured arm with the falling curtain of hair an excluding veil between them.

'I cannot say,' she said. 'I cannot tell you.'

She slipped her hand away and gathered up her bag, flicked her yellow-white tresses across her shoulder, and left the room.

She would of course be reporting their meeting to Marcus.

How did his cousin fit in? What should he assume about Marcus's relationship with Agnete? It would be a curious arrangement at best, with Marcus both her senior professionally and old enough (unlike himself) to be her father.

He could see where this was going. It would take him no time at all to justify a romantic pursuit of this ice maiden. And somewhere inside him he detected an unaccustomed boldness. He liked the feel of it. Though the final decision, after all, would not be his. Nor Marcus's either.

He followed Agnete's instructions to the syllable.

His departure through the Opera House stage door was conveniently masked by a noisy influx of students. He quickly found a taxi and directed it across the Oakland Bay Bridge and southwards to a Holiday Inn remembered from a family vacation a decade before. The motel overlooked a small marina with boutique shops and restaurants; far enough off the beaten track to avoid recognition.

After checking in, he settled outside a waterfront brew pub, with a glass of the house IPA on the table beside him, and gave some more thought to his situation.

It was a strange thing, love. Loving; and being *in* love. Bryn imagined he understood the former. He believed – for example – that he still loved Marion. Being *in* love though: he'd never had any trouble recognising it when he was young, but it all seemed so much a part of that foreign world of the past. So where was he now with Agnete? Not, he thought, merely charmed or bewitched – he still knew what that was like. But in love? How would he recognise that? Some conscious loss of the self, he imagined, like being overrun and occupied. An unbidden image floating in the ocean in front of him. A small troubled smile like a melting iceberg. There even if you looked away up at the sky. A gaze as commanding and as unblinking as a small child. Heroes had fought dragons for less. He would know it if he felt it.

The marina reminded him of Darling Harbour in Sydney in miniature. Bustling with young people full of money and irresponsibility. Parties rather than couples. Soft top BMWs, customised roadsters, 'all-wheel-drive' monsters. One was parked on the cobble walkway directly in front of him, oblivious of pedestrian inconvenience. The biggest and blackest Porsche he had ever seen.

He'd noticed an ocean-going yacht called *The North Star*, with two sails lowered but not yet tidied away, chugging into the harbour. The crew were short and heavily tanned, possibly from a South American country. A blonde man leaned out of the Porsche and waved to them. The yacht was too long to moor up beside the walkway; so it dropped anchor in mid-water and lowered a small dinghy. Some crewmen clambered down and gunned the dinghy's outboard motor towards a slipway and out of sight beyond the behemoth in front of Bryn.

He turned his attention to the contents of his glass. This Californian micro-beer was the most delicious he had drunk in America and, with its rich, dark colour and ten degrees of alcohol, unlike any IPA ever brewed in Burton upon Trent. He imagined introducing Agnete to the quotidian pleasures of his own former life: beer (and, as a Dane, she should be receptive), a favourite local restaurant in London, walks through autumn beech woods in the Chiltern Hills.

The South Americans by now were piling into the Porsche. The blonde man was leaning against it, his back to Bryn, talking to a taller South American who might have been the yacht's captain. Both climbed inside and the Porsche pulled away, leaving

Bryn finally to an uninterrupted vista of the sun setting over the poorest suburbs of San Francisco.

He pondered Marcus and his world view. He was right of course to treat the Lassen isotope as such a serious threat. But it reminded Bryn a little of a scaremongering story from the newspapers, with screaming headlines attached; the kind of overcooked account that modulated with time into something rather less alarming, until finally it was no more than a footnote in some politician's memoirs. Perhaps you really had to be on the inside of events to know their true significance.

The sunlight flared on the edge of his beer glass. He put out his hand to drain the last couple of inches, and a tiny concentric ripple spread outwards from the centre.

And disappeared as if it had never been.

Chapter 12

There was a slight hiccup when he came to pay his bill in the morning. Neither Bryn nor the previous evening's receptionist – when she'd taken the usual precautionary imprint – had noticed that his credit card was missing a signature. The morning shift was an obese young man the size of a schooner. He was more alert.

'No signature, buddy boy,' he said, tapping the back of the card in case Bryn didn't understand American English.

'Stupid,' he confessed, and reached for the motel ballpoint.

'Need to see your ID,' said the young man, folding the card back officiously into his capacious palm.

'I'll pay in cash.'

'You're darn right you will. If'n you can't pay on your card.'

'Can I have it back, please.'

'Nope. Not without ID. City law.'

He considered for a moment surrendering the card, but decided that was too perilous an option. If the motel passed it on to the police, his false Hathrill identity could be rapidly exposed. Then it occurred to him that his new driving licence and passport must already bear some kind of signature. The trouble was that he did not know what it looked like. And he'd never practised it.

There was no choice but to busk it.

'Here you go,' he said, fishing out the new passport. 'And it's got a fine picture of me.'

He thumbed the page open helpfully, long enough to get a quick look at the signature, and passed it over. Small, rather scribbly writing, with the single initial 'G'.

The large young man looked at him narrowly, checked the photograph, looked at him again, looked at the photo again, and finally ran the card through his reader.

'Sign it now, buddy,' he said, as he returned it with the credit slip.

'I will,' said Bryn. 'I will. Thank you so much.'

He did it rapidly and confidently with a flourish, replicating the loose character of the original. The receptionist had already moved on to the next client.

He found a taxi rank on the marina and gave the Mexican driver Mighty Motors' address. The driver had never heard of the company, and was so unfamiliar with the locale that Bryn had to read out the zip code so he could tap it into his GPS system.

He sat back and studied the new documents more carefully. It was apparent now that, even had he been obliged to forge the Hathrill signature sight unseen, he would still have passed the test with flying colours. It was, chillingly, in his own handwriting. How this could have been achieved, he could not imagine.

Or maybe he could.

Some years previously, he recalled that he'd tutored a young man of that name – one of the new history intake at UCL. At the start of each first term, it had been his custom to scribble out on a sheet of paper the names of all the freshers, to help him memorise them: always the single initial and the surname. Someone, presumably Marcus, must have come across this and copied it. How long had he been planning to make use of it? Serendipity again? He did not think so.

The taxi had crossed the Oakland Bay Bridge back into San Francisco City and turned south. It followed the line of the waterfront, down a long, straight, traffic-busy thoroughfare overhung by tall buildings, with few pedestrians. The driver turned off towards the Bay and the buildings shrank back to two storey height. The road system was rigidly grid patterned; tiny balconied houses shortly gave way to rows of decayed repositories, each with a bolted roll-up door and a four-digit number painted alongside it. There were more people now on the sidewalks, but they were all men and all African-American.

They drew up in the last street before the sea.

'Hunters Point,' said the driver, looking closely at the GPS display. 'Sure is a dump, mister.'

He did not hang around.

Bryn was on a square peninsula jutting out into the Bay. Container vessels stood at anchor in the quiet waters beyond. There were signs of an initiative to upgrade the area – a couple of wall posters proclaiming future plans and an estate of bright new apartment buildings a quarter of a mile further down the coastline. But where he stood, all was windswept, rubble-strewn and derelict. Low-hanging power lines, which invariably announced the underclass districts of the city, criss-crossed the crumbling, pot-holed street.

There was a small car lot nearby, with a solitary dirty Chevrolet sedan parked up against the wall. A wooden fire escape led up the side of a building to an open office door. Beside the door was a signboard: Mighty Motors.

No one was inside. On a shelf by the entrance lay a set of Chevrolet car keys, attached to a piece of torn envelope with the word Hathrul (sic) scrawled upon it. Bryn waited.

Ten minutes passed and no one came. He remembered Agnete's easy-going instructions: 'They won't ask for ID'. It was too hot to wait any longer. He scooped up the keys.

As he descended to the sidewalk, a fat man emerged from a mobile toilet further up the road, tucking his sweat shirt into his jeans. If he showed any interest, Bryn did not detect it.

He sat in the driver's seat, trying to figure out how to drive the vehicle. It was a disappointingly bottom of the range, GPS-free model, gear stick already worn down to the white plastic, with no air-conditioning and smelling of sweat and floral cleaning fluid. For the first time in his American driving career, it came with manual instead of automatic transmission. He could start the engine easily enough, but he needed the reverse gear to allow him to leave the parking space and he could not work out how to engage it.

Deep in the recesses of the glove box, past the discarded candy wrappers, was an instruction manual. A previous owner had wrapped it in a protective black plastic that had decomposed in the California heat to a nasty stickiness. He tracked down the advice about shifting into reverse but, when he attempted to return the book to the compartment, he had to detach each of his fingers, one by one, from the wrapper. As he did so, a plastic slip containing a CD fell away with them.

It was an album of, of all things, recorder music.

He turned it over. The bewigged portrait of an obscure baroque composer called Pezel adorned the paper cover. He vaguely remembered the name from when he used to play tenor recorder with a group of friends, back in the days before the move to America. He chuckled. It was the last thing you'd expect in the derelict back end of San Francisco.

He was on the point of tossing the CD into the door bin when a peculiar dawning surmise held back his hand – as if his brain had just caught up with a processing overload. He took a closer look at the disc cover. As he suspected, Johann Christoph Pezel was not at all what he seemed.

Someone had, really quite subtly and professionally, photo-shopped a more recent image into the space between the wings of the composer's full-bottomed wig. A photograph he'd seen before, though not perhaps for twenty years. He sat back and laughed. It was the face of his dearly beloved Shropshire aunt, whom he had last visited that summer, before Bayreuth. And – of course – not only his aunt but Marcus's also. Clever bastard.

He switched on the car's audio system and dropped the CD into the tray. What a surprise: no sweet sound of recorders; not a trace of Herr Doktor Pezel. Instead, the voice of Agnete, quiet and close to her microphone. He was conscious for the first time of her Scandinavian accent, albeit the faintest, most teasing trace of one. He adjusted the sound to the minimum level necessary to hear, and composed himself in concentration.

'Good morning, Bryn. I hope it is morning.'

'Yes, it is,' he said.

'And first I must apologise for the car which may not be what you are used to. Its virtue is that it will not look so much like a hire car. And I am sure, in all the circumstances, you would not wish to stand out where we shall be sending you.

'I will be giving all the instructions you will need. The car's CD system has a pause control. Will you locate it now please.'

There was a long gap, vexingly more extended than necessary, while he found the right button.

'Use it at the end of each instruction. I will give you a few seconds to practise it once now.'

He did not bother.

'Good. Now listen very carefully. You must not, repeat not, attempt to hear my instructions more than once.'

As if he would dare.

He was to return to the main thoroughfare, Third Street, and turn left. Three blocks further down he should release the pause button, but otherwise maintain speed and carry on southwards.

'You must press it in now.'

He pulled away from the car lot, relieved at last to feel the air flowing through the open windows. But while the Chevrolet might have looked well-worn, it turned out to be a good, strong runner. The gear shift worked quickly and smoothly. Within a few blocks, he felt at ease.

He remembered to release the pause button at the third intersection. Agnete had now adopted exactly the kind of dull tone a passing driver might expect from a satnav commentary. A nice touch.

'Hello again. Do not worry but if you look in your rear view mirror you will see you are being followed by a green sedan. I will need to speak to you again when we join the freeway. Press pause now.'

The only vehicle visible behind was a yellow San Francisco cab. He wondered if Agnete's sophisticated command system had already gone awry. But within a block, the cab pulled away to the right and a small green sedan disclosed itself on the highway beyond. With Agnete – he fondly imagined – at the wheel.

The sedan followed at a safe distance until they began to approach the feeder road to the main north-south Route 101 freeway. Bryn was preparing to ease across into one of the access lanes when it suddenly disappeared from his mirror.

He craned back through a rear window and saw the sedan accelerating away down a side street, with a squeal of cornering tyres. A taxi overtaking on his offside blared its horn as he wavered into his path. By the time he looked again, a black car, similar to the giant Porsche he'd seen the previous evening, was coming fast down Third Street, sweeping past the rest of the traffic. He eased aside to let it through, but it braked and fell into line behind him.

As soon as he was on the freeway, he reactivated the CD.

'Hello. We will stay on the freeway for a few miles,' said Agnete's calm, official voice. 'Perhaps you could switch your emergency lights on and off very briefly to indicate that you have understood everything so far.'

He did not follow his instructions. There was no green sedan in sight. The black Porsche continued to keep pace a regular hundred yards behind, regardless of whether he speeded up or slowed. Candlestick Park passed by on the left, and then San Francisco International Airport. Still the Porsche held its place.

He thought he could take a lesson, though, from Agnete. He increased his speed again and drifted across the freeway to the left. The Porsche did the same. He decelerated but remained in the outside lane while less patient drivers overtook on the inside. An interchange was approaching. When it was almost too late, a momentary gap in the flow of traffic gave him his chance, and he swerved across the lanes and away. The Porsche swept on with the crowd towards the south.

He had arrived – in this city of huge and sudden economic contrasts – in another run-down, grid-planned precinct. The streets were lined with bungalows and second-hand cars. There were trash bins outside the houses and piles of uncollected rubbish on the sidewalks. All the residents in sight were Hispanic or Latino, slow moving and elderly.

The roads were too badly maintained and uneven for him to keep up his previous pace and he dropped his speed by about half. After a long series of random left and right turns, he felt confident that any pursuer would be as comprehensively lost as he was, so he pulled up outside a shuttered drug store to take stock. He left the engine running while he fished a street map from one of the car door pockets.

He had been studying it for barely a minute when, on some self-preserving instinct, he glanced up at the street ahead.

A black Porsche was two blocks away, driving slowly towards him. A man's head emerged from the passenger side window, and an arm. Bryn slammed into first gear – thanking God for the manual box – and shot away down a side street, engine roaring, tyres squealing.

He had no idea when he finally shook off the Porsche. He was too riveted on last ditch turns and the avoidance of oncoming traffic to give time to his rearview mirror. Sometimes as he cornered he thought he caught a glimpse of it, mostly not. He drove like a movie driver, through pot holes, bouncing over kerb edges. Whenever the lights were red, he took a sharp left and sped on through, in the alarming and legal American way. The Chevrolet finally careered across a side walk, down a service alley, through a building site and onto a wider street with shops running down either side. His tyres should rightly have shred and burst. But – like they do in the movies – they survived.

A police squad car was parked on the high street ahead of him and he decelerated, eased in behind it and stopped. There was no sign of the Porsche.

He tried the CD again.

'After the airport, you will pass a golf course.'

He held the pause button down for a few seconds and tried to recall when if ever he'd seen such a thing.

'You will need to turn off west at the next intersection.'

He allowed Agnete to continue a little while with her series of notional lefts and rights; and paused her again. He had found a bay-side municipal golf course on the street map, and also the turn-off he suspected he should have taken. But where he had now arrived was a mystery. Probably best not to ask a policeman. He drove slowly on.

The high street was in serious disrepair, cracked and roughly patched with tar, its road markings worn out and invisible. There were as many open spaces beyond the walkways as there were buildings. The overhead cables of urban decay hung again like washing lines by the roadside. He thought he might have been in Mumbai or Istanbul.

He passed the first street sign he'd seen for some time.

El Camino Real.

There are many *Caminos Reales* in the Americas. Bryn knew them as the Roman roads of the New World. So this drab, decaying highway slipping diffidently through the suburbs below San Francisco must once have been the most pre-eminent on the West Coast: the centuries-old mission trail that linked Mexico with northern California.

'You are on Route 82,' said Agnete's voice.

He took another look at the street map lying open on the passenger seat. There it was: the '82' clearly marked, on a road running north and south with, in bracketed letters almost too small to be legible, its historic title: *Camino Real*. The Royal Highway.

Agnete apparently wanted him to continue south for 'a further eight miles'; and look out for a parking lot to the right of the road. But eight miles from where? He carried on. Nothing. Nothing still after five, eight, ten miles. He had almost given up when he saw ahead of him an isolated, white-faced building set well back from the road. With a car park.

He tucked the Chevrolet in amongst several well-used models of similar vintage, where he reckoned it was least likely to be noticed, and released the pause button for further information. The CD refused to play. He tried to run the last passage again in case he had missed something and the disc expelled itself. He pushed it back in and tried a second time but the CD whirred noisily, ground to a halt, and resisted all efforts to release it. He remembered Agnete's prohibition on repeat listening. It was not the sly joke he'd thought it was.

The white building was a bookshop, much the grandest he had ever seen. Even out of season, the presence of students was unmistakable. A car by the entrance had a sticker in its rear window advertising an 'ASSU Senior Pub Night'. A young couple cycled past with laptops, tennis rackets and study files in their panniers. He guessed he might be somewhere near Stanford University, in which case he had travelled a long way south from San Francisco.

The front part of the shop was given over to a coffee lounge, and armchairs, settees and low tables. Summer course students and a scattering of (no doubt) professors were sprawled about, mug of coffee in one hand and a book in the other. He ordered a cappuccino abundantly sprinkled with sweet chocolate powder, and settled in with them.

He was feeling remarkably relaxed. He loved bookshops. They were his natural environment. If Marcus' and Agnete's grand scheme had finally ground to a halt and this fortuitously was to be his journey's end, he could happily while away an hour or so here, amongst the cherished tools of his profession.

There were half a dozen hardback books strewn about the coffee tables. One of them was the first volume of Shelby Foote's excellent history of the American Civil War – to which his own recently published monograph about the confederate generals had paid respectful *homage*. He picked it up and flicked through the familiar pages.

And put it down.

A theme seemed to be emerging in this day. Playing the recorder; the Shropshire aunt; the university bookshop; even the historic *camino real.* And the happy coincidence (or not) of Shelby Foote's book. In brief, the stuff of his life. As Marcus, in particular, would know.

He picked the book up again and looked through it more carefully. No turned down pages or underlinings or hidden messages. He put it back on the coffee table and a shop assistant tidied it away onto a small trolley, with a pile of other books she was returning to the shelves.

He watched her shuttling up and down the aisles. The Foote, a good-sized tome almost too heavy for her slender hand, was the last to leave the trolley. She slotted it into a space in a well-stocked section with the stack heading: 'United States History – 19th Century – Civil War'.

From where he sat, he was confident he could identify most of the display. But there were a few works he did not recognise. This was not necessarily unusual. What concerned him more, though, was what was likely to happen if he went up and had a closer look.

In Bryn's world, a good hardback book was like a bottle of fine wine. Paperbacks and, heaven forbid, internet downloads were the equivalent of an off-licence purchase. The books he most prized were not easy to track down and often needed to be sourced from specialist suppliers. They defied new technologies, sold for more than he could afford, had to be treated with respect and love, and opened *very* carefully. The best would keep for years.

So, generally speaking, a fine bookshop was a place of peril. He never intended to buy what he browsed. He never intended to browse. But he always did. With inevitable, and costly, consequences.

And so it was that on this pleasant morning, when he had finished his cappuccino, he found himself wandering over to the shelves to check out what was on display.

He ran his fingers along the title spines – Finkelman, Foote, Neely, Russo, Smith – until he came to his own recent volume about the Civil War generals; and contentedly pulled it out. An irritating vandal had taped a slip of paper across his name on the front cover. He peeled it off. And noticed that something had been written on it. A single word: Laura.

In Marcus's handwriting.

His first response was one of pure exasperation. If the message was intended for him, as it had to be, then his cousin's method of conveying it was ludicrously hazardous and whimsical. No better than a childhood treasure hunt. How could Marcus know that the paper would fall into his hands? Could he not have contrived a more direct means of communication?

And yet, somehow, it had been successful. And he knew exactly what was meant. Once when he was very young and Marcus already a teenager, his cousin had taken him on an illicit visit to the cinema. Marcus had probably decided he needed to widen Bryn's horizons. An old *film noir* was showing, far too sophisticated and grown-up, starring Vincent Price and an actress with whom both of them fell instantly in love, called Gene Tierney. It was the kind of experience a small boy never forgets. The film was called *Laura*.

He went back to the coffee area. Some young men were using the shop's free Wi-Fi system. Bryn asked a relaxed looking, long-haired student if he would mind him doing a quick internet search on his MacBook.

'Sure,' replied the young man, as if it was a request he received every day. 'And the usual trade, bro, is a Toffee Nut Latte. A Big One.'

'It's a deal,' said Bryn.

He searched on 'Laura' and 'San Francisco cinemas' without success. The hairy student looked over his shoulder.

'Try Palo Alto. The University Theater,' he suggested.

The University Theater it was: *Laura* was scheduled to play there that afternoon, in a double bill with *The Big Heat*.

He bought the student a twenty ounce *Venti* serving of his sweet smelling beverage and left the bookshop – for once – without any further purchases.

Chapter 13

The University Theater was a plain, white, Mission-style building on the outside, and a claret and gold extravaganza within. The exact, confident, unreconstructed, art deco auditorium of his earliest cinema-going memories. He bought a ticket, took a seat at the dead centre of the empty back row, and settled down for whatever awaited him.

The traditional red curtains, in their heavily ruched folds, were still drawn across the screen. Deep in the background an orchestra was playing the theme from *Limelight* on multiply divided strings. Two young couples whispering to each other were all the rest of the audience. It could have been an early afternoon thirty years ago in the suburbs of London, except for one thing: that all-pervasive, pungent, inescapably American aroma of stale, unsweetened popcorn.

The violins segued into the cascading harmonies of *Charmaine*. The auditorium faded to darkness and the music dwindled away into the distance. For a moment there was absolute silence. Then with a roar of Rodgers and Hammerstein and a brilliant blaze of light, the Mighty Wurlitzer rose like a dolphin from the depths. For an instrument barely larger than an upright piano the din was extraordinary. The ball-gowned lady organist bouncing on the bench seat seemed likely to be around for a while, so – regretting the diuretic effects of too much coffee and his old familiar weakness – Bryn stole out for a few moments' relief.

When he returned, a second person was sitting in the back row.

Agnete had camouflaged herself in jeans and a scarlet Stanford sweatshirt. Her long blonde hair had been folded up inside a floppy hat – except for the few artfully fugitive strands that trailed beside her cheeks. He doubted he'd ever seen a less unnoticeable student in his life. She looked like a fusion of Annie Hall and Greta Garbo.

He took the seat alongside her.

'Hi.'

'Hi,' she responded coolly, as if to an importuning stranger.

The *Carousel* overture succeeded a medley from *South Pacific*. And gave way in turn to a bells-and-percussion rendition of 'Oh What A Beautiful Morning'. The floodlight on the Wurlitzer slowly contracted to a single spot. Two rows in front, a student couple melted into an oblivious embrace.

He badly wanted to kiss her. It was the moment. Would an arm around the shoulder be welcome – or should he take her hand first? He had not felt so much at a loss since he'd been a teenager, and for the same reasons. He had thought about the moment too long, the penalty for failure had become too great, he could not guess how the lady would react. Whatever adult skills he might have acquired were now as rubble.

And so, while he procrastinated, it was Agnete who made a first move. Her left arm crept towards him and his heart soared. And as quickly returned to earth: an envelope lay in his lap. From the weight and feel of it, it contained keys. Three or four, one of which belonged unmistakably to a car. He reached a hand across and grasped hers.

'I have to go now,' she said sharply.

'Can I ask you something first?'

She did not reply. Her hand lay coolly within his grip.

'Why do I need a second car?'

'You'll get instructions,' she whispered, so quietly he could barely hear her.

The organist had embarked upon a final peroration and was sinking out of sight. The red curtains parted. The search-lit 20th Century Fox logo filled the screen.

'Agnete,' he whispered back. 'No one is listening.'

'I must not be seen with you.'

'Are those *your* instructions? Or Marcus's?'

The film had begun and its images flickered on Agnete's face. Her bleached profile, trained on the distant screen, was as cold and as incomparable as a Grecian marble.

'When will I see you next?'

'I do not know.'

'I want to see you again,' he said.

She drew in a deep gust of air and gathered up the scarlet hood of the sweatshirt and pulled it over the back of her hat. It was the last opportunity he might ever have: he slid his arm impulsively around her shoulder and kissed her.

There was no resistance. No response. He held the moment for as long as he could, until her lips began to quiver and he realised the vehemence of his embrace might be preventing her breathing in. She disengaged with a gasp and stared back at him unreadably – bewilderment, anger maybe. And eased out of her seat and departed the cinema.

The post-mortem lasted through the second reel of *Laura*. A dour battle for the high ground between his maturer self and the teenager in the back row. At least, he finally agreed, he had attempted to do something. No sin – no matter your age or wisdom – was greater than the failure to act. Clumsiness was an operational hazard; a peccadillo. No success was ever achieved without failure and Agnete was an experienced woman who must have endured many more inept encounters.

The recall of it made him shudder.

Good might – nevertheless – come out of it. Maybe, as the cinema dust settled, Agnete would find she'd discovered something... not unwelcome. And there was plenty of unfinished business. Further instructions. Further opportunities. Time to prove his mettle. The cause was not lost.

As he was passing through the curtained door at the back of the auditorium, he noticed two stocky-looking men – certainly not students – buying tickets in the lobby. There was little enough about them to alarm him. They did not look in his direction. They were not wearing three-piece suits with unsightly pectoral bulges. But he was beginning to get into the habit now of elaborate exits. So he retreated up a corridor, pushed open a door at the end and made his way round the building to the car park at the rear, where his Chevrolet should still have been.

It was not. He checked around in case he'd misremembered its location; but it was already obvious what he was supposed to do. One of the keys in Agnete's envelope had a tag attached to it, and a number. The matching vehicle turned out to be a newish Ford Focus similar to his own car in Salt Lake City, parked near the exit. Sitting on the backseat was his overnight bag – which he had last seen when he'd thrown it in the boot at Medford – packed with all his clothes and belongings.

The Ford was an automatic and needed no instruction this time in how to manage it. He drove out of the lot and dog-legged around for several blocks until he could be confident no one was following. He returned and drew up in a tree-shadowed side street where he had a view of the entrance to the cinema car park; and settled in for Agnete and further instructions.

It was another very long wait. After an hour, during which there was no sighting either of Agnete or of the two stocky men, or indeed anyone else who might have concerned him, he fell once more to searching through the car for guidance. In the glove compartment he found a hard-cover map book of San Francisco and the towns to the south, and worked his way through that for clues. Nothing. It was so crisp and clean he wondered if it had ever been opened.

He scoured the car. There were a few grubby signs of previous use – an unopened pack of lady wipes and some parking tickets in the driver's door bin; and a discarded sandwich wrapper and a half-drunk bottle of grape juice in the other. Otherwise – again – nothing.

There was one other obvious place to check. He climbed out, looked both ways up the street for strangers, and cautiously raised the tailgate. Under a piece of carpet was the promised fold-up trolley, a range of metal tools including a crowbar, a hammer and some chisels, and a pencil torch. But there was no sheet of paper, no cell phone, or scratched message, or anything else that might have helped to enlighten him.

It seemed to him he'd stayed long enough. He drove away, past Stanford's great green campus with its grand, impeccable lawns and avenues of palm trees, and headed south from Palo Alto until he arrived at an all-day Pancake House on the San Antonio Road. He ordered a takeaway coffee and a pie-like dessert called a 'Dutch Baby'; and sat in the Ford Focus with his supplies.

The only item still unscrutinised was the envelope containing the keys. He held it up to the light and squinted at it from different angles for hidden writing or a similar clue. He even sniffed it and thought he detected the fragrance of Agnete. There was nothing left to do but sit back and let his brain process everything in its own good time.

He finished the pie and stuffed its crumpled plastic tray into the door bin. Then – as he sat and sipped his coffee – from the darkest recesses of his memory the solution began to emerge. A possible solution only, he told himself; but he knew he was right.

He leaned across to the front passenger seat and retrieved the old discarded paper sandwich wrapper from its bin. First he held it up to the daylight, already fading with the approaching evening. He had not really expected anything; and there was nothing to be seen. He smoothed out the wrinkled paper on the cloth of the seat, silently apologising for what he was about to do. It was a game he had used to play with Marcus, taught him – as usual – by his cousin. He twisted the top off the half full grape juice bottle and poured the contents over the wrapper. The liquid was a deep, purple colour, and left a stain on the seat cover which could probably never be removed.

A rubric slowly resolved itself, as indistinct as a wraith, but – for one moment – legible. 72 D20. Like the CD before it, the wrapper started to dissolve and disintegrate until all that was left on the ruined seat was the faint smell of grape juice and baking soda and a soggy mass of what might once have been brown paper.

He picked up the map book and looked up page 72. Letters of the alphabet ran down the side and numbers across the top, and he followed them with his fingers until he arrived at the confluence of D and 20. There, very faint and missable unless you happened to be looking directly at it, was a tiny pencilled circle within a grid square. The page covered Professorville, a district a few blocks north-east of Stanford University.

Bryn closed the book and gazed at the setting sun.

'So we meet again, Professor Williams.'

Of course he'd heard of the place. It had been built around the same time as Stanford and was not, as a person might reasonably imagine, a stopping point on some ride around Disneyland populated by munchkins in mortarboards. It had been created – quite literally – for the purpose proclaimed by its name.

Was this, however, a coincidence *too far?* Bryn had never thought of his cousin as a particularly humorous person, but the adventure was taking on the character of an elaborate and rather extended joke. Maybe it was time to recognise a signal to a wiser man than he – not perhaps the first such signal – that the game was no longer worth the playing.

Unless… that is… Marcus and his people really did take it all seriously. An *Alice in Wonderland* world as opaque as a *Guardian* crossword. Secrecy, riddles and complexity. Boys' games as a way of life. Lapel transmitters, hidden cameras, ciphers, codes and dead letter boxes. Power plays and betrayals. Where people even killed each other in novel and ingenious ways, with poisoned sushi and toxin-tipped umbrellas.

Agnete's world also.

He opened the map book again. No harm in playing the game a little longer – it was not as if he had yet committed himself. It would be prudent to avoid a direct route to Professorville, and

144

better still to keep off the main thoroughfares. A detour to the east through Mountain View should do it, past the naval air station and back west to Charleston Meadow and thence up the dormitory side streets past Rinconada Park, to the objective. No harm in trying it out...

The approach to the block discreetly circled on the map was down streets so tightly lined with trees and high-grown hedges that the houses were only intermittently visible. The few he could see were set well back behind their defensive greenery, and built in the now-familiar white-faced, decorated Mission style. They were all huge and magnificent. Either construction costs were exceptionally low in those days or Stanford academics were exceptionally well paid.

He had arrived at the circled spot. On one side of the street was a high wall with a double gate set into it; on the other, what looked like a private tennis club, with some courts beyond a car park. He parked the car in a space designated for the club Vice President, conveniently below an overhanging acacia bush.

He sat at the wheel for a quarter of an hour. No other vehicle or pedestrian came down the street. In the dying evening light, the site was as dark and silent as a burial ground. He could feel himself becoming excited and apprehensive and ready for action. He climbed out of the car and collected the pencil torch from the boot.

The wall on the other side of the unlit road ran the full length of the block. A security camera was mounted alongside the gates, pointing at the ground in front of them. He edged up on the tennis club side, keeping in the deepening shadow of the trees, and crossed and approached the camera from behind, hoping to get a glimpse of the house within. But even when he crept up to the gates, all he could see were wide lawns and dense, excluding shrubbery.

Chapter 14

There was a mail box in the wall by the gates, immediately below the camera. Not the usual open-fronted design, but a stout, black steel canister with a letter slot set into a lockable flap. A number of bricks had been removed – not a difficult task since the wall was already flaking with age – and the box had been cemented into the space created.

He pressed back against the wall beyond the camera's field of view, and tried to slip a hand through the slot. It was stuffed with envelopes; and he struggled to force his fingers far enough in to grasp one. The gap was too narrow and the thick gauge steel too brutally unyielding. He tried teasing an envelope out with a ballpoint pen but managed to lose the pen in the box's maw. He found a twig by the roadside and wriggled it around. It shortly broke in two. The problem needed a little more thought.

He edged back up the street, crossed in the darkest part, and worked around again to the car. He took out the map book and ripped off its front cover, folded the cardboard down its length and flexed it to and fro until it became two pieces. He returned with one to the mail box.

It required time and patience but eventually he managed to force the cardboard into a shape with which he could lever up the topmost envelope inside the box. With some wriggling and shaking, it slid to the front of the open slot and into his grasp. A disappointment. In the slim beam of the torch it revealed itself merely as a circular letter from a local real-estate agent, addressed to 'The Property Owner'.

He tried again. This time the process took even longer. The outcome, though, was everything he could have hoped for. This second envelope was from The Academy of Motion Picture Arts and Sciences and was addressed to a Mr Ricky Gaunt. *Serendipity*... He tore it open. Inside was a leaflet listing the events and exhibitions available to Academy Members during the forthcoming year. No further information; but that was enough.

Bryn recognised the name. Ricky Gaunt might be well forgotten these days. There would be no tourist charabancs drifting past *his* celebrity residence, or fans hanging around for a brief glimpse of the one time star. Occasional bit parts in Japanese *yakuza* films, as an elderly Mafia don or the millionaire American father of a kidnapped heiress, were currently his main source of employment. Yet Ricky had once been the beefcake hero of a series of massively popular teenage *Beach Party* films – forty years ago and more.

Bryn had even attended a season at the British Film Institute in London two years since, when half a dozen of his derided money-spinners were brought together for a celebration presided over by the great Ricky himself. Bryn had thought him remarkably well preserved, if a little expanded at the waist. A testimonial to liposuction, Botox and permatan.

He studied the keys Agnete had given him. Attached to the car key was a smaller one, cut from hard plastic, multi-pinned as for a high security lock. It could not be for the mailbox or the gate, which was activated by a key pad set in the wall, and too well protected by Ricky Gaunt's camera to risk attempting. The plastic key had to be for some later lock.

He went back to the car and collected up the crowbar, the hammer and a chisel, though not – for the time being – the fold-up trolley. He felt his way along Ricky Gaunt's nine foot high curtain wall until he found, about a hundred feet beyond the gate, a point where the mortar was at its most decayed. He threw the crowbar over and waited for its impact in the soft earth on the other side. He tossed the hammer over a little further down to avoid a clash of metal on metal. It took a few minutes' quiet chisel work between the bricks to excavate the foot holes needed. He scrambled up with assistance from an overhanging tree branch, and dropped into the darkness beyond.

There was still no sign of a house or any building. He seemed to be in an enclosed country estate, surrounded by groves of mature rhododendrons, camellias and azalea. He followed the light of his torch down a narrow winding path between the towering bushes, to a clearing. Ahead of him – at last – stood a mansion three storeys high with a single gable spanning its frontage. Beneath the gable was a covered verandah and a flight of steps – all as wide as the house. The whole edifice floated on a sea of billiard-flat lawns, gleaming in the evening moon like a silver galleon.

He hung around amongst the rhododendrons, searching for security cameras. There were none that he could see. He worked through the bushes until he was opposite the right flank of the mansion, where the overgrowth came closest and hidden lenses might be least likely, dashed across a stretch of lawn and edged along the house until he reached the front entrance.

The darkness under the overhanging gable was so intense that he could not make out a lock in the door until he had switched the torch back on. He tentatively inserted the plastic key; and at once it began to turn.

And at that point he stopped. Old fears about the credibility of the enterprise began to rise again.

The lack of security inside the perimeter wall was, to say the least, surprising. Unless he had missed something. It was unlikely that the owner could have placed all his reliance on one camera covering the gates.

He crouched down on his haunches, watching and waiting. Silence. No dogs, no alarm bells, no arriving police car.

What would happen when he turned the key fully and the door opened? He shone the torch through the leaded window lights. In the entrance lobby, a couple of yards away, a control panel was fixed to the wall. Its style and four digit code pad were familiar from the homes of Bryn's wealthier Salt Lake City friends. He'd even seen them in London. He squatted down and pondered again.

The plastic key was a chimera. There was no point in utilising it if he could not switch off the inevitable alarm. Maybe it really was time to recognise that this was an adventure fraught with too many problems, and call it a day.

On the other hand.

One thing he'd learned from security-conscious friends, particularly the older ones, was how dependent they were upon something memorable to put into that code pad. And the older they became, the more likely it was that those numbers – those four digits – would be the same easy-to-remember sequence. With a maximum of sixty seconds before the alarm sounded and the police were on their way, it was almost inevitable that they would fall back on the one set of numbers they could all, always, recall whatever the pressure. Security companies counselled against it, but still they put it in: the year of their birth.

And Ricky Gaunt was no spring chicken.

Add to that the near certainty that he – an ageing Hollywood star – would be systemically vain and self-obsessed. How likely was it that he could invent a code that was not, in some way, himself? Bryn was as sure of this as he could be. If, in the event, he was wrong and all the bells burst into evening chorus, he could still beat a retreat before the Palo Alto constabulary arrived. And register a proud defeat.

So when exactly was little Ricky Gaunt born? What was the year of his birth?

He, like his co-stars, was famously a teenager when the first of the *Beach* Films was released. He looked mature even in those days, so let's say he was nineteen. That would make the date around 1945. In fact, now he considered it, Bryn was sure that was the year he'd seen recorded in Ricky's own, self-generated entry on the imdb.com website. It was worth a try.

He inserted the key again in the lock and turned it all the way. The door swung open and he hurried through to the panel. It was already counting down, but – alarmingly – from forty seconds only. He held his breath in fierce concentration and carefully put in 1… 9… 4… 5…

The countdown continued relentlessly.

Should he try a year later, making Ricky eighteen at the time of his first film? But what star would claim publicly to be older than he really was? He put in 1946 anyway. Still no effect. And only ten seconds left. Should he leg it down the drive or try an earlier date? He stabbed a final time at the code pad… 1… 9… but disastrously missed his aim and put in a 3 where he'd intended a 4. He wildly hit one last digit and fled.

Bryn was already well out of the door when he realised that nothing had happened. No ringing of bells. No screaming of sirens. So either the police had been silently alerted and were already on their way.

Or.

He crept back and looked at the face of the device. The countdown had stopped with two seconds remaining. For a moment, before it faded away, the small LCD window showed the last code tapped in: 1938.

He closed the door and walked through to the main part of the house.

He was in a vast sitting room, also stretching the width of the building. It was less dark than expected. With floor to ceiling windows on three sides, and heavy tapestry curtains drawn back, the full moon bathed the entire saloon in a soft, silver light. The décor reminded Bryn of the interior of the Frank Lloyd Wright houses he'd once visited near Chicago with arts and crafts detailing on the furniture and around the massive open fireplace and on the oaken stairs at either end leading to the levels above.

But there was work to be done. He pointed the torch at the floorboards. They were great polished oak beams half a yard wide and as thick as railway sleepers. Each one ran unbrokenly the length of the room. He could not see how, short of industrial scale equipment, he could ever hope to raise a single slab. By the same token, it seemed supremely unlikely that any proud owner would have ever wanted so destructively to secrete a safe beneath one. In front of the fireplace and under the Model D Steinway at the far end of the room, a few expensive Persian rugs had been shaken out onto the boarding. So he lifted them all, just in case, to see if there might be a hidden cavity below. It was a predictably futile endeavour.

In the distant opposite wing from the grand piano, a rosewood table had been laid as if for dinner. There were eight settings each of white porcelain, white napkins, engraved crystal glasses, heavy silver cutlery. How remarkably tasteful Ricky had turned out to be.

Bryn picked up a champagne flute to check if, nevertheless, the star had celebrated his name in the engraving. He noticed that the glass – and the rest of the table – had a light mantle of dust, as fine as the powder that had covered his car in Lassen Park. The place could not have been visited or cleaned for weeks. He pulled out one of the tapestried dining chairs and settled back, like Miss Havisham at her wedding feast, and looked about him.

At the dining end of the room, the star had hung several framed photographs of himself on the wall. Three or four showed him receiving awards: not Oscars, and none recognisable to Bryn. Another photograph had him with California Governor Arnold Schwarzenegger, each with an arm on the other's shoulder. There was even a picture of him shaking hands, rather stiffly, with George W Bush. Every one of them looking much younger.

He lifted each picture up and checked the wall behind. Entirely cavity-free.

Perhaps the dust might give a clue. Interestingly, there was far less on the polished floor than on the dining table. No indication of any footprints apart from his own. He wondered if, when the isotope was brought in – if it had been brought in – some attempt had been made to erase the traces. That might explain the dust on the table and its relative absence elsewhere.

He pointed the torch at the exposed cross-beams in the ceiling. Mahogany evidently, with lighter floorboards on top. He climbed one of the flights of stairs to explore.

The upper storeys of the house were quite empty and unfurnished. It appeared that Ricky might have moved out some time ago and sold or removed most of the furniture, leaving the ground floor perhaps as a display case for any prospective buyer. If indeed there had ever been one.

He spent a further hour searching. A dozen upstairs floorboards fruitlessly raised, chimneys explored, fittings removed, until the beam of the torch expired. He retreated finally to the kitchen. It had retained its charming early twentieth century fittings, with a minimum of modern adornments – a dishwasher, mainly, and a tall American refrigerator.

The refrigerator opened with such a blaze of light that Bryn slammed it shut again. He went back to the saloon and pulled down a curtain to drape over it so that he could have another try without giving himself away. The fridge was empty except for half a dozen nicely chilled cans of a micro-beer new to him. He snapped one open. Not bad at all.

By now a stubbornness was setting in. He had been in the house for the best part of two hours and was damned if he was about to give up. The whole thing might well be a wild goose chase – and maybe no isotope had ever been here or, for that matter, anywhere else either. But if it *was* here – then he was bloody well going to find it.

He gave himself another thirty minutes. No more.

In the movies, the correct routine is to put yourself in the mind of your opponent. How clever might Ricky Gaunt, or his security advisor, have been? Might they have been crafty enough to hide the safe box somewhere utterly unpredictable – specifically avoiding all those obvious places he'd spent so much wasted time exploring? Or should he be looking for something more in tune with the personality of the Hollywood icon? Somewhere a bit cute and flamboyant, for example? But showing unexpected taste.

As the half-hour deadline approached, and Bryn was no nearer his objective, he returned his third empty can to the refrigerator and paid his second tedious visit of the evening to what polite Americans, he reflected, quaintly called the bathroom. Or restroom, powder room, comfort station, washroom, John. Anything of course to avoid addressing its actual function.

This particular small room was windowless, with illumination which for once he could switch on. After a few minutes in the happy relief of a trio of beers well spent, he took to studying Ricky's white Ferrara marble tiles, light-filled ceiling and minimalist chrome fittings. He could have been adrift in a shadowless space capsule æons from anywhere, like the final survivor in Kubrick's *2001*. A small fortune had been spent to make it all so clean and pristine. Even the cistern had been hidden out of sight behind a false marble-faced wall. The one thing disturbing its uncluttered smoothness was a discreet little handle to flush away the last memories of the visit.

He took a closer look at it. The grouting of the surrounding marble tiles was a slightly, subtly, different shade of white from the rest of the room. He flushed the toilet a second time, but much more energetically. There was a perceptible 'give' in the handle. He tried levering it in the wrong direction: up rather than down. At first it felt immoveable, but – when he put all his weight and both hands behind it – the entire cistern wall shifted half an inch towards him.

He leaned into the handle with every ounce of his strength, forcing it upwards until, with a conclusive click, the handle settled into a position pointing directly at the ceiling. It needed a quite modest exertion to pull backwards on it; and an entire panel, three feet by three feet, swung out – soundlessly cantilevered on a single stainless steel bar. Behind the familiar working parts of the cistern there was a recess and, deep within the recess, a safe.

It was quite modest in size and may have originally been intended for cash or jewels. But if Marcus had expected its removal to be a simple matter, he had been sadly misinformed. It was efficiently cemented in on four sides. Neither the crowbar, nor the hammer and chisel, nor Bryn's most strenuous efforts to drag the beast bodily from its hiding place, made more than a trivial impact upon it.

After much struggle, he leaned back against the opposite wall and contemplated the scene of defeat.

There was a small door on the front of the safe, shinier than the rest, as if it had been added more recently. At its centre sat a little bevelled dial, as inscrutable as the Sphinx. The kind with an inset window which, if you spun the dial clockwise, offered the letters of the alphabet and the numbers one to ten.

He tried a few half-hearted combinations. There was less likelihood of hitting the right one than winning the national lottery. With the lottery, at least you knew how many elements to put in; and could probably assume they were all numerical. He tried the star's name, his birth year again, the titles of every film of his that he could remember, and the names of some of his co-stars.

After that he went out and had another beer.

He stood on the verandah and watched a thin wisp of cloud, or the vapour trail of a jet plane, drift across the full moon, like a stripper's veil. The darkness and silence of the streets beyond the house belonged more to the deep countryside than the suburbs of an American city. Even the birds were mute.

It occurred to him that if the safe door and its dial had been added since Ricky Gaunt moved out, the unlocking combination would be even more unguessable. He wondered if Udell Strange could have arranged it himself. Judging by his car plate, he was every bit as solipsistic as the ageing Hollywood star. And what was that he'd said in Bayreuth?

It's my 75th birthday tomorrow. We can celebrate it. You can bring your new girlfriend.

Hah! It was a trick he had pulled once, maybe he could again. Go for it.

He was sure he'd remembered the date correctly. But neither the year nor the day, nor any combination of those elements, worked the oracle. He tried variations on the 4th of July 1776,

American Independence Day and the cell phone number on Strange's card, still in his pocket. The mocking tolerance of the dial kept him going: there appeared to be no limit to the number of times you could put in an incorrect sequence of numbers or letters.

He returned to the saloon. The street beyond the gates was glowing in the headlights of a stationary car. He was out on the verandah at once, ready to bolt. But the car started up again and its beam flickered between the trees as it drove very slowly down the road. At the end of the block, where the curtain wall turned a corner, it stopped and waited, headlights still full on. Bryn stayed where he was, ears straining, until – after several minutes – the headlights finally eased away and disappeared.

It may have been nothing. Merely a fortuitous reminder that he needed to move on. He went back to the toilet to retrieve the tools. It seemed sensible to restore the cistern to its previous condition, and he was halfway through swinging the false marble wall back into position when he recalled Udell Strange's boastful car number plate and, on a parting whim, dialled in the letters. USPATRIOT.

The shiny little door clicked open about five millimetres.

He slipped his fingers into the gap and tugged till it swung all the way back. There was one object inside. No lead-lined flask or steel cylinder. Just a simple wooden box containing, according to the label, a bottle of 'Reserve Ten Year Old Canadian Club Whiskey'.

He took the box out. And nearly dropped it. It was even heavier than Marcus had predicted. So heavy that it needed to be supported with both hands. But what a neat idea to disguise the isotope as the kind of homecoming gift a tourist might buy in duty-free. Though the weight, surely, was a bit of a give-away.

He closed the door, spun the dial, replaced the false wall, reset the household security system, and crept out of the house. He retraced his steps through the camellias and the rhododendron bushes, hauled the box over the wall and returned to the car.

Chapter 15

For a moment, with a churning rush of alarm, he thought the Ford Focus had vanished – so embedded was it within the shadows and the acacia branches. Only the moon gleam on the body chrome gave it away. He opened the boot and laid the Canadian Club box under the piece of carpet; and took out the tools and the fold-up trolley and threw them into a patch of overgrown woodland on the other side of the car park.

When he came back, he realised that a small package had been taped to the front windscreen. A parking ticket, no less, courtesy of The Professorville Tennis Club. He tossed it onto the passenger seat as a souvenir for his cousin – with a contented chuckle at the idea of Marcus being pursued through the Californian courts, long after he was gone.

Then, as he turned out of the car park, he caught a glimpse in a side mirror of some movement by the gates to the mansion. No sooner seen than it dissolved back into the shadows. And whether male or female or even human he could not be sure; but cared so little to find out that he floored the accelerator and bolted towards the freeway with the blood beginning to pound again at his temples.

He was now facing an unexpected problem – one that should have been anticipated had he taken the likelihood of success more seriously – the sheer insubstantiality of Marcus's putative exit plan. What was he required to do next? He needed to contact either his cousin or Agnete and divest himself of his alarming booty. But where? When? How in all this vast land were they supposed to find each other?

An hour or so north of San Francisco he drew up at a roadside diner. Since leaving Professorville, he had obsessively watched his rearview mirror for any sign of a pursuing vehicle. There'd been one or two scares with drivers sitting in behind for longer than seemed natural; but they had all eventually overtaken or turned away. Now he wanted a final certainty that he was on his own. While he waited, a couple of cars did draw up, but one contained a young family, the other a gangly youth who let himself into the diner through the kitchen door to noisy shouts of welcome.

He should persuade himself to relax.

The absence of any clear hand-over arrangement was – on consideration – more than a tad insulting. Surely they'd had some faith that he might succeed? He checked under the bonnet and around the vehicle for any sign again of Marcus's tracking equipment. None: they had not bothered even to take that precaution.

They must in that case have intended to follow along behind and make contact at a convenient time. The present moment, for example. It was a pity that they'd not thought to alert him to their intentions, because they had now clearly and comprehensively lost him. He had no phone number or one-time cell phone; or any other means of communicating with them.

He debated going back to San Francisco and hanging around some of the locations where Agnete might look for him again: the Opera House or the university cinema or the coffee shop. The prospect chilled him. San Francisco, with thirty pounds of isotope and a bunch of assorted murderers searching for it, was not where he wanted to be.

An alternative option was to travel north up the Cascades and hang out for a couple of days near Mount Rainier, where they'd managed to discover each other before. But if that failed, what could he do? Cross the border? Try for a flight home? *With the isotope?*

It looked very much as if the game was over. Perhaps he should consider finding the wooden box a new hiding place. Lassen Park appealed to him – a neat irony – somewhere near the peak. And one day, who knows, Marcus might pick it up.

The overnight hold-all was still on the back seat where Agnete had left it. He burrowed around till he found his orange vinyl Harrods bag, full now with his dirty clothes; and emptied them on the floor. He retrieved the Canadian Club from the boot. The old carrier would amply serve the purpose if anybody saw him with it: quaintly and unsuspiciously English, and – crucially – sturdy.

He was zipping the carrier and its new contents back inside the hold-all when he noticed that the unwanted Tennis Club parking ticket had fallen into the passenger-side footwell. Something was loosely wrapped within it: a document of some kind. He scooped the package up, slit open its plastic envelope and unfolded the enclosure.

It was a single Business Class e-ticket from Calgary to Heathrow. In the name of Hathrill. Someone – possibly Agnete – had written across the top in capital letters: CARRY ON BAGS ONLY.

He apologised for his cynicism. Either she, or Marcus or both, would be at the airport waiting for him, poised to relieve him of his fatal cargo.

He checked for anything else. Just a card for the fast track service. The flight, however, was scheduled for next evening. That left him a little over twenty hours to travel thirteen hundred miles. Even without sleep that would require an average speed of sixty-five miles per hour. Time to get a move on.

He took off up Route 5, aiming for Oregon. This would be the fastest part of the journey and a chance to eat up the miles. Because it was so late in the evening, the highway traffic was light and he was able to plant himself in the outside lane at a constant eighty-five to ninety, slowing when he thought he might have glimpsed a police vehicle. With one stop for petrol and some leg stretching, he was already east of Portland seven hours later.

And dog tired. He could not afford the time to find a proper bed, so he hid the car in a crowded motel car park, curled up on the back seat and fell asleep immediately.

When he awoke, the dawn was already upon him. He breakfasted on pies, biscuits and coffee from the motel's dispensing machines, freshened up in the washroom, and took off again to the east. There were about twelve hours left to accomplish the second half of the journey. The fear was that, as he approached the Rockies beyond Spokane, the fast freeway would give way to much slower mountain roads. He also needed to slip into Canada by one of the smaller country highways: the kind with the least heavy border security. He would be lucky to keep up the sixty miles an hour average required to get to Calgary in time.

A problem not anticipated was the rising sun. His early start meant that the roads for the first couple of hours were virtually bare of traffic; but the glare of the sun ahead transformed his windscreen into an opaque, speckly shroud and forced him for periods to travel more cautiously than he'd intended. He did not pass Spokane till noon. Then, as he got closer to the mountains, the road began to sweep round some soaring rocky outcrops and through heavily shadowed canyons and he had a chance to make up for lost time.

He avoided the usual and shorter route up the west side of the Great Divide and crossed the Rockies through Glacier National Park. He turned north up the smallest road on the map and arrived at the border in the late afternoon.

It was everything he could have wished for. The American side had no interest in him at all. The Canadians were pre-occupied with a South Asian family whose loaded station wagon was being sifted through by three punctilious Mounties. He hoped that meant they'd be correspondingly relaxed about the contents of a white middle-class Englishman's car; and he was not disappointed. A Mountie confined himself to checking the Hathrill passport and asking if he'd been on holiday. He pointed towards the car window shelf and the Glacier Park entry permit he'd paid for a few hours earlier. The Mountie waved him cheerfully through.

He reached Calgary Airport with time to spare. He abandoned the Ford Focus in a long-term car park and printed off a boarding pass from an e-machine. He had remembered Agnete's clear instruction not to check his bag in. So he stood by the entrance to the fast track channel, and waited.

It was a reasonable assumption that Marcus, or possibly Agnete, would intercept him before he passed through security. The fast channel was the obvious rendezvous. But after an hour hanging around the entrance, with time beginning to run out, neither had turned up and he was becoming concerned that officials might start taking an interest in him.

He wandered around the main concourse in case Agnete and Marcus were waiting somewhere else. His confidence in his cousin, never particularly robust, was beginning to sag again. He flogged his memory for any clue he might have missed as to his intentions. He could think of none. Surely Marcus could not have expected him to take the wooden box onto the plane? Apart from anything else, there was the well-publicised ban on liquids of more than a hundred millilitres, and a battery of security checks. He wondered if he should abandon his cargo in a wastepaper bin. Or simply walk out of the airport. Both seemed to him unacceptably feeble conclusions.

He was out of time. There was nothing left but to make the best of a bad job. And hope, against the evidence so far, that this had been Marcus' intention all along. He found a food store off the concourse and – with his cousin's mountainside advice in mind – bought a bunch of bananas and half a dozen doughnuts for good measure. He packed everything into his bag, put further rational thought on hold, and marched through to security.

Again: no problem with the passport. He passed through the metal detector and received the usual intimate pat-down, without incident. But when he arrived at the far end of the luggage conveyor belt to retrieve his hold-all, an official was already standing over it.

'Would you care to open this, sir?' he said.

Bryn tried to look bemused.

'Is there a difficulty?'

'You've got something in there, sir, that's setting off the machine. I need you to take the contents out and put them here on this table.'

Bryn was on auto-pilot. He removed the Harrods carrier from the hold-all and stood it upright in front of him; and started building a neat pile alongside it of shirts, underwear and pyjamas.

'That'll do, sir,' said the official. 'But you can't take those bananas through. Or the doughnuts. No food.'

'Drink?'

The official was inspecting the contents of the carrier bag. He looked up condescendingly and shook his head.

'You know you could have sent this through in your checked baggage? What a pity you didn't do so, sir.'

And he lifted it up, carrier bag and all, with no apparent effort, and placed it in the confiscation basket at his feet.

Bryn was paralysed. He watched as the man returned to the table and ran his hands over and through Bryn's most private possessions before reinserting the whole pile, more or less, back into the hold-all. Except for the bananas, the doughnuts and the Harrods carrier bag.

And that was it.

He picked up the hold-all and walked away into the departure lounge with a wild, heady euphoria. Relief that his task, however fruitless in the end, was at last concluded. His flight had been called, so he shifted the bag over his shoulder and marched directly to the departure gate to join the embarkation queue.

The final walk to the aeroplane took passengers down a short corridor and past a row of tables where sealed and wrapped duty-free purchases were set out for the claimants to retrieve. A few random travellers were being asked – one last time – to show their passports and tickets. Bryn had already walked through when a man in a business suit, who'd been standing apart from the proceedings, stepped forward and put out a restraining hand.

'Would you wait a moment, sir,' he said.

Bryn handed him his papers and the man gave them a cursory glance and nodded. A second, uniformed, official produced an old orange vinyl Harrods carrier bag from the back of a row of purchases and planted it carefully in Bryn's hands. The heavy box-shaped object inside had been wrapped in plastic and sealed, and had a duty-free sticker attached.

'Move along, please sir,' said the first, deftly dropping Bryn's passport and boarding card into the top of the carrier.

At Heathrow, he passed unchallenged through the Nothing to Declare channel. When he emerged into the narrowing final corridor, two familiar figures were standing waiting in the middle of the lane. Marcus did not look at him. His gaze was fixed on the bag weighing down Bryn's left hand. As he reached him, he lifted it tenderly from his grasp.

'So we meet again, professor,' he said, in a tremulous whisper. 'Well done indeed.'

'It's heavy,' Bryn warned.

'Ah yes,' he murmured contentedly. 'Why don't we step aside and have a coffee?'

Agnete led them to a table in a coffee shop nearby.

While she was buying their cappuccinos, Marcus made some small talk about mutual friends and barely remembered aunts. But his mind was on other things. From time to time he glanced down at the bag between his feet; his fingers never left its handles. It must all at last have got too much for him because, as soon as Agnete and the coffee returned, he hauled the bag onto his knees under the sheltering edge of the table, dived into it with both hands and energetically began to strip off the wrapping inside.

'Keep talking,' he said quietly.

Agnete asked if Bryn's coffee was satisfactory. He replied that it was not so good as the last time, and she laughed. Marcus tore away until the box of Canadian Club appeared. He ran a penknife along its edge and, very delicately, slid the top aside.

He went *white*. Bryn had never seen a man so shocked. His own first reaction was to assume some terrible accident with the isotope and he jumped to his feet and started to back away. Marcus flung the carrier bag on the table in front of them and forced both sides of it down, fiercely, with the open palms of his hands. A bottle of Canadian Club whiskey lay serenely within its wooden coffin: seventy centilitres of Ten Year Old Reserve, just as the label had promised.

And evidently not what Marcus had expected.

He abandoned all discretion. He tossed the wrapping and the Harrods bag on the floor and tipped the bottle out on its side. A lead weight had been strapped to the base with duct tape. Through the clear glass could be seen, not liquid at all, but a quantity of light brown sand. He ripped out the cork and upended the contents on the table. A piece of paper, held in a tight roll by a rubber band, floated out on a tide of silica and fell to the floor.

Agnete leaned over, picked it up and opened it. She giggled and passed it to Marcus. The complexion of his face as he read it darkened from ashen towards deep crimson.

'Fuck,' he said, and threw the paper at Bryn.

It had a simple, if dyslexic, message:

Hapy drinkin, sukker

'Wilson?' queried Agnete.

She did not appear to be taking the reverse too seriously.

Marcus rose to his feet and brushed the sand off his trousers.

'Fuck,' he said again.

And: 'Sorry, Bryn.'

And with that he marched off; followed after a few seconds by his companion. As she turned into the main concourse, she looked back at Bryn, and blew him a kiss.

He retrieved the discarded bag, did his best to tidy away Marcus's mess, stuffed as much as he could into a waste bin, apologised to the waitress, and set off for the Piccadilly Line for West London and a good night's sleep.

The English and America

The Origins of Our Species

Brynmor Williams PhD

PREFACE

I am writing this in West London. Unlike, say, urban California – from which I have recently returned – this is a placid part of the world. It has a low crime rate. There is an extremely modest risk of earthquakes. Few beggars sleep on the pavements or squad cars lurk by street corners. Extreme wealth and hapless poverty co-exist far less frequently. There is a strong sense of community, underpinned by networks of schools, clubs, societies, groups, parties, centres, educational classes, religions – and public houses. This is Brentford, Hounslow and Ealing: the aptly named 'dormitory' suburbs of the metropolis.

It may be difficult therefore to accept that *civilisation*, even here, is the product of violence. Like the bones of our ancestors, death and destruction are never more than a few layers away. Nations in general are not created by the people who were here first, but by those who forced their way in later. By the invaders, the 'pioneers' and the settlers. In this monograph I shall be addressing a theme which I hope may have as much relevance to the present-day English as to America.

Let us begin by rolling back the centuries to a time when the 'New World' – that is to say, its accessible eastern territories – was mainly forest and the first natives met by the incomers were those living in communities on the sea edge. The history of what happened next remains sketchy, though we know it to have been brutal.

We know that, as their ambitions became greater, the settlers began to move inland. They split up into groups large enough to protect themselves: ten well-armed men seems to have been the norm. A few of them were able to travel on horseback. They carried a range of weaponry of which the commonest was a small cutlass with a single edge, a heavy blunt back and a sharp stabbing point – an effective defence if local inhabitants were to come unexpectedly from the dense forest.

They moved in scattered bands united by their own separate pledges of loyalty, but these people had a common purpose: to claim the best land for their own. They showed little mercy. In the words of a popular historian of this period: '[their] methods of settlement, though extremely practical, and perhaps not wholly at variance with the methods of later colonists, were not distinguished by much regard for the conquered.' [1]

But whatever criticisms we might have from a modern perspective, we cannot doubt the pioneers' courage. They had committed everything. They had come huge distances from the countries of their birth to the east, and sea travel – all travel – in those days was protracted and hazardous. The further inland they progressed, the more hostile the terrain became. Literally the fittest survived.

Of course the incomers were better equipped for conflict than the locals and more ruthless and determined. This was their last and best chance of making a successful life for themselves. They were better organised and knew what they had to do. The native inhabitants, by contrast, were mostly ignorant of the impending danger and fatally unprepared.

We may imagine such a group, travelling one day along the valley of a small river, led – let us say – by a tall yellow-haired man in his early forties who is shouting to keep up the spirits of his companions. It is summer, because in those days that was the season for long journeys. The river is shallow and sluggish but treacherously prone to fill up in heavy weather and inundate the land surrounding it. They need, nevertheless, to keep it close by because it provides their only reliable reference point within the anonymous canopy of the forest. There are bears still, and wolves; and also deer that they can kill for food.

[1] C E Vulliamy p225

After weeks of travel, with little sign of any indigenous communities, they cross at a natural ford and emerge into open meadows and are surprised at what now presents itself to them. Fields cultivated for crops beside the river. A cluster of simple dwellings. Honey bees in wickerwork hives. A hunting dog sprawled in the sunshine and a child approaching, naked except for the woollen breeches drawn tightly around his ankles. It has been described as a vision of paradise.

But for these people, the new arrivals, it is what they have come to destroy. Farming and the cultivation of land – the historic enemy of mobility and enterprise and the reason why history has always favoured rootless invaders.

Perhaps, if the natives are lucky, the arrivals will merely subdue them, kill their leaders, and force the rest to labour as slaves in – what for centuries had been – their own fields. And there will, at least in the earliest days, be a degree of inter-racial mingling. Not to put too fine a point on it, invaders tend to be short of women.

But history is always written by the conquerors. Traces of the previous inhabitants, even their language, will be progressively erased. A place will be given a new name, for example to celebrate a prominent pioneer. In this particular case, it will commemorate the loud blonde man who has led them to these meadows.

That is why this site – the site that now most interests us – became known first as *Gylla-inghas*. It has been suggested [2] that *Gylla* in the language of the blonde man's people meant 'the shouter'; *inghas* meant 'his followers'. The name metamorphosed and shortened through the centuries until it became *Eal – ing*, a suburb of West London. Similarly, other conquered locations such as Reading, Woking, Barking, Worthing and Epping still reflect the names of those Saxon leaders whose followers subdued or killed the existing native tribes and settled there themselves.

A reader may possibly have assumed my narrative to have had some other location in mind. If so, I make no apology. This could have been a story about America, or of many other countries. It is nevertheless about the *ancestors* of those Pilgrim Fathers who, a

[2] Neaves p61 ff

167

thousand years after Gylla, set out once more to seek a better life – making a similar journey across water and land to create what, in both cases, was to become the New England.

The standard carried by the Pilgrim Fathers was the Cross of St George. Gylla's was the White Horse. He and his fellow invaders raised it on the hillsides overlooking their newly subdued territories. One such eminence overlooks Ealing to this day and on modern maps is called Horsenden Hill: the Hill of the Saxon Horse. The sluggish little River Brent still meanders through the parks and golf courses below, and in the heaviest weather wells up and inundates them. The great primeval forest disappeared long ago. The rich farmland, however, survived well into the nineteenth century, when it was buried progressively beneath rank upon rank of peaceful suburban housing.

*Standing in the middle of the road
is very dangerous; you get knocked
down by the traffic from both sides.*

Margaret Thatcher

Chapter 16

It was good to be back.

The semi-detached he and Marion once shared in Ealing had long since been sold, but old friend Dieter quickly stepped into the breach. In his insistent way, he loaned Bryn his own nearby home while for a few weeks he spent filial time with his ageing parents in Baden-Württemberg. It was a kind gesture, and an unusually touching one. Meticulously clean and tidy, the house was exactly as it had been when Dieter's much-loved partner had died the previous year – exquisitely furnished and lit, not a pot plant or a cushion or a photograph out of place. A challenge to any guest.

The sense of relief, however, soon began to fade. At first Bryn put it down to too many memories of life hereabouts with Marion; or even to the strain of keeping up with Dieter's (and Graeme's) impossible standards. But something felt wrong. He wondered if the American experience had left him in delayed shock, or rendered him slightly paranoid.

He was half-convinced that the house was being watched, or that his calls on Dieter's artistically antique – and crackly – telephone were being intercepted. He was unnerved to discover that both Dieter's bedside clocks were eight hours slow, as if they had been set to Pacific Standard Time – a mirror image of his experience in Yosemite. There would be a perfectly innocent explanation of course; if he could think of it.

He badly needed to get out.

He made himself busy with practical issues, the kind that allowed him to hop on buses and lose himself in crowds; and he was the better for it. He set about getting a replacement passport in his real name.

He had not thought this through. First there was an issue of how he had managed to return through Heathrow – which he finessed by claiming he had lost the passport subsequently, while rescuing a dog from the River Brent. That ushered in a fresh complication, because the London office could find no record of the document's most recent use. It occurred to him, a little late in the day, that it was only a matter of time before they caught up with the news from San Francisco: the SFPD might even report possession of an undrowned document. When – fortuitously – it turned out the passport was due to expire in a few months anyway, he conceded that he could, after all, wait till then.

He was beginning to feel trapped. It worried him also that there was no news from Marcus, or from Agnete. He could see no way of resolving the complications, or staving off the inevitable follow-up enquiries, without some help from them.

There was no reply on Marcus's work number. An attempt to reach him through the switchboard was also fruitless. Bryn could remember, more or less, where his cousin lived – or used to live. So he took the Underground to Belsize Park Station on the Northern Line, and walked up the hill towards Hampstead Heath until he found the familiar leafy cul-de-sac with a tall, detached Victorian house at the end of it.

For a long time there was no response. He backed away for a better view of any signs of life within. A check-shirted man passed by on the other side of the road and lingered briefly: a neighbour, perhaps, wondering what his business was.

Marcus's wife opened the front door.

Fiona and Bryn had never had a comfortable relationship. At the root of it, he'd always suspected, was the absence of children. For Fiona, who came from 'county stock', breeding was a social necessity. She and Marcus had undertaken all the usual tests but no explanation had ever been forthcoming. Maybe they were incompatible. Or had left it too late – Marcus's ambitions (and Fiona's for him) had postponed the business of building a family until well into their thirties. Meantime, Fiona had watched as Bryn and Marion's offspring, the product of student indiscretion and no forward planning at all, noisily grew into adolescence. If she had found all this unbearable, she never said so.

There was also the disastrous event that took place when Fiona had just turned forty. They were celebrating with some friends in this same Hampstead house and had all got drunk, none more than Fiona. At some point late in the evening, she had intercepted Bryn on the stairs and insisted he accompany her to the third floor ('I need to show you something'). In a spare bedroom intended, as he knew full well, for the children they had never had, she pressed him against the wall and embraced him and, as he responded, slipped a hand down the front of his trousers. Bryn had reacted as if bitten by a wild animal. He jumped back; her face flushed crimson; and in the time-honoured phrase, he made his excuses and left. Scuttled away down the stairs. The whole incident concluded in a matter of seconds.

He doubted if she had ever forgiven him.

'Good morning, Bryn.'

'Hi, Fiona. Good to see you.'

'This is a surprise. I don't suppose you're here to visit me.'

'Well. I thought it might be nice.'

'Bullshit, Bryn.'

'Aaah. Fiona. How long is it since we last talked?'

'I don't know, Bryn. You tell me.'

She stepped aside and waved him towards the sitting room. It was Surrey translated to north London. Heavy chintz-covered

173

settees and armchairs, framed paintings of country scenes, an alabaster mantelpiece with photographs of Fiona and Marcus in the company of the great and the good. And on a side table, two pictures. Marcus receiving an honour from the Queen. And Marcus and Fiona in white tie and ball dress at some grand embassy reception, standing beside a tall man wearing a white and silver star on his left breast and a slim, blonde woman in a stunning, figure-hugging gown.

'Very dear friends from Geneva,' said Fiona, returning from the kitchen with coffee and a Victoria sponge. Pleased in spite of herself that he'd noticed.

They sat down opposite each other.

'So you came to see Marcus?'

'Well. Yes. Partly.'

'Of course you did, Bryn.'

'Yes.'

'Pity. I wish I knew where the fuck he was.'

'He isn't here?'

'In London?'

'Yes.'

'No, Bryn.'

'But he was here a couple of weeks ago.'

'I don't think so.'

'Are you sure?'

'Believe me, Bryn. I haven't seen my husband since July. Business.'

She pronounced the word as though it were a term of abuse.

'He's in America,' she added. 'Probably.'

'He certainly *was* in America. I saw him on the West Coast.'

'Did you really?'

There was a pause. Marcus's kind of pause. So long that he wondered if she had lost interest in their conversation.

'Business or social?' she said at last.

'Oh. Social. Definitely. I ran into him in… in… '

'You can't remember?'

'San Francisco.'

It was a confusing game. A sort of battle of discretion – how much each could appropriately reveal to the other. But there was an additional subtext and Bryn thought he could guess it. Fiona's next remark left him in little doubt.

'Really? San Francisco. And who was with him?'

'Oh. A colleague.'

'Professional?'

'Absolutely.'

She could not have made her scepticism more apparent if she had chalked it up on a blackboard.

'You can tell me, Bryn. Did this particular state secret have long legs?'

He tried to suppress the colour rising to his temples.

'I wonder if I could leave a message?' he said.

'You can try.'

'Tell him I'm in Ealing again. Perhaps he could get in touch.'

He wrote down Dieter's address and telephone number on a paper napkin and she folded it away under her coffee cup.

'If I see him, I'll tell him.'

As an experiment, Bryn thought he would return to Ealing on the Overground – the little-publicised, cross-London system used by the metropolis's more sophisticated commuters. Hampstead Heath station was a couple of blocks away and the link to West London took less than twenty minutes. With a taxi for the last leg, he accomplished the journey in half the time it had taken him to travel in the opposite direction.

A window cleaner was packing up his ladders when he arrived. Bryn watched him while he sat in his cab, making calls on his mobile. He wished he'd had a German telephone number for Dieter – he could have discovered if the man had a contract with him. As soon as he was indoors he found Dieter's copy of the Yellow Pages and looked up the name on the side of the vehicle. He could find no reference to it.

Late in the afternoon he went for a stroll. There was a park along the Brent river that he'd enjoyed in the days when the family had a dog. It seemed a good place to reflect on his predicament.

And try and put his accumulating concerns into perspective. Consider what he should do next. And in the meantime try to think about Agnete rather than Marion.

A heavy shower set in – a phenomenon he'd not experienced since Bayreuth. He withdrew to the shelter of a pergola at the north end of the park and sat for a while gazing out through the curtain of rain. His thoughts wandered away – to a dead figure in the snow and an unforgettable image of a small hole in the base of a man's skull. He shivered again at the memory of the murderer, hiding barely yards away. Waiting for an opportunity to complete unfinished business.

A man was coming towards him through the downpour. He wore a flapping, old-fashioned, belted raincoat and had pulled a grey trilby over his eyes. But this time Bryn recognised him before he had a chance to speak.

'Hello, Marcus.'

His cousin settled on the bench beside him and shook the water from his hat.

'I hear you've been to see Fiona,' he said.

'That's correct.'

'Bit unexpected.'

'Are you here to tell me you'd rather I hadn't?'

'That's entirely your affair.'

'Hardly so, Marcus.'

Two dog-walkers joined them in the pergola and Marcus fell silent.

The rain began to ease and the dogs and the ladies moved on.

'In any case,' he said, 'that's not why I'm here.'

'Why didn't you phone me?'

Marcus shrugged his shoulders as if the question barely merited a response. He circled a finger round the brim of his hat and watched the water trickle from it to the ground.

'How are you doing financially?' he asked.

'Fine.'

'You have a joint account with Marion, don't you?'

'I do. As it happens,' Bryn replied, irritated more than puzzled by the intrusive enquiry.

'Judging from your response, you haven't been checking it recently.'

'Why should I? There's plenty enough in it. More than I need.'

'Oh, is there?' said Marcus.

There was a pregnant pause as he waited for Bryn's reaction. He stubbornly declined to comply.

'So you will not be aware,' Marcus continued, 'that the other account holder two weeks ago cleared every last cent out of it. Every last penny.'

Bryn hated his cousin. Life was too short to enumerate the ways he had, in a single sentence, embarrassed and confounded him. And he had – no doubt of it – orchestrated this moment for one reason alone: to soften him up. To make him more amenable to whatever next he would require from him. He wondered what had happened to the ten thousand sterling Marcus had promised on the mountainside.

'I don't suppose you came all the way here through the rain to tell me that,' said Bryn.

'No,' he agreed. 'I thought you'd like an update.'

'Not really.'

Marcus dug into a pocket of his raincoat. He pulled out a pewter hip flask and flicked off the screw top. The sweet aroma of fine cognac floated across the pergola. He took a sip and offered it over.

'You're breaking the bylaws, Marcus. No alcohol in the Park.'

He hung the flask out for a few seconds more. It was the usual test of power, and Bryn ignored it.

'We under-estimated Strange,' Marcus continued. 'He laid us a false trail. Not just for us: everybody.'

He sipped again at the brandy. Bryn wondered if he had ever seen Marcus roughing it without some similar consolation to hand. Or maybe he did it for pure egotism: like an executive with a Montecristo cigar and leather braces. To remind himself he was important.

'So you think he had other safe houses?'

'Maybe. Maybe we got the wrong one.'

'Or maybe he rumbled you, Marcus. Did you think of that?'

He shrugged his shoulders.

'Certainly it was not your fault, Bryn,' he said briskly. 'You did a fine job. We have nothing to complain about there.'

How soon before the other shoe dropped?

'Actually,' Marcus continued, 'I think the problem was with his own security. He didn't trust it enough. With some reason of course since that's how we found out about the Professorville house. Bad luck the isotope didn't happen to be there.'

'So where is it? Exported already?'

'What do you mean?'

'On the cocaine route? '

He glanced at Bryn sharply.

'How would you know about that?'

'You told me.'

Marcus frowned.

'Did I? Well, things have moved on and if we don't intervene very soon it will assuredly be too late. The latest intelligence is that Strange has set up a deal and an exchange is imminent. I'm guessing it's more than one deal, involving both sides because that's how arms dealers work. Double your money and prevent one side being better armed than the other. After all you don't want one of them to win the war. The whole Middle Eastern market would collapse.'

He glanced at Bryn again.

Bryn put out his hand and took the flask. It was predictably excellent. Light, smooth, aromatic. You could drink it forever. Wherever did he get his stuff from?

'So – I'm guessing, Marcus – they're moving the isotope and there's an opportunity to slip in and steal it. And once again you need someone below the radar to do the job, am I right?'

'I wouldn't want you to do anything you were unhappy about,' said Marcus smoothly.

'Good,' said Bryn. 'Because "unhappy" would not begin to cover it.'

'And yet,' the other mused, 'you did such an excellent job last time. Nobody knows you're a player. It's a chance to work with my assistant again… '

Marcus's expression was as inscrutable as hers had been.

'There's very little danger,' he added. 'All we want this time is for you to be a courier. No more break-ins or dramas. Why don't you think about it?'

A small card materialised in his left hand and he tucked it into the breast pocket of Bryn's jacket. The exact same gesture as Dieter's when he had handed over those fateful Bayreuth tickets so many long weeks ago.

Bryn returned the flask.

'You cannot seriously believe, Marcus, that I would fall into that trap again. Professorville was a one-time stupidity. You knew the dark place I was in. And how vulnerable I was to your schemes. But now that I am back home – in England – I will *never* do anything as insane again. And if it's of any interest, I am through Marion now. I'm in the business of putting my life back together.'

'Oh right. And I don't suppose you've any idea what you are going to do next?'

'None. Yet. But whatever I do, you will not be a part of it. You and I are over too, Marcus.'

How many ways did he have to tell him?

'It'll be a lot of money this time. And you have an opportunity to make a real difference, Bryn. Make history.'

'Please, Marcus. It's all so transparent. I don't want any more manipulation. No more nasty tricks. I've learned more about your cousinly feelings in these last weeks than in the rest of our life together. And I do not like them. I do not like *you*, Marcus. I'm sorry. But that's the way it is.'

'You're not going to help me?'

'No. I'm not. I'm not going to help you. End of story.'

Marcus had so far appeared to absorb it all with his accustomed suavity. But now his face tightened into a mask and he jammed the screw top back onto his hip flask.

'You will regret this, Bryn,' he muttered fiercely. 'Seriously regret this.'

There were no further words to be had. Bryn left him sitting alone. A lost soul, much more disturbed than he was. He wondered if the cousins would ever meet again. And whether, in the end, he was sorry – or glad – to be free of him.

Chapter 17

The first thing he did was to close their joint account. Marcus had not been entirely truthful. Marion had visited it once – a couple of weeks past – and cleared out everything bar a few dollars. But a more recent salary transfer had been left unmolested. He decided to move what remained into a fresh account, and at a different bank so there could be no confusion. For good measure, he chased up two or three small savings Marion and he had also shared, removing from each exactly half, and putting his own moiety into a single account in London.

And straightaway ran out of momentum. There was something deeply enervating about unpicking the accessories of a marriage. At least (he told himself) there was no house to sell or young family to be concerned about. Their two children had long since grown up and scattered. They had – nevertheless – been the centre and purpose of pretty well his entire married life. Telling them it was over was, for the moment, unimaginable.

And Marcus had been right yet again when he doubted he'd any idea what to do next. He fell into a pattern of sleeping, walking in the park, eating in pizza restaurants, and watching the news till he fell asleep again. He stopped worrying about inquisitive strangers or officialdom or the crackling telephone line or his cousin; or about anything particularly at all.

Disengagement as complete as this was a new experience. As time passed, it began – a little – to intrigue him. He had all his life been a busy person, fearful of the moral vacuum that the alternative represented. How long might it be possible to embrace this drug of idleness – this listless state that in the middle ages they called *accidie* – before it consumed him and became a life style? How fragile indeed were the conventions of work?

And yet at his lowest ebb he recognised that something was still ticking over inside. As he slouched in front of the television, with a takeaway and a bottle of red wine on the table beside him, he found he was turning more obsessively than ever to the breaking news. To images of a world outside going to hell in the proverbial hand cart.

Not that there were any echoes in North Ealing. The old ladies still walked their dogs, mothers took their children to the little school by the park, the hairdresser and the fishmonger stood outside their shops on the Pitshanger Lane gossiping with the passers-by. It was a world as impenetrably tranquil as the electronic version was demented.

At the centre of events, as so often, were the Middle East, and America. Secret State Department correspondence, leaked on the internet, had revealed a network of deceit, of diplomats intriguing with both sides of the Arab-Israeli divide in an attempt to preserve a neutralising balance of power. Trust had collapsed, and been replaced by threats and ultimata. There were rumours of a lethal new generation of weaponry in the hands of Islamic militants, sourced variously (according to the latest story) from Burundi, Armenia or even California. Israel had threatened unilateral military intervention if no action was taken by its allies.

On the other side of the Atlantic the President had eyes and ears exclusively for domestic affairs. But a speech by her Vice President, praising New Left principles of non-interventionism, was widely taken to be a signal that the President would oppose any form of American military action in the Middle East, however critical matters became.

Meantime, she had battles enough of her own. Her proposal to introduce a beefed-up version of the 1933 Glass-Steagall Act, to prevent the banks gambling with depositors' money, had incited Wall Street to a new level of outrage. A threat to move financial operations to unregulated Moscow was being taken seriously by the pundits.

He watched a Fox News programme devoted to a panegyric of the Muscovite oligarch life. More stretch limos and traffic jams than Hollywood. Hotel lobbies with as much mink and sable as a furriers' convention. Headdresses glittering with diamonds. Bodyguards with ten thousand dollar watches. Apartments of Italian marble and polished chrome. An annual 'Millionaire Fair' for oligarchs only. The commentator explained that Moscow now had more than fifty billionaires, while the millionaires were uncountable. The last rash official who'd attempted to impose bank regulation in Russia had been gunned down in 2006 as he left a football match. What was there not to like?

And then there was the White House's stubborn determination to impose political balance on the American media. Dissension within the President's own party meant that her 'Fairness' Bill was in danger of being filibustered – unless she agreed to open up some of the National Parks to mining companies so they could ease the nation's critical shortfall in mineral resources. One of the Parks targeted for exploitation was Lassen.

Bryn took his usual early walk through the park. Overnight downpours had left the sky clear except for some light clouds at its western edge. Its china blue bowl was marred only by the vapour trails of Boeings and Airbuses sliding in towards Heathrow. The air was warm and fresh and he sat down on a bench at the furthest end to enjoy it.

Half a mile away, poking through the trees, was the steeple of a church. Behind him, the quiet drone of the A40: the susurrus of ceaseless traffic. The sun had brought the midges out from the woods by the River Brent – with their own competing murmuration, higher and fainter than bees, and more irksome. The park was empty and busy at the same time, small and intimate and embracing. A possible metaphor for England in general. He made a note for later use.

He closed his eyes and dozed.

When he awoke, a small film crew had assembled a couple of hundred yards away, where the river curved sharply to the north-east. It was a common enough occurrence: there was a new university a mile to the south, with performing arts and media courses and doctorates in cinema semiology. The students were probably shooting the week's assignment. He had always been struck by how long they took to achieve a single brief scene. So much discussion, camera adjustment, checking of light.

Today was the same. Two of the group wandered off into the woodland, another sat on a log with his ear to a mobile phone, while the shortest student mounted the camera on a tripod and swivelled it around looking for angles. Bryn watched the wandering couple till they melted out of sight amongst the horse chestnuts and tangles of ivy, down a path he had travelled himself many, many years ago. In a different world.

He realised that the young man with the tripod was now photographing *him*. Or at least had settled on an angle which placed him dead centre of his frame. The morning idyll was over and he hauled himself up from the bench. By the time he reached the path leading towards the park's iron gates, the young couple were already returning across the grass and the cameraman had begun to pack away his equipment.

Twenty minutes later, as he meandered through the sleepiest part of Ealing, where the houses were double-fronted and the cars all German, he arrived at Longfield Walk. He'd often used it as a – notional – short cut. He liked its name, its echo of the countryside as it used to be. He liked the way it slipped between high garden walls, a slim half-secret avenue for pedestrians and the occasional cyclist. It was delightfully unnecessary – the main road ran parallel to it a hundred feet to the east. Two fingers in the air to modern planning.

Usually when he passed down it in the morning, there was someone in a downstairs room at the northern end practising her vocal scales: too good for a student – a professional opera singer maybe. Today she was tacet. The solitary being within sight or earshot was a drunk slumped against a wall with a suitcase beside him, fast asleep in the sunshine.

Bryn was about halfway down when a man stepped in from the street below and stood across his path with arms akimbo.

He stopped instinctively. Immediately a door opened in the right hand wall and a second man emerged. Something about his face was familiar and in a moment of puzzled incomprehension Bryn delayed for a fatal second or two. Then just as he turned to flee, a canvas bag swept down from nowhere over his head and shoulders, straps were snapped tight round his body, and he was helpless.

He tried to shout but a hand clamped the foamy inner lining of the bag across his face so that he could scarcely breathe. He was aware of being whisked back through the wall into the garden beyond, down what must have been a service alleyway and into the boot of a waiting car. A needle came through the canvas and into his arm and after that he remembered nothing.

He awoke to complete confusion. For a while he barely had a sense of memory, let alone an inkling as to where he might be. He was like a frightened child waking in the night except there were no clues at all: no moonlight edging round the curtains, no sounds of distant traffic, footsteps on the landing. It was so pitch dark he could not at first tell if he was indoors or out.

The first thing he identified was a smell of urine; and he discovered that his jeans were wet with it. His shoulder ached – bruised, he supposed – and when he tried to stand up both knees crumpled beneath him. The floor was unlike any he had ever walked on before. As he sprawled across it, he could feel with his fingers a soft, undulating, pitted surface like a beach after the tide had withdrawn. He crawled along until he bumped into a wall; and followed it round in an attempt to establish the shape and size of the place he was in. A room perhaps twelve feet by twelve. Everything in it was padded.

A door slammed open. A silhouetted figure in boots, tucked-in trousers and loose shirt stood in the space; then he was gone, the door slammed shut again behind him. Followed by a terrible blaring cacophony – music louder than he had ever heard and, of all things, Wagner.

A bank of ceiling arc lights crashed on. He could feel their heat; and the brightness was so intense that even when he squeezed his eyes shut and covered them with his hands he could still see the pink outline of his fingers. The noise, meantime, was equally intolerable. He had to settle in the end for a crouched position with his head against the floor and his thumbs deep in his ears.

The door burst open again and two men rushed in and whipped his hands from his head, cuffed them behind his back and rammed a heavy baton between his elbows. And began to shake him and shake him and shake him. One on either side each holding an end of the baton with gloved hands. Wrenching him rapidly back and forth until he had no idea which was the most unbearable: the excruciating pains rushing up his spine, the surging headache and gagging dry vomit, or the certainty that if this continued much longer he would surely die. He caught a brief glimpse of their faces – or that part of their faces visible between their heavy ear-defenders and black-lensed industrial goggles – but he could not this time mistake the dark and aquiline features of the Mediterranean.

He passed out.

When he came to he was alone again, lying in a doll-like heap. He made a vague effort to raise his head and one of the tormentors instantly returned with a hessian sack and threw it over him. The pain of the past half hour had begun to abate but also sufficiently to make him more acutely aware of the new ordeal. He tried to shut out any sense of what the sack must contain: horse manure, dog crap, human faeces – but *shit* by any other name. He choked and gagged and vomited. The more he tried to shake the monstrous object off his head, the more it clung to him. He could not breathe. He could only, and almost with relief, weep.

Someone eventually came into the room and pulled the sack off. A hand – almost tenderly – wiped the mess from his face and dropped it in a bucket, and passed it to someone else for removal. His wrists were unshackled and the baton put aside. He was now wholly unrestrained but, when he tried to stand or move, his limbs folded up as if they were jelly. His hands and fingers had become a twitching collection of pins and needles. He fell sprawling to the padded floor; and lay there.

'So you'll tell us everything now, will you?' said the man and Bryn nodded.

He realised that he recognised the voice.

'I know you,' he said fatuously.

'Of course you do,' said the man, amiably. 'We shared a table in the Volcanic Park last month, did we not?'

The hikers. Walking the Pacific Crest Trail; flirting with the ladies from Sacramento; quizzing him about his intentions.

'You can still call me Eyal. Though that's not my name. Any more than yours is Hathrill. You don't make a very good spy, whoever you are. You didn't even recognise me this morning, did you?'

Bryn nodded again. Even a tiny movement was painful.

'But there are many things about your involvement in this affair which puzzle us. You will be helping us, won't you?'

Another nod.

The other man returned. Again Bryn realised, with a sigh of despair, that it was a familiar face. The little photographer in the restaurant in Bayreuth. The cameraman in Pitshanger Park. And Eyal, or whoever the first one was, was probably the student he'd seen sitting on the fallen log, setting this whole thing up on the phone.

'Let's get down to business,' said Eyal, and gave a hand signal to his companion. The other grabbed one of Bryn's wrists and pressed it inwards in an agonising lock. Bryn gasped.

'It's not necessary,' he whispered.

'Well, we shall see,' said Eyal.

'All we need,' he continued, 'is for you to tell us everything you know about the isotope. Who your contacts are, where it is now, what plans have been made, where you meet. You understand that?'

Bryn nodded again.

'Let's start with who you're working with.'

Out of the fear and pain some small clarity was emerging. It must have been Eyal he had passed climbing the cliff path out of Yosemite, and whom he'd seen later under the Douglas firs at the summit. And it followed that if Eyal's group had been onto him from such an early stage, it could only have been because of his Bayreuth dinner with Strange.

In which case, he guessed he was one on a whole list of Strange contacts, all under surveillance. Networks of agents searching for the isotope. What a chilling affirmation of the monster's power.

And they might have lost interest in him if he'd not stumbled upon Sidney Stratton's body. And run into Strange outside the Opera House. By the same token, they might know nothing at all about Marcus – always absent from these conjunctions – and almost nothing about Agnete. Nor should they. Ever.

He considered trying to bluff it out. Explain his association with Strange on the entirely truthful basis that no business was ever involved. Purely social acquaintance and a mutual interest in opera. He was an innocent member of the general public. Then he remembered Eyal's earlier comment about his identity. Eyal knew about the false passport. How could he explain that?

The cameraman tightened his wrist lock and Bryn gasped.

'I think the man you want is called Udell Strange,' he whispered.

'You're working with him?'

The pain again seemed to clarify Bryn's mind.

'I have done.'

'In what kind of way?'

'I... I... shift currency around for him. And drugs. I'm a bagman.'

'A bagman, are you? What was the last job you did for him?'

'Cocaine. I took some cocaine through to London.'

'Through Heathrow?'

'Carry-on baggage. No problem with Customs.'

'You paid them off?'

'That's right.'

Eyal nodded to the other man and he released Bryn's wrist and left the room.

'You're not taking us seriously, are you?' said Eyal quietly.

'Of course I am.'

'Because you've never worked for Udell Strange in your life. You've met him twice and we have a full record of both those meetings. You have been working for someone else. And we need to know who it is.'

The cameraman returned, this time carrying what appeared to be a stretcher, which he placed full length on the floor of the room. No one spoke. Bryn was hauled to his feet and slung face upwards on top of the device, and bound at the shoulders, hips and ankles with heavy straps. One end of the stretcher was raised so that his head was a foot or so below his heels. The whole assembly – wood struts, canvas, straps – had been soaked with water and was ice-cold.

Eyal looked down on him.

'If we cannot trust you to tell the truth,' he said, 'maybe we should give you a cleansing bath.'

'Wash his mouth out with soap and water,' said the other, in a thick Germanic accent.

'I'm sure you know what awaits you,' said Eyal. 'Something we learned from the American Department of Homeland Security. Just to remind you… we apply water to a cloth which is lowered over your nose and mouth. If that is insufficient incentive, we pour more water from this large watering can, from a distance of twelve or twenty-four inches above your face. This we will do for about half a minute. At that point we may allow you to catch your breath – two or three full draughts should be enough – before we start the whole cycle again. The back of your throat will seize up. You will believe you are drowning. Oh yes. Your chest will heave – people are even known to break their ribs against the canvas straps. Your lungs and your sinuses will be on fire. Do you want me to continue?'

'No,' said Bryn.

'Then tell me who you are working for.'

'MI6.'

'Oh really. Give him a drink, Feivel.'

The cloth was lowered over his face and, after an interval, he heard the water begin to trickle onto it from the watering can. He had sufficient time to take a massive breath, reckoning he could last forty-five seconds, perhaps a minute. But a minute and more passed and still the water flowed, and continued to flow, till his head and lungs were on the point of explosion. But when he could hang on no longer and tried to gasp for air, the cloth had become as impermeable as cellophane. He could feel his lungs collapsing. He struggled to cough and retch and every muscle of his body screamed in spasm – until a great dark cloud began to gather around him and the agony receded and faded away and he knew that he was dying.

The cloth had fallen from his face. He was conscious for a long time before he felt able to open his eyes. On the periphery of his vision a couple of figures were standing in the opened door of the chamber. One, probably Eyal, was talking to someone very quietly. He looked as though he was holding a small mobile to his ear.

Both men went away and the door was closed. Bryn attempted to lift an arm but the slightest movement shot him back into his valley of pain. If anything, his hips were the most aflame – all that convulsive twisting against the straps. As for the straps themselves, they now lay on the floor around him, each in its own little pool of water.

The ceiling lights were on, but dimmer now. Wagner still played – quietly – through the loudspeakers in the walls. He could even recognise the work. The composer's last opera, *Parsifal*, slow

190

and relentless – a five hour fable about an innocent fool out of his depth in the real world. He would not care if he never heard Wagner again as long as he lived.

Eyal came back into the room. He was carrying a long hypodermic syringe filled with some yellow liquid. This was it. He had no strength, and scarcely any will, to oppose him.

The Israeli rolled up Bryn's left sleeve and – very professionally – rubbed up a vein with his thumb. Bryn could barely feel the tip of the needle as it sank in.

'Is it all over now?' he asked. 'Is this what you guys call a termination?'

Eyal glanced up at him and smiled.

'No,' he murmured. 'Kill a friend of Marcus's? Never.'

Chapter 18

The first thing he saw was the fox. Probably a teenager: slender and delicate, with a tail hardly bushier than a cat's. It stood a couple of feet away, staring at him with unblinking amber eyes. A black streak swept back along each side of its slim snout, luring Bryn's gaze towards two bat-like ears, forward-swivelled as if to focus all of the creature's hypnotic force upon him.

He gazed at the fox. The fox gazed at him.

Eventually he must have moved slightly, because the creature skipped back, like a fallen leaf caught in a gust of wind, and drew its head back towards its shoulders in darkest suspicion.

'Hi,' he said.

The young animal turned away and trotted off down an avenue of oak and horse chestnut trees; and Bryn turned reluctantly to the business of exploring his body and his environment.

He was out in the open air and soaking wet. The ground beneath was greasy but hard and flat. He had been dumped within the curve of a decaying log screened off on three sides by a tangle of brambles and ivy. The moon and the stars were so clear and bright, and the night so silent, that he thought at first he was somewhere in the English countryside. But a few yards away he could make out some low railings and a municipal children's playground. He was back where the horror show had started. In Pitshanger Park. In Ealing.

He could not get up. Even dragging an arm around for support required an effort of will. The sudden shift of balance rolled him onto his face and he lay helplessly with his mouth full of dirt and grass. His head ached; the pressure of ribs and hips against the hard clay made him gasp with pain. But a little strength was beginning to seep back. Sufficient to lever his body onto the ivy-smothered log and settle for a few moments into a pain-free sitting position. In the light of a full moon as bright as a winter day, he craned his head left and right until he was certain that he was quite alone. Even the fox had disappeared.

His brain began to spin with a wild relief. Dying and returning to life! He could hardly breathe for the elation. And yet, after all he'd been through, how bizarre to rejoice. Had he really died, he'd have been no less content. It seemed as rational as a man acclaiming his good fortune for escaping from *bad*; or praising the Almighty for delivering him from an Act of God. He must pull himself together.

The first priority was to make an itemisation of what he'd been left with. He forced his trembling fingers into the pockets of his jacket. He could feel a wallet still, stuffed and bulky: money, credit cards and driving licence for Hathrill, even the fake passport. A pair of spectacles in the top pocket. Handkerchief and change. Notebook. Keys. They'd not even taken the keys. Did they have time to copy them; or had they no longer any use for them?

He tried to stand up. His limbs were still shaky, but already becoming stronger. A more commonsense mood was beginning to replace the early adrenalin. Whatever he might fear, what he needed was a bed. Change out of his cold and soaking clothes. Sleep.

Covering the quarter of a mile home through the empty streets turned out a labour of Hercules. It was slightly uphill from the river, but as tiring as the Yosemite cliff climb. Every few minutes he found himself obliged to sit on a dustbin or a garden wall, and wait for energy to return to his flat-lining batteries. The last block was the hardest and it was the fear of discovery and recapture that chiefly drove him on. On the inside of Dieter's front door were two chains, plus a bolt and a night-latch; and he slapped on every one.

He slept through till next evening. Even when he awoke he had no desire to leave his bed. Every muscle, from his neck to his ankles, ached. He could move around alright, take himself to the toilet for a trickling pee, eat some fruit or cheese from the fridge; but the effort soon exhausted him and he shuffled back again to bed. His second sleep lasted into the following morning.

He had been out of touch with the news for two full days. Long enough for another major development in world events. All the news channels were buzzing with speculation following the shockingly unexpected death of the American Vice President. A widower, he had recently remarried a much younger woman whose glamour and vitality had – by all accounts – reinvigorated him politically and physically. The circumstances of his death were still obscure. The strongest rumour was that Vice President Flaxman had expired while engaged in some unusually energetic marital activity – the details of which of course could not be shared with the daybreak audience.

The wider implications were serious. With the rising threat of war in the Middle East, the President had become very dependent upon her VP for his reassuringly *macho* presence in the White House. Without him she was exposed. A one-time pacifist, she had never been persuasive in the role of commander-in-chief, as national opinion polls persistently reflected.

Some of the media speculation concerned Flaxman's successor. One candidate, a retiring four-star general fresh from a successful conclusion to yet another campaign in Afghanistan, was the subject of a blog and twitter campaign to draft him into the post. In the view of a breakfast pundit, commenting live by satellite from Washington, public opinion might make it impossible for the President to resist his appointment. In the meantime, her – apparently – grief-stricken withdrawal from public view and refusal to address either the VP issue or the Middle East crisis had created a political vacuum, which was being vigorously occupied by her opponents.

Bryn was feeling better now. A short walk to the shops on the Pitshanger Lane convinced him he was fit enough to make it down to his old doctor's surgery south of the Broadway. He booked an appointment around lunchtime.

He had given no thought to the route and was concerned only, in the absence of convenient public transport, to get there as directly as possible. But he had over-estimated his physical strength and – critically – his resilience to the emotional effects of his ordeal. He realised there might be a deeper problem when he was approaching Longfield Walk and heard – very faintly ahead of him – a woman's voice practising her scales.

The sound froze him where he stood. He felt nauseous and dizzy. Perspiration started to run down his face and he put a hand against a street lamp to prevent himself falling over. Only after a period of deep breathing did he feel able to turn aside and travel the long way round to the surgery. By the time he walked into the little consulting office, he was regretting his decision not to spend the rest of the day in bed. He sat beside the desk as the doctor scrolled through a database of his previous medical history.

'How are you today?' said the GP cheerfully – still peering at the computer screen. 'Looks like I haven't seen you for a while.'

'Not so good. Depressed.'

'Sorry to hear that.'

The doctor swivelled round in his chair. He was an overweight, middle-aged man with a florid complexion who looked as though he could do with some medical advice himself. Bryn had known him for more than twenty years and visited him perhaps six times. He had forgotten to take himself off the surgery's list when he'd moved to America; but he doubted if his absence had ever been noted.

'What appears to be wrong?'

'I was beaten up two days ago. I don't know how serious the damage is.'

The doctor unfurled an inflatable cuff and wrapped it round Bryn's upper arm.

'You were attacked?'

'Yes. That's right.'

He pumped away thoughtfully and made a note of Bryn's blood pressure in his database.

'You've been to the police?'

'No.'

No. Not after the passport debacle.

'Don't you think you ought to?'

'Maybe.'

'Take off your shirt and trousers now, please.'

Bryn stood up while the other circled and peered and squeezed him. A few times he gasped involuntarily when a muscle or a rib protested too much. After a thorough inventory, the doctor gestured to him to put his clothes back on and typed some more notes into his PC. A body-mapping template disgorged itself from his printer and he began to mark up Bryn's injuries.

'So you were beaten up, you say?'

'That's right.'

'Well, you've got some bruises on your shoulder and on your hips. The kind some people get when they take a tumble. Not much worse than that. You didn't collide with a door, say?'

'No. Two guys beat me up.'

'Only joking. Pity you didn't tell the police.'

'What about the muscle pain?'

'I can give you something for that. A bit stronger than Nurofen.'

The printer hummed again.

'And the injections?'

'The injections?'

Bryn explained about the hypodermic syringe and the yellow liquid. The doctor looked puzzled. He inspected Bryn's offered arm and typed another entry into his database.

'Any nightmares? Flashbacks? Trouble sleeping? I can give you a mild sedative if you're feeling depressed,' he murmured, studying his notes. 'And of course something for the pain.'

There was a chemist's shop down the road from the clinic and Bryn had the two printed prescriptions filled immediately. He swallowed the first round of pills in the taxi on the way home. By the time he had propped himself up in front of the television set he was feeling decidedly more comfortable.

The craggily handsome face of four-star General James Scott was on every news channel. The hero of Afghanistan had hit the ground running. He proclaimed himself flattered that people should think him vice presidential material. But he was *merely* a military man with no aptitude for Washington, no experience of politics. All he could offer was leadership and a proven record as a winner. In a long, exclusive interview, a Fox journalist asked him if he had ever had a role model, and he acknowledged that yes, there was one. That fine soldier and great American, General Alexander Haig.

Bryn was not the sole observer to find this remark intriguing. Haig had been Richard Nixon's White House Chief of Staff during the final Watergate-enfeebled months and had managed to accumulate powers more substantial than anyone in American history who was not actually President. Journalists on other, non-Fox, channels sought further elucidation. But General Scott had withdrawn 'for foreign and domestic policy briefings' to the Texas ranch owned by one of his supporters – a member of a group of concerned Americans calling themselves the Friends of the Right. Matters were taking an interesting turn.

He left the television on and went into the kitchen for a sandwich.

He had not forgotten Marcus's reference to the Friends of the Right, during their conversation on the mountain. The likelihood that his cousin knew significantly more about these events than the news channels inflamed his interest. He had no reason since their last meeting to be less wary of his cousin. But he remembered Marcus's invitation in the park… just a telephone call. There could be no harm in that.

He checked the breast pocket of his jacket for the card Marcus had dropped into it. It wasn't there, or in his other pockets. He had almost given it up for lost when he found it neatly tucked into one of the credit card pockets in his wallet. Someone had written in ballpoint across the top:

תאצל ול ונתנ

He did not need to understand Hebrew to register its significance. A decision of some kind: probably to release him. Whoever made the note must have rung Marcus on the cellphone number on the card. How long had his ordeal endured before Eyal and the cameraman discovered the connection? Did they stop because they feared to spoil a good relationship with MI6? Exactly at what point had Marcus become involved?

Another good reason to speak to him.

But when Bryn dialled the number himself, all he reached was an anonymous voice inviting him to call later or leave a short message. He tried several more times that day and the next until, in the end, he left Dieter's telephone number and a request for 'someone' to call back.

The pills had done an adequate job of relieving the muscle pain and after a couple more days he was moving around freely. The effect of the sedative, though, if indeed it had any separate effect at all, was more transient. His absorption in the news had diverted him for a while, but now – with too much time for his own thoughts – he was already beginning to fall back into his slough of despond.

Memories of the padded cell persisted like unhealed wounds. He had a troubling sense of loss, like a bereavement, as if he had left part of himself behind, a more innocent and self-confident part. And he could not shake off a presentiment of continuing vulnerability. There seemed to be no one in this morass to whom he could turn for trust or protection. He considered visiting the police again – but there was still that small matter of illegal entry, and a general shortage of witnessed credibility.

Then one afternoon, the telephone rang.

It was Dieter's house phone. No one had ever rung in on it before, not since he'd moved in. If it was Marcus returning his call, he was not even sure now that he wanted to pick it up. He let it ring till it died.

A few minutes later it rang again. This time he did lift the receiver.

'Bryn?'

It was the last person he'd expected.

'How are you?'

'I'm fine,' he said.

'Are you sure?'

There was a note of concern, that he had only once and fleetingly detected before. A similar remembered hesitancy.

'I have had some trouble,' he confessed.

'Tell me about it, Bryn. Everything.'

He found it exceptionally difficult to come to the point. The first attempt at his story was a brief throw-away outline, as if he did not expect her to be interested or to believe him. She pressed for more and it was the evident sympathy in her voice that unmanned him. Hard as he tried to censor out any self-pitying detail, some of the pain began to spill over the barricades.

Mostly she listened in silence. Twice, when he paused, she repeated his name as if to encourage him to keep going. Even his bare-boned version was much longer than he'd intended. By the end, though, he was relieved to have at last got it out. But he wished it had not been Agnete who had to hear the sorry tale.

'I'm fine now,' he said. 'Been to the doctor. Nothing to worry about.'

'Where are you, Bryn?'

'Ealing.'

There was another silence.

'Where in Ealing?'

He told her.

'Stay there. I'm coming over. About an hour.'

Chapter 19

One hour gave him little enough time to shower, clean up the rooms, make himself more presentable. In the event Agnete was late and he was impatient for her arrival. He was watching through a bedroom window when a taxi arrived and she clambered out, packages cascading around her.

She was upon him before he could step through the door; only the framework kept him upright. He'd not experienced so enveloping an embrace since childhood. It was as if she meant to squeeze every last remaining breath – and ache – from his body. But when he tried to return the favour, she detached herself and kissed him lightly on the lips.

'I've brought you a meal,' she said. 'I don't suppose you've eaten properly in days.'

She gathered up the bags and strode through to the kitchen as if she'd known the house all her life.

While she pulled out pans and plates, bowls and cutlery, he busied himself opening and emptying the packages. There was a bottle of Billecart-Salmon Rosé ('put it in the refrigerator – *now*'), a cool bag of cold meats, salads and desserts, and an oven-ready meal from some upmarket delicatessen.

'Do you know how the cooker works?'

'Of course.'

'Can I trust you to heat the moussaka?'

He watched her squinting short-sightedly at the packaging. The mystery of her enigmatic, spell-binding gaze was solved. Not witchcraft after all.

'Forty minutes at 180.'

'I can do that.'

He persuaded her, with some difficulty, to leave the rest of a not very complex operation to him. She cast around until she found a key to the French windows, and went out onto the garden terrace.

When he brought out the champagne and two glasses, he found her sitting at Dieter's picnic table with her hands folded demurely in her lap and her eyes closed. He thought about pilfering a kiss. He still did not know quite where he stood.

He laid the tray on the table and started to open the wine. By the time he had finished pouring it out, he was conscious that Agnete was watching him.

She picked up a glass and held it towards him.

'*En skål på venskab og måske… mere end det.*'

He had no idea what she meant.

She smiled. Not a wide-lipped English smile at all – but the same small private smile he'd seen not more than a couple of times previously. Ice blue eyes and cool command. But the thought that she might be seeing him in soft focus, too proud for lenses, made everything now seem more possible. He brought his glass up to hers and leant over and kissed her.

'Whatever you said, I wish it too.'

'*Mere end det?*'

'That's not fair.'

'Look it up on Google. Tomorrow.'

She laughed and produced an iPhone, box-fresh still in its translucent plastic cover.

'I want a picture of us,' she said. 'Before the bubbles die.'

The sun was already descending into the taller trees at the bottom of the garden. He set up the phone so the pair of them could pose together – artistically – with the light glinting on the glasses in their hands. Dieter would have approved. Agnete circled the terrace taking snaps of the house and of Bryn, while he laid out the feast she had brought with her.

It was a voyage of discovery.

If he had ever thought she would be the conventional echo of her boss, the evening quickly disabused him. Agnete was something more frightening and entrancing: an independent woman. The first shock was her politics. How she fitted into MI6, he could not imagine.

'I blog a lot,' she said cheerily. Between mouthfuls. 'Kochadoodledo.'

'I'm sorry.'

'Kochadoodledo.com. You're really ignorant, Bryn.'

He was happy to be so.

'It's a US-based blog dedicated to challenging anti-democratic arguments. It started off as a counter to the Koch Brothers, the boys behind the Tea Party. You must know *them*. Anyway, we've moved on from that. There are hundreds – radical blogs and websites. The problem is keeping them clean from trolls and rightist hackers. People have got to control their own destiny.'

'Ah yes,' said Bryn. 'I know that argument.'

She frowned sternly.

'Are you trying to patronise me?'

'*Au contraire.*'

'It's a new world, Bryn. Pay attention. Twitter and Facebook were the start. We have the levers of power if we can learn to use them properly.'

'I can't imagine Marcus would go along with this.'

She smiled back at him contentedly.

'Fuck Marcus.'

As they sat, drank, talked and ate, he found his own convictions – such as they were – under increasing pressure. He'd read Marx, Engels and Lenin as an undergraduate and later – in the line of duty – Luxemburg, Gramsci and Althusser. But he had never managed to get far beyond a detached academic interest in radical politics. This was not good enough for Agnete.

'I know you're on our side,' she said. 'You're just too frightened of leaving the middle of the road.'

'It's an intellectual thing. Objectivity. Balance.'

'Bollocks. It's a middle-aged thing.'

She must have recognised that this was below the belt. She at once leant over and kissed him on the cheek; and changed the subject. Very slightly.

She began to talk about Udell Strange. It was her first acknowledgment of the evening that she and Bryn had a pre-history. She was much more informed about Strange than he was. She talked about his campaigns for political and legislative change and the clandestine funding arrangements that supported them. About how much of the darker, reactionary side of the web – what Bryn had taken, with all its faults, to be the natural downside of grassroots democracy – was, in fact, paid for and promoted by Strange and a small circle of his allies. Bryn wondered how deeply embedded she was in her political activism and what dangers she risked. He did not believe that the myrmidons of Marcus's shadowy trade could be ignorant of this side of her life.

'The older a man gets,' she said, 'and the more power he accumulates, the less interest he has in other people and other people's opinions.'

'Power corrupts.'

'Tends to corrupt. You've read Spinoza?'

Steady on.

'The greatest of the great Jewish philosophers.'

'Of course.'

'"God loves no one and hates no one, too full of power to let anything exist other than himself". Well, it's the same with Strange. Only, immortality for him means imposing his world on future generations *after* he has gone.'

It was the kind of academic dirty talk he loved. It was intoxicating; and he realised how badly he had missed it over the past year. The Danish ice maiden had vanished. He could see fire now in her cheeks and – as the last embers of the setting sun faded behind her – flames in the glowing corona of her hair.

They got up from the table and went through the house to the sitting room.

'Put some music on,' she commanded.

There was a sound system in the corner, and a rack of CDs. Dieter's collection – pretty well all opera – was unlikely to be what she had in mind but he found a recording of Puccini's *Tosca* near the top of the pile and put on a disc of the Third Act. He hoped the tunes would be good enough for her not to object.

She did not even comment. She had kicked off her shoes and was waiting in the centre of the room. When he went to embrace her, her unzipped dress slipped away from his hands onto the carpet. He backed away like a man caught with a shattered vase.

She placed a hand on the top button of his shirt.

'Am I going to do everything tonight?' she said.

They made love where the garments lay. Uncomplicatedly and unhurriedly. As if they had known each other all their lives. The world dwindled away. Clocks, traffic, music – all the surrounding sound – faded to nothing. Time suspended itself. Only the moment existed.

When it was all over, and he had returned to earth, he become aware of the opera on the CD player and of the half-completed tenor's aria.

> *E lucevan le stelle*
> *e olezzava la terra*

Appropriate words, appropriate melancholy.

He took her back to his room and she fell asleep in his arms, while he lay awake exploring his thoughts. Why – when he should have been purely happy – did he feel so uncertain? Spinoza, famously, would have put it down to a universal animal *tristesse*. He suspected a different cause. If he was sad it was because of unfinished business: something the sex had merely – and for its duration – postponed.

> *Entrava ella, fragrante,*
> *mi caddea fra le braccia.*
> *Oh! dolci baci, o languide carezze,*
> *mentr'io fremente le belle forme discogliea dai veli!*

So many questions he should have asked her.

He looked down at Agnete, perfectly at peace in his arms, sprawled across his chest with a hand against his cheek and gossamer strands of hair floating on the eddies of her breath. He marvelled at the capacity of women to sleep so soundly, at such a time. *Oxytocin.* The uniquely female hormone released at the moment of climax – creating a calm spiritual contentment and sense of trust and security. It did seem unfair.

He ran his fingers lightly down her spine. Wishing he could tap into whatever she was having.

'That's nice,' she said.

The fingers jumped away.

'Don't stop.'

He started to speak but she placed a hand fleetingly on his lips and rolled away on her back. They lay side by side, like alabaster statues on a tomb, until he thought she must have drifted back to sleep; and raised himself to look at her.

The sapphire eyes were wide open and fixed on the ceiling.

'It'll spoil everything if you ask me.'

'I won't ask you then.'

She turned her head and stared at him.

'I came here because I wanted to say I was sorry.'

'Why should you need to?'

'And to make it up to you.'

In the next room, the music – with a mechanical click – came to an end. Bryn eased off the bed and went through to switch the sound system off.

When he came back, her mood had darkened.

'I'm so sorry, Bryn. I am so bad at this. I want you to know you won't be involved again. The wretched *stof* is on its way to Europe.'

'The *stof*?'

'The isotope thing. They're smuggling it in.'

'The cocaine route.'

'How do you – '

'Marcus told me.'

'You're really not supposed to know about the cocaine route.'

'Well I do. I expect Marcus is hoping to intercept it. Would that be Ireland? Or Iceland perhaps?'

She turned away from him and pulled a coverlet up over her shoulders.

'Is that why you are here in London, Agnete – waiting for his instructions?'

'Please don't ask me any more questions, Bryn.'

It was a long night.

He considered moving to another room, where he might be less troubled by her proximity. When he did doze off alongside her, it was for no more than an hour or so. She stayed in the same foetal position, deep in a silent slumber. He could feel the satin smoothness of her skin. She had a natural, unperfumed smell now – that made him think of open country and cornfields. He could bear it no longer.

He pulled a spare blanket from a drawer and carried it through to the sitting room. The floor was littered with the crumpled evidence of their love-making. He picked up Agnete's dress and hung it across a chair. Her tote-bag was open beside it: it was one of those carryalls likely to be popular with pickpockets, loose and bulky with only a flap to protect their contents. Two or three papers had fallen half out of the bag and he began to push them back in. One was an envelope. Scrawled on the outside in a familiar, confident, broad-nibbed hand were the words *Darling* and *Agnete*.

He stood for some time with the envelope between his fingers. It had clearly been opened and read and he could feel the folded letter inside. In the next room all was silence. It was one of those moments upon which life hinges. Minutes passed. He made the decision to pull the document out.

It needed only a glance.

Marcus was – with palpable warmth – thanking her for the weeks they'd spent together – their wonderful summer – how he'd been rejuvenated, counting the days to the next time. Bryn refolded it and returned it to the envelope, leaving the rest of the letter – for a second time – unread.

He was surprised that Marcus – in his position – could be so careless with an affair. Agnete evidently meant a great deal to him. He remembered Fiona's bitter comment about 'state secrets with long legs.' Perhaps sexual indiscretion in these enlightened times no longer rang official alarm bells. He was still a bastard though.

Amongst the other papers was a train ticket – for the next evening's 21:15 sleeper from Euston to Inverness – and a couple of other letters. Bryn didn't look any further. He already felt ashamed of his intrusion: and he'd got his just deserts.

He found it very difficult to settle down on the couch.

The revelation – or, to be honest, confirmation – that Marcus had a prior claim had left him again bemused. He must have mistaken the signals she had given him through the course of the evening. He had not thought there was a serious gap in years, but now it seemed a gulf. Was this 'modern' woman, unreservedly playing both ends against the middle? Or was it a Scandinavian thing? He reflected on the propensity of Danes to treat divorce and remarriage as the social norm; with family holidays of step-children, ex-husbands, ex-wives, ex-lovers, all contentedly vacationing together. Maybe his main deficiency was in being British.

But what was it she said?

'I came here because I wanted to say I was sorry.'

'Why should you need to?'

'And to make it up to you.'

Quite simple really. Last night must have been his pay-off.

He went back to the bedroom and watched her sleeping. The coverlet had fallen to her waist – or she had unconsciously pushed it away in the heat of the summer night. The moonlight made her more like an alabaster statue than ever. Venus de Milo with arms. He wished she had a less dangerous profession. He doubted her other SIS contacts would be as reliably harmless as him. Did Marcus worry about this at all? Probably not.

He returned to their bed and – worn out, perhaps, by too much thinking – slept till morning.

Agnete was already sitting up against the pillows.

'Did you set the clocks?'

It took him a moment to realise she was referring to Dieter's Pacific Standard Time bedside alarms.

'They were like that when I moved in. I've never bothered to reset them.'

'Have you noticed anything else peculiar?'

'No, no. This is Dieter's house, Agnete. It's all peculiar.'

Later they made love again. The focus and simplicity of the previous evening was absent. There was a more conspicuous passion, as though they were both trying to make up for something that was absent. At the end, she held him in silence, enfolded in her arms, until he fell asleep again.

When he awoke, she had already showered and dressed. He could hear her moving quietly through the other rooms of the house. By the time he had thrown on a dressing gown and emerged from the bedroom, she was in the hallway. He was just in time to see the front door closing behind her.

Chapter 20

Hardly any trace had been left behind. Even the remnants of their meal had been tidied out of sight into bins and cupboards. Only her natural fragrance – the barest hint of it – still hung in the bedroom and the living room. In the garden, though, abandoned in the long grass like a difficult memory, he found the iPhone with which she had photographed them together.

He sat outside in the cool morning air, with a mug of coffee, and examined it. It seemed unimpaired by its night under the stars. He wiped off the dew and checked the last picture she had taken. Two glasses on the table, a hand – his own – putting a plateful of *prosciutto* beside them, her shadow unprofessionally in frame. He put the phone away in a jacket pocket. He would find her and return it to her.

He still had Marcus's card with its mobile number. He called it again, and again got no reply. He considered visiting Fiona, but concluded it would be a wasted journey. There was one other way of tracing Agnete. Marcus would not be grateful for it, but needs must...

For a Secret Service, the huge MI6 Headquarters on the Albert Embankment was remarkably anxious to draw attention to itself. From across the River Thames it made a startling if confusing show: a lego pyramid, a tower of babel, an ocean liner, a Babylonian ziggurat. If however, like Bryn, you approached from Vauxhall Underground station on the southern side, it was an altogether more modest affair. With its squared off ranks of blank windows, it was much more like the anonymous office block one might reasonably have expected.

A trickle of men and women who looked exactly like office workers were passing through an open gate, some – not all – showing an identity card to the uniformed security officer standing beside it. Bryn fell in with them.

The officer stepped forward with a raised hand.

'Yes, sir? Can I help you?'

Bryn gave him Marcus's name and handed him, for good measure, Marcus's card. The man spoke into a wireless telephone and motioned him to stand aside.

There was a very long wait. Twice, the security officer took calls on his phone. Twice, Bryn had to repeat his name and business ('I'm delivering a report. He'll be expecting to see me personally'). Finally, a second officer appeared and took him to a waiting room outside the wall of the main building – a kind of quarantined halfway house with a woman sitting inside behind a glass screen. Bryn smiled at her. She ignored him.

A well-used copy of the *Daily Mail* lay on a low table by Bryn's armchair and he flicked through it. Time passed. The woman behind the screen lifted a telephone and spoke inaudibly into it. Without any warning, a tall young man strode into the room and extended his hand.

'Professor Williams,' he said. 'Please come with me.'

He grasped Bryn lightly by the bicep, and ushered him out again into the sunlight and through to the reception area of the main building.

'I'm Marcus's cousin,' Bryn confided, as they negotiated an airlock-like security barrier.

'I know who you are, sir, thank you.'

A public schoolboy, perhaps fresh out of Oxford. A future Marcus. He wondered how much the Service had changed since those famous, fictionalised Cold War years.

The young man guided him through to the lift lobby, up several floors, through a set of keypad controlled double doors, and down a final, carpeted corridor. He stopped at the entrance to the last office.

'Do come in, Bryn,' called a voice.

Not Marcus's.

A man had stood up behind a desk at the far end of the room. Bryn did not recognise him at first. He appeared taller than when he'd last seen him and he was now wearing a sleek three-piece suit – in considerable contrast to the baggy well-used DJ affected on that previous occasion. His hair – collar-length before – had been trimmed back and his manner was less gently clerical and more briskly business-like.

'I was hoping you would call me,' said David Burton.

'Ziggurat Exports.'

'Indeed. Most people find it rather obvious. But if you had rung the number you'd have come straight through, without all this palaver.'

'I was hoping to talk to Marcus.'

'You can talk to me instead.'

Bryn waited for the explanation that was bound to follow; but Burton merely smiled. Something was amiss. Marcus had hinted on the mountainside at opposing factions within the intelligence service. *'If all this gets out, I'm stuffed.'* On whose side was Bryn's now not-so-fortuitous San Francisco acquaintance?

Burton walked round from behind his desk.

'I see you're wearing the same jacket as last time I saw you,' he said.

He leaned into Bryn and deftly plucked something from his lapel. He held it for a moment frowningly between his fingers: it was a pin with a small round head.

'Very unreliable,' he said. 'Czech manufacture.'

He tossed it disdainfully into an open drawer.

He sat down in one of two well-worn leather chesterfields and invited Bryn to do likewise. He laid a pen and a small notepad on the arm of his chair.

'When we last met in San Francisco,' he continued, 'I was merely keeping an eye on you. Killing two birds with one stone.'

'Marcus didn't tell me. Never mentioned you.'

'We are a discreet organisation.'

'Really.'

Bryn looked around at Burton's office. More austerely furnished than he suspected Marcus's might be. No sign of a drinks cabinet.

'So how can I help you?'

'I need to speak to Marcus.'

'Ah. There, I fear, we have a problem. Marcus is on leave and I am looking after his desk. But there's nothing you could tell him that you can't also tell me.'

'No secrets within the service.'

'Quite so. And what's been happening to you, old boy? Who have you been seeing? Who are you in contact with?'

'Surely you must know all that already, David.'

Burton made a brief note on his pad.

'I thought maybe you had some shipping news for us. No?'

'No.'

He made another note.

'So why did you come here, Bryn?'

'To talk with Marcus, David. Only Marcus.'

He was surprised at his own loyalty. The other's opacity was beginning to irritate him. He sensed the feeling was mutual.

'I think I should tell you something about your cousin,' said Burton, with the deliberate enunciation of one who expected to be paid close attention. He leaned across to his desk and pressed a button. The tall young man returned and took a seat to the side of the room.

'Your arrival here today,' he continued, 'suggests my colleague Marcus may not have been entirely honest with you. You should know that your cousin has not been employed by the Service for some little while now.'

He waited before moving on, but Bryn resisted any impulse to respond.

'Opportunities do arise in our profession to make something on the side – even minor secrets have a monetary value, you understand – and Marcus had rather an expensive lifestyle. He has been on gardening leave for six months now. During that time, regrettably, he has contrived to drop below our radar and for several weeks we've been trying to re-establish contact with him. All this against a background of some very worrying reports.

'We've known of course about you and Udell Strange. And about Marcus's own interest. The reason I was in San Francisco was because we hoped you might lead us to your cousin. Well, that and the heaven-sent opportunity to hear Nina Stemme as Brünnhilde. Unfortunately, Marcus has managed to avoid meeting you anywhere we could have intervened. So what we would like now is for you to help us to find him.'

Bryn felt his stomach turn. What Burton was saying sounded credible enough. But why, in this world of mirrors, should he trust this man rather than Marcus? At least one thing was now clear: the two of them were on quite different sides. With which of them, however, should he align himself?

'If I knew where my cousin was,' he said heavily, 'I wouldn't be here.'

'He may contact you,' said Burton. 'More likely you than us. Call me on this line if he does.'

He wrote a number on the pad, tore it off and passed it over.

'This one will find me wherever I am. You'll be performing a national service if you contact us the instant you hear from him. Now is there anything else you want to tell me?'

'No.'

'Are you quite sure?'

'Yes.'

'Just remember to keep in touch.'

He rose from his armchair with his hand extended and his gaze locked on Bryn's – as if he intended to leave a permanent imprint of his final few words. Bryn returned with the young man to street level. As he left the building a light flashed from the window of a passing car. It was probably nothing more threatening than a tourist memento of the Spy Palace.

He travelled the Underground back to Ealing Broadway. He now took it as axiomatic that his movements were being monitored. When a man in a suit followed him out of the station, he turned into a Tesco Express and made a great show of buying a pork chop, a small bag of potatoes and a bottle of cheap wine. There was no obvious sign of a tail during the twenty-minute walk home. But a small saloon was parked opposite the house, and a man in the driving seat was talking on a mobile telephone.

Everything seemed precisely as he had left it. He checked the telephone, the toilet, the kitchen and the bedroom. If there were any microphones, he suspected they'd have been there for some time. He found none – though he knew that was hardly conclusive. He remembered Agnete's quiet tour of the rooms early that morning and wondered whether she too had been searching for bugs; or had been removing them.

A trawl of the rest of the house was no more successful. He was reluctant to prise away skirting boards or pull out light fittings for fear of interfering with Dieter's lovingly realised décor. But when he peered behind a framed Burne-Jones print hanging on the sitting room wall, a dusty card tumbled to the floor. At first he ignored it. It was only later, when he picked it up to tidy away, that he noticed that a phone number had been scrawled on it. Marcus's mobile number. In Dieter's characteristically German handwriting.

It took him a few seconds at most to work it out. Bayreuth tickets that were not so serendipitous after all. The all-round convenience of Dieter's house to everyone concerned, state of the art bugged and ready prepared for him. An address ('*Where are you, Bryn?*') with which Agnete would already have been familiar. A web of deceit that he could barely begin to unravel. He was even more determined to find her.

There was still time to pack a bag and catch the 21:15 from Euston to Inverness. He was half-way through dialling National Rail for a ticket when the full absurdity of the situation overtook him. Not only were MI6 undoubtedly tapping the line – but also conceivably MI5, the Israelis, Marcus's people, even the BND. All of them united by the imaginative assumption that he might actually know something. He put the phone back in its cradle.

There was no point in using the front door. He decided to slip out through the French windows and try the service alley at the bottom of Dieter's garden. It ran about fifty yards to the end of the block. From there he was able to work his way circuitously back to the Broadway and load up at a cash point, using his Hathrill card. Marcus, interestingly, had not cleared the account. Doubtless he was monitoring to detect any withdrawal; but he had to assume that no one else would know about it.

He returned to the house by the same route. He packed a few things in a rucksack and borrowed a velvet slouch hat and an anorak from Dieter's wardrobe, as well as his birding binoculars. For the fun of it, he went into the front upstairs bathroom, put on a pyjama top and stood by the open window for a few minutes brushing his teeth, yawned ostentatiously, drew the curtain across and switched off the light.

This time, after leaving the alley, he went northwards down the narrow ways past the allotments and over the golf course, and across the main west road until he reached Perivale Station. He took the train out as far as the northern branch of the Central Line allowed, hired a car from a small private garage, and set off up the M40.

After the distances he'd become accustomed to in the American West, the drive to Scotland was a breeze. Aside from refuelling at a motorway service station – paying cash again – he did not need to pause until he was well past the border.

He pulled off the road north of Moffat for a doze. It was still a few hours before sunrise. The bright achromic beauty of the

215

moonlit landscape could merely hint at the oranges, yellows and reds already suffusing the Lowlands hills. Even so, it was not until a cloud drifted across the moon and the forest fell into shadow that Bryn was able to close his eyes and sleep.

By early morning he was on the A9. Edinburgh to John O'Groats, the longest road in Scotland. And for a historian, one of the most resonant highways of Europe. You could trace the narrative of Scotland through the great battlefields that lay beside it. Mons Graupius, where Agricola subdued the northern tribes; Bannockburn, where independence was won from the English; and Culloden, the death knell – until the present century – of Scottish nationhood.

He had arrived at Inverness. And he was too late.

The night train from Euston had been and gone. He parked up in the station yard and wandered around. There was not a person to be seen. He spotted a car rental across the road and went in. A red-cheeked middle-aged lady smiled at him from behind the counter.

'I know this is a very silly question,' he said. He could hear the Englishness echoing back at him.

'I dinnae mind silly questions.'

'I want to check if my wife managed to rent a car here earlier.'

He pulled out Agnete's iPhone.

'I've been trying to get her all morning on her mobile but either she's got it switched off or there's no signal.'

He showed the lady the photograph of them posing together with champagne glasses in their hands.

'Honeymoon photo,' he said bashfully.

'You wouldnae get her anyway,' said the lady. 'There's no signal where she'll be now.'

'Oh dear.'

'Did ye not know that?'

'No signal at all?'

'Depends how patient y'are of course.'

'How patient do I need to be?'

'Och, it'll be fine when she gets to Lochinver.'

'Lochinver?'
She looked at him curiously.
'D'you no ken where your wife's goin'?'

Chapter 21

For much of the journey it was an 'A' road in name alone, winding and slow, frequently single-track with 'passing places', bleakly surrounded by a harsh, unyielding country of rocks, marshes and tiny rushing streams. For an hour and more at a stretch, there was no sign of habitation and just occasionally of sheep or other livestock struggling to crop the bald terrain. Even the sky was devoid of birdlife. Savage, isolated crags of weathered granite loomed above the approaching horizon like pieces of Henry Moore. But though he started probably not more than an hour behind Agnete, drove as fast as he could and had few vehicles to pass, he never caught sight of her.

It was well into the afternoon before the road finally petered out and he reached Lochinver, a small grey town on the edge of the Atlantic Ocean.

The breeze coming in across the water was, unsurprisingly so far north, bracingly fresh. He put on Dieter's anorak and the velvet slouch hat, slung the birding binoculars around his neck and went for a stroll. There was one main street and hardly anyone about. No clues at all as to where Agnete might be. He switched on her iPhone in the vague off-chance she might try ringing it from a landline to trace its whereabouts. The lady in

Inverness had been right. At least there was a signal in Lochinver, if not a very strong one.

It took him barely an hour to explore the town to both ends, twice. He found a teashop and settled in the bay window with a pot of strong tea, a slice of banoffee pie and the previous day's *Guardian*, to watch for comings and goings. Pensioners chatted outside the greengrocer's; fishermen in chest waders came up from the harbour with boxes of fish and ice; cars dawdled through the town; time passed.

A young family was taking tea at the far end of the room. Father, mother, girl and boy a year or so apart. Without thinking, he picked up the iPhone to dial his own daughter's number and for a minute or more his finger hovered over the keys while he struggled to suppress the dawning conviction that – the instant she lifted her receiver – every intelligence agency in the country would be triangulating his position. He laid the phone down on the table and turned away to gaze morosely out of the window.

Someone had parked a dirty Ford MPV on a double yellow line on the other side of the road, outside the public library. He had glanced at it once or twice, wondering how long it would be before the Caithness and Sutherland police intervened, when it occurred to him that the MPV was the sole vehicle in Lochinver – apart from his own – without a Scottish 'SX' or 'SY' prefix on its number plate. Instead it bore an 'L', for London.

He did not have to watch for much longer before a slightly built man, in an anorak very like his own, emerged from the building carrying a small MacBook. It was Marcus – fresh from a session, he guessed, plugged into the library's broadband connection. He moved quickly to the MPV and was away while Bryn was paying his bill.

Slow-changing traffic lights at the junction east of town held the Ford up long enough for Bryn to catch up while they were still on the main highway. He held a position a couple of hundred yards to the rear as the other vehicle turned north up a small coastal road which shortly deteriorated to a tarmac track, snaking round the sides of sharp, rocky outcrops and through a tumbled domain of boulders and narrow valleys, sheep and hooded crows. The one passing place sign was pitted with gunshot.

Once or twice, the MPV slowed its pace as if suspicious of the following vehicle. When it veered sharply right up a rutted path too challenging for an ordinary saloon, Bryn accelerated on down the main track. But – as soon as he was out of sight – parked up within the lee of a drystone wall; and scuttled back.

Marcus's path ran over the crest of a rise and down towards the coast. Directly ahead was a tiny cove, squeezed between granite promontories. Twin ramp-like blocks rose out of the ocean at its entrance, their inward faces a perfect match as if, millennia before, a single monolith had split and drifted apart.

Tucked into the curve of the bay was a solitary house. It had been built in the modern, cosmopolitan style with floor to ceiling sliding windows on the seaward side, and looked out upon a landscaped terrace of benches and summer barbecues. On the landward side there was a gravelled stand for four-wheel drive vehicles, and a small parked car.

Bryn ducked behind a drystone wall and watched.

Rabbits chewed at the grass. A Wheatear pecked at some tiny dark-blue berries. Somewhere out near the shoreline, Oyster Catchers shrieked.

Marcus had driven his MPV onto the grass below the terrace and was standing on a wall, peering out to sea. He hopped down and entered the house through one of the sliding window doors. For a while Bryn lost sight of him – until he arrived in the kitchen, immediately below his hiding place. A second person emerged from an inner room to greet him. It was Agnete. For a moment they were framed against an open window: he kissing her briefly on the lips, she resting a hand lightly on the side of his face. Then she placed a finger on his mouth, as if sealing an important message.

He felt no better than a Peeping Tom. He slipped down from his eyrie, retraced his steps to the car and drove away along the curve of the ocean until he reached a headland north of the bay. There he found a small walled cemetery nestling in the lee of the high ground. He left the car and went in to find some solace in other thoughts.

Maclean, Macdonald, Mackay, Matheson, Macrae, MacAuley, MacLeod, Mackenzie. Sturdy headstones of granite enduringly inscribed. A roll call of the western clans. The names of families – the last two in particular – that had ruled this wild land since the earliest middle ages.

And little change since to the surrounding landscape. Too windswept and exposed for anything better than a scrawny kind of grass, full of salt and sand, nibbled at by little wiry sheep. One low wall snaking across it – millennia old – constructed not of conventionally horizontal dry stone but of sharp vertical rocks, like giant's teeth. Wild yellow irises. Bogs and fields of white flowers with blossoms like cotton tufts.

He wandered towards the sea and back down the shoreline. Another battlefront of tumbled boulders, bleached flotsam and tangled vegetation wrenched from the ocean. A landscape of violence. Who could not admire the resilience of the people who had made their home in such wilderness?

Where the coastline swerved up towards the cliff edge, he came across a pile of rocks more densely packed than the rest. They all seemed to have been roughly squared off, like gargantuan dice, and covered an area not much smaller than a football pitch. He walked round them until he found a narrow pathway leading towards the centre.

It was a *broch*: a two thousand year old circular tower built by the local Celts against rival tribes. Its original height could be guessed at by the quantity of stone jumbled around what remained of the central structure. Thirty feet perhaps. High enough to look across the ocean for a threatening enemy.

There was a small entrance in the low landward wall with a triangular stone lintel across the top. Modern six-foot man could just about enter, bent double. Inside, the ground floor was well preserved with a low stone-ceilinged corridor and a couple of rooms leading off it. The most macabre feature, though, was the killing room.

221

Two or three feet within the broch, where an interloper might wait for a moment while his eyes adjusted to the gloom, a hole had been let into the ceiling. And above that, a secret space embedded within the walls, wide enough for a small man – or a mature boy – to wait invisibly, knife in hand...

In the spirit of historical enquiry, Bryn crawled on down the corridor. The origins of the brochs remained shrouded in mystery, with historians and archaeologists arguing to this day about whether they were for military defence, or merely a safe winter lock-up for crops and livestock. The first room was too full of fallen rock to make a guess at its size or likely use. He crawled on to the second.

This room's flagged ceiling was high – higher than necessary for storage purposes – and the daylight through a collapsed hole at its apex illuminated the broken corpse of a large ram. All the flesh had been eaten away from the skull and legs. The fleece though was intact and gently vibrating, as an army of tiny creatures worked busily beneath it. A strange, sweet odour caught his nostrils and he withdrew the way he had come.

A barely altered iron age land. What else might he find? A broch was such a major investment, it would be surprising if there were not other fascinating remnants of its ancient community nearby. He continued on down the coastline, wishing he'd been more alert.

A few hundred yards further on, in a tight curve of the shore and near the water's edge, he came upon a diamond-shaped carpet of rounded stones. Too recent and tidy to have any historical significance. But intriguing nevertheless. He climbed down and explored around the carpet in widening circles, until he arrived at a clutter of wooden staves jammed between some rocks. He dragged out a couple.

There was a short flight of stone steps behind them, leading to a small padlocked wooden door. He tried the lock but it was too new and robust to shift, so he returned to the shore. It was interesting to speculate what lay beyond the door. There would once have been a natural cavity deep within the cliff where the rock-face had, over æons, fractured and crumbled. Dug out and cleared to make an iron age *souterrain* perhaps – a more practical and secret storehouse for the community's winter food than the broch, and a likely companion to it. He wondered who might be using it now.

The daylight was beginning to fade. He had forgotten how quickly dusk fell in the north. Time to get back to the car and maybe find somewhere to stay in Lochinver or Ullapool. As he reached the top of the cliff, he looked back across the sea and noticed for the first time an ocean-going yacht riding at anchor a quarter of a mile out. A small black rubber inflatable emerged from the seaward side and started heading his way.

He slid out of sight behind a rocky outcrop and focussed Dieter's birding binoculars on the men in the dinghy. They were short, square and tanned, and very familiar. He tilted the glasses up to the yacht. It had been given a fresh coat of paint since he had last seen it in the San Francisco East Bay. And it had a new name: *Stella Polaris*.

The dinghy beached in the middle of the cove and the men fanned out like a searching party. One of them came upon the stone carpet and whistled quietly to the others. The rest went back to the boat while the whistling man paced away from the diamond towards the cliff face, directly to the souterrain entrance. The staves were cleared to the side and several shiny upright black bags carried from the dinghy down the stone steps. The men stood for a while on the beach conferring together before finally clambering back into the dinghy and returning to the yacht.

Bryn waited. The yacht continued to sit at anchor, its sails down, its crew invisible below deck. Apart from the distant undulating *chur* of a nightjar somewhere on the moor behind him, everything – the land, the sea – had fallen into a death-like slumber.

He crept down to the shore. No attempt had been made to replace the staves, which lay in a pile beside the storehouse entrance. Though the padlock was hanging on the door, no one had bothered to click it back into place.

223

It took him a while to become accustomed to the darkness inside. The room was roughly cube-shaped with concreted-in stone walls, and wood planks for a ceiling. A number of black waterproof canoe bags stood together on the rock floor, sea-water wet. He undid a buckle on the first of them and pulled back the velcro seal: the bag was full of shiny foil-wrapped packages, about the size of small, fat, French baguettes. He fished one out and ran a thumbnail across the foil. Some coarse white powder spilled out. He became rapidly very nervous; and returned the package to its bag, sealed the whole thing up again, and started for the exit.

A blonde man was standing at the top of the steps with a small hold-all beside him. He did not seem at all surprised to see Bryn.

'*¿Es usted el inglés?*'

Bryn took a flyer on the one word he thought he could recognise.

'*Inglés. Si. Yo soy.* I am indeed the Englishman.'

And, on an inspiration:

'Have you got something for me? *¿Para mi?*'

The blonde man laughed and produced from the hold-all a parcel, gift-wrapped like a Christmas present.

'Careful,' he said, in English.

'I expect it'll be heavy,' said Bryn.

The man laughed again and Bryn grasped the packet to his chest. Markedly heavier than the last time, requiring both arms to support it.

The blonde man was already returning to a small outboard motorboat bobbing at the water's edge. Bryn gave a friendly wave as it gunned away towards the anchored yacht.

As soon as he felt it safe to do so, he made off as fast as he could – along the shoreline, under cover of the rocks, until he reached a path leading up to the broch. He found the lintelled entrance, and crept inside. Moonlight was now filtering through small gaps in the ceiling and he settled down to catch his breath and explore the new acquisition.

Inside the Christmas wrapping was a sturdy wooden box. Inside that was what at first sight looked like a solid cube of lead; but which, once out of the box, revealed itself as two separate halves. As he carefully lifted the upper one, a glass jar appeared. Thick, opaque, and a dark, possibly amber colour; with a heavy glass stopper partly shrouded in industrial strength duct tape. He did not explore further. He gift-wrapped it anew and half-crouched, half-crawled his way back to the exit.

Where the heavens descended upon him. As he passed under the lintel, he was crushed suddenly and violently to the ground. A choking ligature materialised around his throat. A body, with the silence of a ghost, had plummeted from the space above the entrance and lay so heavily across him that he could not move. On either side of his face fists were jerking at the ends of a leather belt. He could not speak, even gasp. The pain was excruciating. The only sound he heard – as unconsciousness overtook him – was a rasping high-pitched whisper close against his ear.

'See y'in hell, dawg!'

He awoke with a paroxysm of coughing and retching. Every intake of breath raked at the muscles and tendons of his throat. The belt had fallen to the stone floor. The murderous incubus lay across him, as still as a windless day. Very slowly, as the pain began to recede, he was able to wriggle himself free and climb shakily to his feet.

He could see a small tear in the middle of the man's shirt, six inches below the shoulder blades. Blood was spreading from it across the cotton. A San Francisco baseball cap had tumbled away across the grass and the dead man's face was tilted towards the moonlight, open-mouthed and glassy-eyed. A kitchen knife, bloody to the hilt, lay on the rocks beside him.

Twenty feet distant, propped up against the outer wall of the broch, was Agnete.

Her smock was heavy with blood. Blood glistened on her right forearm. Her breathing, as he approached her, was shallow, fast and uncontrolled. He crouched down to put an arm around her and she shrank against him with a shivering judder that almost tipped him to the ground. Her breathing gradually slowed and relaxed and she lay, eyes closed, against his shoulder.

They might have stayed like this for some time, but he was worried that Wilson might not have come alone. Others would surely follow to find out what was happening. His concern for Agnete meantime seemed to have a positively therapeutic effect. Her shock had absorbed his own and left him with a welcome clarity of purpose. He rolled up his anorak and eased it under her head and stood up.

The landscape was empty. No movement, no lights on the horizon, not even a yacht at anchor. He dragged Wilson's body into the broch, as far inside as his strength allowed, and covered it in stones; if they were lucky, it might not be discovered for weeks. He tied the knife to the leather belt to make a slingshot out of it, and tossed it from the edge of the granite cliffs into the darkest, furthest, deepest waters beyond.

By the time he had returned, Agnete was on her feet. Neither spoke. They walked together back to the walled cemetery and the parked car, and drove away south, towards England.

Chapter 22

The worst part of the journey was the beginning. In such a bleak, empty landscape, they could not risk giving themselves away by using the car's headlights. It would have been difficult enough driving quickly in the day-time. At night, even with a full moon, Bryn could barely make out the edges of the road. And only by pressing his face, like a small child, against the windscreen.

For a long time there were no other vehicles on the road. Until they came to the most hazardous stretch, where the route wound through tumbled boulders and precipitous bends. Agnete was aware of the oncoming car before Bryn. She threw a hand at the steering wheel and he swerved immediately into the single passing place. All he saw at first was an orange glow intermittently lighting up the distant hillside. Then the glow resolved into a Ford Galaxy travelling at a speed far greater than the road was ever intended to allow. As the headlights swept towards them, Agnete caught his head in both hands and drew him down to an embrace so sudden and desperate that the ravaged muscles of his neck screamed in protest.

'That was nice,' he rasped through the pain.

When he eventually raised his head back above the windowsill, the MPV had disappeared from the car's mirrors.

'Drive now, please' she said. 'Headlights on. As fast as you can. *Please*.'

She said nothing further for nearly two hours. But as they were nearing Inverness she began to glance back as though at any moment she expected pursuers to materialise behind them. He pulled into an all night filling station and she jumped out of the car and ran into the public rest rooms, with his rucksack clutched tightly to her smock. He had forgotten how much dried, hard blood there would be on her.

He filled up and paid and was ready to go when she reappeared. She looked even more like Annie Hall than that day in Stanford. She had dug his spare jeans and a sweat shirt out of the rucksack and tucked her hair away under the velvet slouch hat. A little of her confidence seemed to be returning. She had bought a road map at the petrol station and was studying it as they pulled away.

'I don't want you to go the normal route.'

'OK.'

The ligature had left his vocal cords so bruised he could barely speak.

'Go down Loch Ness to the coast. No one will expect that.'

'It will take forever.'

'Let them fly on down the A9. We have time.'

And so they worked their way past Fort William and down the west side of Loch Lomond, across the Clyde beyond Glasgow, through Ayrshire and Nithsdale, until they crossed the border at Gretna Green and found themselves approaching Carlisle around mid-morning. She instructed him to pull up outside a clothing store in the town where (disappointingly for Bryn) she proposed to buy herself some more conventional apparel…

'Have you ever seen a red squirrel?' she said, as she re-emerged.

'No.'

'Well we're going to see some now.'

She had made a real effort to return to normality. She was wearing a sleeveless cotton sundress of a simple whiteness that set off the honey-coloured glow of her skin. She wore no makeup

228

apart from a trace of eye-liner. She had managed also to rinse through her hair and a few damp strands of it clung to her cheeks and shoulders. There was still a febrile intensity; but she was making the best show she could of reclaiming her usual, business-like persona.

'The manageress was helpful. There's a farm a few miles further on which will suit us fine. Relatives of hers. She's already telephoned ahead.'

They turned off the main highway south of Carlisle and drove through several villages of square little houses and square stone-surrounded windows. The lanes became narrower and more winding and the trees crowded together in a progressively darker canopy. At the bottom of a hill, where floodwater from a recent storm was streaming across the tarmac, she directed him up a stony track towards a white building set alone against a ridge of elm trees, and almost invisible from below.

It was one of those medieval hall houses that have been standing on the same spot for a thousand years, serving at different times as a refuge for animals, a grain store, a family home, or all three functions at the same time. The small square windows of the region were outlined in black stone. Black and white stones alternated up the four sides of the building, glistening from the recent cloudburst. In front of the house, running sharply downhill towards the road, was a long, close-mown lawn, bordered with rhododendron bushes. A pair of mistle thrushes stood blot upright in the middle of the grass, monitoring the newcomers' arrival. A spotted flycatcher was making sharp little sorties from a telephone wire. Bryn could not imagine a more secret or private or welcome place.

The owner was an economically distressed gentleman, public school educated naturally, hoping to eke out a living from his small pig farm by entertaining – not too frequently – passing tourists. The Carlisle shop manageress was his cousin.

There was no special frontier between owner, wife and guests. Agnete and Bryn's bedroom lay on the same long corridor as theirs. Their shaggy, friendly dogs roamed freely, even in the bathrooms and dining room. The hospitable routine was explained: guests were expected to share a sherry or a glass of madeira in the sitting room before dinner, with coffee and (if they felt like it) a round or two of bridge afterwards. They would, however, have their own, separate, dining room.

Bryn badly needed to sleep. Agnete, who had been able to drift off on the long journey south from Inverness, left him to it. She needed some air, she said. He wondered vaguely why she also needed his rucksack for a walk in the woods, but he was too tired to care. His main concern was the Christmas-wrapped parcel, which he'd carefully stowed in an art deco tallboy in the corner of the room.

He did not wake till she returned to the room in the late afternoon. She was standing by the closed door, the rucksack dangling lightly from her hand, watching him. Her eyes were bright and hectic. He wondered how long she'd been there.

'How are you feeling?'

'Recovered, I think.'

She sat on the bed and ran her fingers over the bruises on his throat.

'Does it hurt?'

'A little.'

He lied. The skin was still tender and any neck movement a punishment. Sleep, though, seemed to have restored his voice.

'We need to talk.'

'Not yet.'

She kissed him on the lips, a slow, open kiss that left little doubt of her intentions. He raised his hands to restrain her but she placed them deliberately upon her breasts and slipped the cotton dress away from beneath them.

'Don't move.'

It was not wise and not the time. But she was in a strange, dangerous mood and he rapidly lost command. She brought her knees up on either side of his chest and settled in upon him; and rose and sank until he could bear it no longer and caught her up in his arms and turned her into the sheets for a final fierce homecoming.

Much later, after the pains briefly banished by ardour had seeped back, and he opened his eyes, he found her gazing unblinkingly at him as if contemplating something she could not quite comprehend.

'We need to talk,' he said again.

'Do we?'

'We do.'

Somewhere deep within the house, a school handbell was ringing. It was much later than he had thought.

When they descended twenty minutes later, showered and sleek, the owner and his wife – George and Caroline – had already made some headway with the decanters. Agnete was not accustomed to the strange, sweet, fortified wines of the British upper classes; but George, quite unfazed, produced a half-bottle of amber-coloured Aalborg akvavit and poured her a mighty slug. The portions continued to be of such generosity that Bryn began to wonder how their hosts could ever make a profit. But that, perhaps, was not altogether the point of the exercise.

They were hugely interested in both their guests; but especially Agnete. Bryn learned more about her, her family and background than all the conversations they'd ever had together. George and Caroline were delighted to discover that Agnete's father had been a senior Danish diplomat and that her mother was a Hambro – a titled Danish family with connections to British banking (George had been at school with one of its British sons). Such was their enthusiasm that Agnete was obliged to go upstairs to retrieve her passport – because 'I always keep a picture of my parents with it' – while Bryn made small talk about the state of further education in the western states of America.

'Here,' she said when she returned, unfolding an A4 sized photograph.

'*Min Far og Mor*. My Father and Mother. On this day Papa was wearing the Order of Dannebrog for services to the State. A special honour.'

The photograph was passed around and arrived finally with Bryn. A tall man wearing a brilliant white and silver star on his left breast and a slim, blonde woman in a stunning, figure-hugging gown.

All it required to complete the picture was their two British friends standing alongside in white tie and ball dress.

'So this is why you know Marcus,' he said quietly. 'I always wondered.'

'What do you mean, Bryn?'

He could see she was startled.

'Well it's just that I've seen the photo before – or a very similar one – on a side table in Marcus's house in Hampstead. Do your parents know about you and Marcus? Does Fiona? How silly of me... of course she does.'

No one was speaking. George had turned away to refill his sherry *copita* and Caroline was studying the garden lawn through the French windows.

'Yes they are all friends still. However, my parents are divorced now.'

She folded the picture back into the passport and left the room.

The three of them talked together – about pig farming mostly and the iniquities of the Min of Ag (as George called it) – until it was impossible to defer dinner further. Caroline ushered Bryn through to a small parlour where a table was laid for two.

'I hope she'll be down soon. Shall I ring the bell again?'

'I'm sure she'll be down.'

The house routine was that guests helped themselves from a side table where three courses had been set in line. A bottle of Argentinian Malbec had been opened and a silver pouring spigot inserted into the neck to prevent red wine stains on the fresh white linen table cloth.

George and Caroline retired to the kitchen to eat their own separate dinner. The arrangements left no necessity for them to wait on their guests – a bridge too far, Bryn suspected.

He had already finished an excellent cold bowl of *gazpacho*, with garnishes and ice-cubes, when Agnete returned. She had been crying.

He was confounded and full of remorse. Something jealous and suspicious had spiked through and taken him by surprise and he would have given anything at that moment to have been able to pull it back. By coming back downstairs again, she had also – rightly – taken the higher ground. He did not deserve her.

He brought her a bowl of the soup and filled her glass with the red wine. She ate in silence.

'I am sorry,' he said. 'And confused. But mostly very sorry. The last thing I wanted was to upset you.'

'Not your fault.'

There was a mini sound system in the corner of the room and he went over to see if he could make it work. A CD of quiet cocktail jazz was in the machine so he pressed a button and let it play.

'I haven't been honest with you, Bryn.'

'It doesn't matter.'

'You know I love you.'

It was more than he could deal with.

'I have to tell you.'

He waited for her to compose herself. There were many questions he needed to ask. He feared the answers.

'Where shall I start?'

'At the beginning?'

'Or the end?'

'Scotland?'

'Not Scotland, Bryn. Not yet.'

'The beginning then.'

She paused again as if preparing for an ordeal. She was still shaken by Lochinver and perhaps less resilient than he imagined.

'This is not necessary, sweetheart.'

But she persisted. She poured more wine into her glass, on an afterthought did the same for Bryn; and began.

'Your cousin is a great man. But he is not the person you think he is.'

'I know he is not working for MI6.'

'He hasn't been working for Six for a long time. Longer than they know.'

'What do you mean?'

'He has been in Udell Strange's pay since before I became his assistant.'

She gave him a moment or two for this to sink in.

'Marcus has been playing a tricky, dangerous game. He's on no one's side. He told me in Lochinver. His plan was always to steal the isotope himself. But not for altruistic reasons. For the money, Bryn.'

Some light was beginning to dawn.

'And I was the patsy?'

'Oh... I think so.'

'I had to do the dirty work so that Strange would not suspect *him*.'

'Not entirely.'

She was reluctant to continue.

They had moved to the second course of their meal before she felt ready to pick up the story a second time.

'You see, Bryn, the whole business in San Francisco was an elaborate double-cross. Strange knew all about you – Marcus had told him. He had persuaded Strange – or thought he had – that he needed a safer delivery arrangement than the old cocaine route. Something that the Feds and the Israelis could not penetrate. Something that did not involve criminals. Clean, and below everyone's radar; and with total deniability so far as Strange was concerned.

'He told Strange that he knew someone who had the right credentials. Someone idealistic – who could be persuaded to 'liberate' the isotope from the arms traders, courier it to London, and deliver it to Marcus in the belief that Marcus would destroy it. Someone unlikely to ask difficult questions. But resourceful enough to cope with emergencies. And controllable.'

She sighed.

'Which is where I came in. Strange of course didn't believe such a person existed or could be relied upon. So – against Marcus's advice that he never be seen with you – he insisted upon a discreet meeting where he could check you out for himself. That was Bayreuth. He concluded you fitted the bill perfectly. Or so Marcus and I thought. The second of the double-crosses was that Strange – without telling Marcus – decided to make your mission a completely fake dry-run.'

She did not need to tell him any more. Bryn could work it out for himself. Strange's teasing questions in Bayreuth about Marion, for instance, when he would have already known the whole story through Dan, his co-conspirator. Maybe Dan had also confirmed the crucial mix of ingenuousness and ingenuity that were apparently his qualifications for courier duties.

And the disappearance of his Harrods bag and the wiping of the iPhone. A belt and braces exercise no doubt to make sure he was 'clean' and could not be connected with Strange. It might have been Agnete herself – in the corner of the restaurant, talking into Strange's earpiece – who had warned him about the little photographer; and arranged for his removal.

She seemed to be near tears again. He guessed there was worse to come.

'So. The whole business of stealing the isotope and smuggling it out of the country was a charade. I was always meant to succeed.'

She nodded mutely.

He supposed it was quite clever in a way. His task had to be difficult but not so difficult that he would fail. It was obvious now, looking back, that all the turning points – the Boy Scout tests of his ingenuity – had been arranged by Marcus, all of them playing to a lifelong knowledge of *him*. Right down to the use of Ricky Gaunt's house. As like as not someone else's house altogether, with a few props added. How predictable he'd become in his middle age. Marcus must have been planning it for months. Years even.

Agnete read his thoughts.

'It was very hard for Marcus to get the balance between setting problems difficult enough for you not to suspect a con – and making sure you would succeed. He never under-estimated you.'

It was kind of her to say so.

'What was Marcus's plan if I failed? That must have been on the cards.'

'I would have had to go in and help you. But I didn't. You did very well.'

'Thank you.'

What a pantomime. The secret messages and clandestine meetings, the pursuing black Porsche in San Mateo, even the compliant officials at the airport. A secret service training exercise – except that no one had told the recruit.

No longer a training exercise now, however.

They left the meal unfinished and returned to their room.

Sometime around three, when Agnete was soundly asleep, he slipped out of bed, went over to the art deco wardrobe in the corner of the room and took out the parcel he had hidden there, carried it to the bathroom and closed the door behind him. Once again he removed the Christmas wrapping, and eased away the lead cladding to expose the amber jar within. The liquid isotope was viscous and slow-moving, as if it had a stubborn mind of its own. It was the genuine article beyond doubt. The certainty of it chilled him to the marrow.

After breakfast they took a walk together. They'd told George and Caroline they wanted to look for red squirrels and received directions so eager and detailed that they felt they had no choice but to follow them to the letter. Before very long they came across a twig-built drey high in the elm trees beyond the house. A squirrel sat on a branch watching them.

It was, quite contrary to what Bryn had expected (and what the books advised), bigger and fatter than the normal American grey squirrel. There were the familiar tufted storybook ears and round monkey face and vast eyes. Backlit by the morning sun, the broad fluffed-out tail had become a translucent chestnut-coloured feather, with a thread of bone running opaquely up its centre.

'We should talk about Scotland now.'

'And Ealing,' Bryn said.

'That too.'

'Are you sure?'

She took his hand.

'Scotland was your fault, Bryn. Marcus thought he could persuade you to be his courier again. When you wouldn't play, he needed me. I should never have been there.'

'Nor me neither. I saw your rail ticket.'

'I know. You're really not a good spy. You have to learn to put things back into people's bags exactly as you find them.'

A couple of smaller squirrels came down from the drey and ran across the ground to a feeding table set among the trees. A nuthatch hung on an elm trunk until Agnete's voice startled it and it flitted away into the wood.

'Marcus knew the Israelis had been following you. That trick of changing the clocks – it's their way of undermining you, like raiding your fridge or using your loo and not flushing – letting you know they're onto you. The Russians used to do it too.'

'It sounds very childish.'

'A lot of the game is very childish, Bryn.'

She came to a halt.

'Tell me more, Agnete.'

'For a while,' she continued, more slowly, 'they assumed – correctly – you were under Marcus's protection. But that changed when you refused to help him. The Israelis were desperate for information. Marcus knew you didn't have any, or at least none that bothered him. So he let them know there was no objection to them taking you in.'

'Which would be my punishment. What a bastard.'

'And I know he regretted it. Almost immediately. I heard him call them off.'

'Later.'

'Yes. Later.'

So she'd already known about the beating and water-boarding when she rang him that day. Those long silences as she'd listened to him, the total absence of surprise...

'Did you know Marcus was intending to hang me out to dry?'

'I didn't know what to do.'

'Why did you stay with him?'

'Oh Bryn. Please don't ask me that.'

She walked on down the path. He followed her until they reached the edge of the woods where a lane ran away down the hill past the pig farm. It was a sadly run-down relic of what it once had been. Rotting wood sheds, rusting machinery, a tyreless Morris Minor buried to its broken windows in rye grass and thistles. The stench of porkers fattening in their own waste.

She had turned to face him.

'Let me tell you the rest of the story.'

Let me tell you a story.

And where had he heard that before?

'Strange decided to use the cocaine boat. Marcus was to receive the package personally and deliver it to the Arab contact in London. But Marcus's plan was for you to intercept it before it even reached him. The Israelis would be accused of the theft, Marcus would have an unbreakable alibi, and another person would be blamed for losing the isotope.'

'Wilson, for example.'

She nodded.

'And no one would connect you – or him – with the theft. That was the plan anyway. Marcus would get the package back from you when it was safe, and do his deal. Probably with the Israelis. A serious quantity of money, a completely new identity, the Bahamas.'

'I can see why he was so cross.'

'That's why I had to help him. I may be the only person in the world he still trusts.'

They walked on from the pig farm and its sweet odours. An incinerator was standing in the middle of a field with a thin cord of black smoke winding up towards the sky.

'The cocaine ship arrived off the Scottish coast a day early. Marcus got a radio message that they'd been seen by a coastguard and needed to unload and move out at once. Wilson was on the boat looking after the package but he had to come ashore to make sure the coast was – literally – clear. Marcus made me hide in the kitchen so he wouldn't see me.

'The original arrangement was for Marcus to meet with Wilson and the captain of the yacht together and receive the package in a sort of formal handing-over. But the captain panicked and brought it ashore early. You were there and of course he thought you were Marcus. I heard Wilson take a call from him afterwards. He gave a very basic description – height, hair, the clothes you were wearing. It didn't mean anything to Wilson. I don't think it meant anything to Marcus either. But I knew it was you. I knew you must have followed me.

'Then Wilson rushed off. Obviously to find you and kill you. Marcus shot away to Lochinver to get a message to Strange and call in the cocaine transport. And I went after Wilson.'

'Thank God for that.'

She was shivering again, just as she had at the broch. He held her until she relaxed.

'I have never,' she whispered, 'never done anything like that in my life before.'

'And never will again.'

She looked away towards the smoking incinerator.

'You see that,' she said. 'There were flames ten feet high yesterday. Someone must have poured petrol into it.'

'Is that where you took the rucksack?'

She laughed.

'I'm afraid we'll have to buy some more clothes, Bryn.'

Over the next two days they became quite familiar with the Cumbrian hills and woods and red squirrels. Bryn learned about Danish customs – the lit candle for a guest, the role of coffee and cake, the songs at Christmas. Even a little about the cocaine trade – its reliance on well-rewarded local fishermen, the regular white van delivery runs to and from London.

They talked very little about Marcus. It was evident to Bryn that Agnete's feelings were still in conflict, and not for discussion. She was opposed to almost everything Marcus did or said, but unchangingly reluctant to condemn him. He wondered how deeply the relationship had run – and how difficult it would be for her to move on.

Their most serious discussions were about the isotope: what should be done with it. Agnete was adamant that Marcus's original argument, however counterfeit, remained the right and true one. The isotope had to be destroyed. Bryn would have been content to bury it in the woods. But he sensed that, for Agnete, its final destruction had now become a necessary expiation for the traumatic events on that Scottish cliffside.

Chapter 23

The idyll had to come to an end. It was the news from Carlisle that triggered the decision. Apparently, some young men – George's cousin wondered if they might be plainclothes police – had been asking questions about visiting strangers and tourists who had not booked ahead. Within two hours, Agnete and Bryn were on their way.

They had resolved their differences about the isotope. Bryn had persuaded her to speak to an old UCL colleague of his – now a retired emeritus professor of physics living in north-west London – who could advise on a safe means of disposal. The problem would have to be a 'hypothetical' of course. Agnete could present as a naïve research assistant.

There was a wobbly period also when Agnete had been inclined to surrender herself to the local police. But she accepted in the end that there would be little chance of destroying the isotope if she wound up in custody. Perhaps, when their task was accomplished, she might turn herself in. But Bryn argued that the police in any case – left to their own uninterrupted devices – were most likely to conclude that Wilson's death was a gangland killing. A cocaine smugglers' argument. There were no witnesses – apart from Marcus, and he would hardly wish to involve the police in his affairs. The only persisting difficulty was Agnete's restless conscience.

They travelled to London down minor roads, as far away as possible from monitoring cameras and highway patrols. It was not safe to return to Dieter's house or Agnete's London pad. Instead they found a small boutique establishment off the Tottenham Court Road which Bryn, in years past, had used to recommend to visiting academics with a taste for English history.

It was a listed eighteenth century building with small oak panelled rooms, period furnishings and dark varnished paintings of Georgian worthies on the walls. The floors were uneven and the bathroom fittings unreliable. The little hotel was as obscure and unlikely a hiding place as they might hope for.

There was business to be done. After a telephone call in the morning, and fifteen minutes on the Jubilee Line, they found themselves in a leafy suburban street north of Swiss Cottage. A few doors past Sigmund Freud's blue-plaqued house, behind a tsunami of shrubbery, was the mansion where the old emeritus professor lived alone. Their gift-wrapped package – a permanent companion now – was in the rucksack on Bryn's back.

Professor Kelp was pleased to see them. He was a little confused – even after the phone call – about who they were. But he received them cordially enough in a downstairs sitting room, between a grand piano and a rosewood dinner table, their surfaces both awash with piles of manuscript and newspapers. A garden of rampant blackberry bushes and nettles could be seen through the open windows. Earl Grey tea was served in china cups and saucers, from an antique silver tea-pot.

Bryn's 'hypothetical' did not bother him at all. Maybe he had already decided they were a couple of mature students with a difficult paper to write and in need of technical assistance. He was happy to oblige.

'Isotopes of the kind you describe have certain common characteristics,' he said. 'If exposed to the air there will first be a blinding blue flash of light, followed by an overwhelming wave of heat. Put bleakly, everyone in the vicinity will be irradiated and is likely to die within twenty-four hours. The Earl Grey's not too weak is it?'

Bryn wondered how the professor would have reacted if he'd known a jar of the terrifying substance was resting at that moment upon his threadbare Persian carpet. With undeterred enthusiasm, he suspected.

'This is what we call a criticality accident. The blue colour is due to the emission of ionised atoms, or the excited molecules of air falling back to unexcited states, producing an abundance of light. I'm sure you know that's also the reason why ordinary electric sparks in the air, including lightning, appear... well of course... electric blue. Sugar either of you? No I'm sure you don't.'

Agnete was gazing out through the open French doors. A fat tabby cat wandered in and started drinking milk from a saucer under the piano.

Professor Kelp was now in full spate.

'Everyone in the vicinity would receive a dose of up to thirty Grays.'

'Thirty what?'

He looked at Agnete sharply.

'Oh dear. Well for your benefit, young lady – not I dare say for your colleague's – that is the modern measurement of absorbed radiation. A dose of thirty Grays would produce immediate nausea and vomiting, seizures, tremor and ataxia and lead rapidly to death.'

Bryn had been making a show of noting down the professor's comments on a sheet of paper.

'So,' he said, tapping the paper earnestly, 'I understand the dangers of such an isotope. But what if – hypothetically of course – I should want to destroy it, how would I do that?'

'I have described its destruction,' said the professor crossly.

'What if I wanted to destroy it safely?'

'Why should you want to do that?'

'Hypothetically.'

'Ridiculous. And terribly hazardous.'

Professor Kelp could see no point at all in Bryn's question. To him it was the very opposite of scientific enquiry. Students these days. He sighed.

'If you insist. There's one solution to that. Get a quantity of sand – several tons should do it – and find a way of burying your isotope deep inside so it can drain out very slowly. Not easy to achieve. The essential thing is that the isotope be deprived of any contact with oxygen and at the same time be allowed to disperse in an inert medium. After a few days it should be safe enough. I hope that satisfies you, young man.'

They thanked him for his tea and advice.

Such an early departure seemed to disappoint him. He had been expecting a longer tutorial.

'Where did you say you were studying?' he asked at the door.

'UCL.'

'Which Professor?'

But they were already, smiling and nodding, halfway down the street. He was still standing on the pavement peering after them when they turned the corner into the Finchley Road.

The interview had left them with as many questions as answers. Even if they found a sufficiently vast quantity of sand, they could see no way to release the contents of a sealed glass jar buried deep within it. No way, that is, that would avoid the outcome Professor Kelp had described with such vivid relish. This was *at least* a two-pipe problem.

At Bryn's suggestion, they took the old Metropolitan Line west from Finchley Road Station. He hoped they might kill a few birds with a single stone.

Within half an hour they were in the Chiltern Hills, West London's greatest secret. Beech woods and rolling farmland, tiny ancient villages, hidden pathways as old as the earliest inhabitants, the finest and most unspoiled pubs in England. Locally brewed beer to die for.

They disembarked at the little country station of Chorleywood and set off for the Chess Valley.

For a while they could think of nothing more practical than lowering the isotope, in its packaging, to the bottom of some disused coal shaft; and filling up with truckloads of sand. It was Agnete who suggested they might instead look for radioactive waste disposal sites – and she Googled them on her iPhone. There turned out to be more than a hundred in the United States alone – thousands of acres of them. But only one English repository, and that way up back near the Scottish border.

She was more struck by the possibilities offered by the *Schacht Asse* pit – a salt mine near the Germany-Denmark border used as a geological repository for nuclear waste, scheduled soon for closure – whose location was familiar to her. How difficult – or expensive – would it be to persuade an employee to lose the isotope in one of the mine's deepest chambers, before it was sealed up for ever?

The bleak topic of their debate contrasted starkly with its surroundings. The Chess Valley was the quintessence of the Chilterns. Tranquil, private, folded around a river as lucent as glass; with watermeadows of marigolds and ragged robin, working watercress beds, hedgerows of blackberries and sloes, and small unexpected herds of grazing alpacas.

They had been walking and arguing for two hours and the burden on Bryn's back was becoming vexatious. An opportunity, he thought, to introduce Agnete to Vales Bitter, Lion Pride – and Wadworths (nothing succeeds like) 6X.

The Red Lion, like so many of England's most cherished public houses, had been an old coaching inn. Mr Pickwick would have recognised and adored it. There was one busy bar surrounded by three or four small drinking rooms. No musak, fruit machines or television screens. Pretty barmaids. A grumpy landlord. All precisely as the genre required.

In a snug at the rear, Bryn found a rack of newspaper sticks including an untouched copy of the *Guardian*. It was nearly a week since his last news fix and he fell upon it like manna.

A spectacular photograph of a dust cloud dominated the front page. American news as usual. The Governor of California had declared a state of emergency after serious earth tremors in the north. Tourists had been banned from the National Parks and residents were being evacuated. The cloud was growing and spreading across the Cascade Mountains and interfering with international air traffic out of Seattle and San Francisco.

It had not prevented one particular traveller, however. In a by-lined comment column, the paper reported on the arrival in London – on unexplained business – of 'one of the most secretive men in American politics'. The visitor it was so intent on flushing out was none other than Udell Strange. And a little less secretive than before.

Bryn showed the article to Agnete. And promptly wished he hadn't. She had begun to enjoy the hushed, gentle atmosphere of the pub and the strange new ales. And for a brief moment – perhaps – pushed her cares aside. Now her good humour seemed abruptly to drain away.

'I think we should move on,' she said.

She remained monosyllabically reticent throughout the journey back to London, staring into space or flicking through an abandoned freesheet. Then she stood up and spent some time at a train window contemplating the passing countryside. Once, when she caught Bryn watching her, she managed a rueful smile. She returned to her seat and placed the freesheet wordlessly in his lap.

It was the *Evening Standard* – the West End Final Edition – with a breaking news story on the front page. So fresh a story that, apart from a photograph, there was precious little detail. A 'world-famous nuclear scientist' had been shot dead in a north London suburb. His name had been withheld by the police; a couple of men had been detained; that was it. Just a picture of the scene of the crime. The house that they'd visited that morning.

The train was two stops short of the Finchley Road.

'I'm going to check it out.'

'No, Bryn. It's too dangerous.'

'I promise to be careful.'

'Be very careful then. I'll see you at the hotel in an hour. No more.'

She carried on alone to central London with the rucksack. She insisted on taking it with her and he was glad to be relieved of it.

The pavement and road in front of Professor Kelp's house had been cordoned off with blue and white police tape. The kerbs had been cleared of parked vehicles – apart from a white van and two police cars – and a single policeman was on duty. A small crowd had gathered and Bryn joined it.

For a while nothing whatever happened. The street remained as sleepy and as suburban as before. The occasional car cruised past. Onlookers became bored and wandered away. New ones drifted over and attached themselves briefly to the group.

He was close to calling it a day when a man and a woman emerged from the house. They were carrying small suitcases and were both dressed in a baggy white garment covering the body from head to toe, along with tight-fitting white latex gloves, a white face mask and white paper overshoes.

'Scene of Crime Officers,' said the single policeman laconically, to no one in particular. 'Nothing very interesting there for you.'

The couple pulled off their masks and gloves and climbed into a white van and drove away.

A few minutes later, a young man drew up in a sports car.

'NUJ,' he said to the policeman, briskly flashing a small photo card. 'Do you mind if I go through?'

'Yes,' said the policeman. And for greater clarification: 'I *do* mind.'

'I'm a journalist,' said the other. 'I'm covering this story.'

'I dare say,' said the policeman.

The young man pondered his situation.

'So you won't let me through?'

'I'm not letting anyone through. Sir.'

A woman in the crowd asked the journalist if he knew anything about the murder. The young man – with an eye fixed on the unmovable policeman – explained that, according to *his* sources, the late professor had been visited that morning by two people claiming to be students. The professor's suspicions must

247

have been aroused because he rang the university and discovered they were no such thing. He had subsequently called the police saying he thought they were terrorists; and the police were actually on their way to interview him when he was killed.

A saloon drew up opposite the house. The journalist broke off his narrative and craned for a glimpse of the occupants. Bryn edged alongside him and tugged his sleeve.

'Have the police caught anyone?'

'Oh sure. There were two men in the house when the cops arrived. They're in custody now. I'm sorry – that's all I can tell you.'

A business-like man in a three-piece suit climbed from the car, ignoring the journalist's feeble attempt to intercept him, and strode on into the house. It was David Burton. Bryn shrank back into the crowd and slipped away.

As he walked back through Soho towards the hotel, a woman hissed at him from a doorway. He increased his pace and she hissed again. He heard footsteps running after him.

'*Bryn!!*'

He turned and saw Agnete. She stepped immediately into another doorway and disappeared. A hand emerged, as in a mime show, beckoning him urgently. He looked around him. The street, so far as he could tell, was full of the normal Soho mix of young people going about their various media businesses. No one and nothing to cause alarm. He strolled back to Agnete's hiding place.

She had his rucksack on her back and was carrying a hold-all.

'Bryn, we have to leave.'

'Why?'

She looked away towards the hotel and took a few sharp breaths.

'When I got back there was a policeman in reception. Asking for me.'

'Did he see you?'

'No. No one saw me. I beat a retreat and hid in the Costa Coffee shop on the other side of the road until he'd gone. Then I went back into the hotel and the receptionist told me he'd been asking about a car rental and she had a phone number for me to call him. You know what this means?'

'It may not mean much at all.'

She snorted with exasperation.

'Bryn. They've found the car I hired from Inverness. I left it at the house by the bay and they'll have got my name from the rental company. That means the body's been found. Otherwise they wouldn't be chasing me up.'

'That's possible of course.'

He was trying hard to be cool and forensic. He was shaken though by the revelation that checking into a London hotel could make their names and location so instantly available to the authorities. At least he had still been Hathrill.

'OK. It could mean a few things. For instance, somebody might have reported the car abandoned. The police would have had to find out what happened to you in case you'd… walked into the sea, or, you know – '

'That's rubbish, Bryn.'

'Or… let's say they *are* following up leads because they've found the body. It doesn't mean they believe any particular lead is significant.'

'Alright.'

She began to speak more calmly.

'I don't think we should chance it. I told the reception lady I would call the police from my room but I gathered all the rest of our stuff, and got out. I think we need to move away from here, now.'

He took the rucksack from her – she was pretty strong to carry that and the hold-all – and set off down the street. A squad car screamed past and they ducked behind some ornamental trees outside a pavement café. The vehicle swerved to a halt in front of the hotel, followed immediately by two other cars. Doors were flung open and policemen raced inside. As all heads on the street turned to gaze, the two fugitives escaped up a side alleyway, retrieved the car from its overnight park and took off towards Piccadilly and the west.

The sky had darkened and it was beginning to rain. Not a regular, steady, depressing London rain but a monsoon – the kind of downpour visited on the capital not more than two or three times a year and which – for its duration – almost invariably overwhelmed public services, transport, drains, even the city's communication systems.

Traffic was already backing up from a set of failed lights on the Brompton Road, and Bryn turned away into South Kensington. At double-speed, the windscreen wipers could barely cope; everything around them had slowed to a crawl. They turned off into a side street and pulled up by a small gastro-pub; and dashed in to shelter from the torrent until it eased.

Chapter 24

A television was on in the corner. Pictures of an ash cloud rising from a volcano. Talking heads speculating on what would happen next.

Agnete was not hungry. She toyed with a *salade niçoise* while he attempted to summarise the options available to them. There did not seem to be many. A bed-and-breakfast, perhaps, where they might expect a lower level of police vigilance – registering as 'Mr and Mrs Hathrill' as an additional precaution. *Unless* of course the Hathrill name had become compromised through association with hers. Even using the credit card to draw cash could give their location away. It felt to Bryn as if a noose was closing on them.

Agnete said very little. At one point she laid a hand on his lips – with a gesture he'd seen before – to prevent him talking further. When she had eaten enough, she took herself off to the ladies' and left Bryn alone in a dark corner of the underlit room, watching the images of the smoking volcano on the television and scouring his thoughts for some proposal that might commend itself to her.

They had deliberately chosen a table where they could keep an eye on the parked car. The rucksack with its package was stowed in the boot and he was as anxious about it as a mother with a wandering toddler. Rain was falling but not in quite such a deluge as before and pedestrians had begun again to scurry through it.

Two men with black umbrellas stopped outside the pub. One of them walked out into the road and paced around the car in a wide, deliberate circle. They chatted together, folded their umbrellas and came into the pub.

Between Bryn's corner table and the bar, a rowdy office party was in full flow – a young woman was leaving for a new job and celebrating with her soon-to-be ex-colleagues. As they stood to drink her health for the umpteenth time, he could see the two men beyond them, interrogating the barman. They were young, well-built, in smartly cut two-piece dark suits. He thought he could detect American accents. The barman waved towards Bryn's table and the men started to turn in his direction.

With a niggling sense of *déjà-vu*, he stole away down the short corridor to the ladies' and opened the door. Agnete was not alone. Two young women were adjusting their make-up at the mirror and a third was emerging from a cubicle with her skirt hoisted round her thighs. They all stared at him in puzzled bemusement.

'Do you come here often, darlin'?' said one. The others cackled.

But Agnete caught his mood at once and took him by the hand back into the corridor.

'Two men,' he said. It was all she needed to know.

The way out was through the main bar. The rowdy office party was still on its feet and Bryn slid in behind them. The two dark-suited men were standing now by the corner table, talking on their mobile phones. Agnete clung to him, and they ghosted through the crowds and through the darkest parts of the room, and out to the street.

They hauled the rucksack and hold-all from the car boot. And fled through the rain. Down Gloucester Road to the Underground station. And down again to the Piccadilly Line – and straight onto a waiting train bound for Heathrow, with no other plan than to put distance between themselves and their latest pursuers. They huddled in a corner surrounded by young people with massive backpacks, shouting in Spanish, German and East European. The carriage rapidly filled up until it was standing room only.

They had not intended to go to Heathrow. Any other destination would have done. But now that they were within forty minutes of the airport, Bryn set about trying to persuade Agnete to take a plane out *alone*. There was no possibility – this time – of smuggling the isotope through. But could she not get a flight to Copenhagen or Germany, somewhere safely beyond reach? He could take his chances by himself, find a way of disposing of the burden, meet up with her later.

She was as stubborn as a mule. He suspected that at base she did not yet trust him; and she may have been right. He could not pretend to her level of commitment. A major part of him was inclined simply to call up David Burton and sort it all out on the phone. The prospect of the isotope falling into the hands of Her Majesty's Government worried him less and less as time went by.

They were still whispering vehemently when they arrived at Terminal 5. They flowed through with the crowd to the main departures concourse, arguing constantly. For him all British Airways' options were open – providing he had Agnete's acquiescence – Copenhagen, Berlin, Chicago, New York...

Agnete had come up with a counter proposal. Bryn should be the one to fly to safety and she would stay on to deal with the package. The argument ran to and fro. He suggested the task was too dangerous for a woman; and she responded with unreserved contempt. When she asserted that a flight was in any case impossible for her because her name would now be on Heathrow's computers, he retorted that 'Hathrill' would be equally compromised. They had arrived at an impasse.

At the height of their dispute, the crowd broke into such a frenzied hubbub that neither for a while could hear the other speak. The departure screens seemed to be in meltdown. Whole sequences of flights began to disappear without explanation. Uniformed British Airways staff moved through the concourse, talking to small groups. One was briefing a line of passengers queuing nearby for JFK New York.

Apparently, the Americans were closing down most of their international airports. There had been a volcanic eruption in California, and a huge cloud of ash and debris thrown across the airways, moving inexorably eastwards. Flights to Europe were also being cancelled, though there was hope they might be restored when better information was available.

'Everything is under control,' said the official several times. 'There's nothing to do for the moment but wait.'

'I do not think so,' said Agnete and grabbed Bryn again by the hand. 'We need to move fast before everybody else does.'

As they left, armed policemen were coming on to the floor and moving through the throng. Some of them talking into radio telephones.

They followed the signs to the car hire counters. The Hathrill credit card and driving licence were both effective and they rented a small saloon. The paperwork was hardly finished before a mob of like-minded travellers filled up the hall behind them. There was no point in checking the car and they left immediately. As they filtered off the ramp into the rain and turned towards the M25, they passed four police cars racing through towards the airport, all lights blazing.

Traffic going south had ground to a standstill. So they drove as fast as they could towards the less congested north. Agnete was the first to speak.

'Do you have a plan?'

'Not yet.'

Bryn wondered how long it would be before their latest registration number had been distributed to the police. How close behind them their other pursuers might be. Whoever they were.

'I have a plan, Bryn.'

'I don't suppose it involves handing the package over to the proper authorities.'

He could see her on the back seat frowning in the mirror. They were like a well-married couple, locked in argument and tied indissolubly together. Rapidly going nowhere.

'Tell me your plan,' he said, more quietly. 'It has to be better than any of mine.'

'We go to Germany. By boat.'

'Right.'

'I'm serious.'

'I believe you.'

'I know what I'm talking about, Bryn. When I was a student, I had a little VW. I used to drive it to Tilbury and take the freight ship home. Cheaper than the ferries or Eurostar and more direct and they always had room for a car or two. Nobody uses them except lorry drivers so there won't be any police watching out for us. It's probably not even listed on their computers.'

'What about customs? Passport control?'

'They never did security checks. A quick look at your passport perhaps but they're not interested. No one will bother with our bags. Once we're on the continent there aren't any more border checks anyway. Not in the Common Market. It's the answer, Bryn.'

'How long ago were you a student in London?'

'It won't have changed, Bryn. It'll still be lorry drivers.'

Shortly after they crossed the M1 they turned south and east, dog-legging their way towards Essex and the Thames. The rain relaxed, and began to resolve into a clear sky. Bryn had conceded that they could at least find out if a ship was available; and make a decision then. Agnete's confident plan was for them to work their way from the port of arrival, across Germany, to the city of Dresden. She had a godmother in Dresden, living on the outskirts of the city. If they were lucky they could be with her by tomorrow afternoon. It was the perfect place to lie low until they were ready to drive to the Schacht Asse pit.

Bryn now had the flimsiest idea where he was. He had been following Agnete's directions through the alien streets of north-east London for some time when she instructed him to pull up. At first he assumed she needed to check their location. He waited while she went to knock at the door of a detached house. A woman – about Agnete's age, blonde and possibly Scandinavian also – came out and embraced her. The pair disappeared indoors and re-emerged five minutes later from a small garage on the side of the building. Agnete returned to the car. She was exceptionally pleased with herself.

'I've got my old VW,' she said. 'I'll drive it and you follow me.'

He watched her back the Volkswagen out of the garage. Old it certainly was. It had been in a few scrapes in its twenty years or so and bore its original Danish number plates. Agnete drove off at a brisk pace and he fell into position behind her.

Their route took them surprisingly quickly into open country and cropped cornfields, and past empty gas holders and new housing estates, until within thirty minutes they were running parallel with the main railway line from London towards the coast.

Like most West Londoners, he'd never been to this part of England in his life. He knew two historical facts about Tilbury. One was that it was here that Queen Elizabeth the First gave her famous speech to the army awaiting the Spanish Armada: 'I know I have the body but of a weak and feeble woman: but I have the heart and stomach of a king.' His other snippet was that the only prisoner-of-war in both World Wars ever to escape from England back to Germany did so by boarding a freight ship – from this very port. Both precedents seemed encouraging.

There were no other vehicles in sight. They were on a long, straight road with a fence of coarse grey concrete planks to one side and an overgrown rose bay willow herb wilderness on the other. Agnete's brake lights came on and she waved at him to stop. He waited while she climbed out and clambered up the low bank and peered across the wasteland. She glanced both ways up the road and returned.

'We need to get rid of your car.'

'Rid of a hire car?'

'It will give us away.'

'What about your VW?'

'We'll use that from here on. It's perfect. I gave it to Anne-Grete and so it's in her name. Nobody will pay any attention to it.'

He cruised along till he found a break in the banking where a couple of concrete blocks had been dumped – presumably to prevent what he now intended. There was more than enough room though to squeeze past and on into the jungle. He emptied the luggage from the boot and bounced the car down through tangles of brambles and ivy and half-grown ash trees until it came up behind an old Ford Cortina long-forgotten in its own private forest of weeds, rusting on its wheel hubs. He dragged some brushwood and ivy across his bonnet, and climbed back to the road. Neither the Cortina nor the hire car were visible.

A heavily built man with a bulldog was coming down the road.

'Caught short wuz ya, guv'nor?' he chortled as he passed.

The dog sniffed suspiciously at Bryn's legs until ('Hey! Chesney!') it turned aside and trotted after its master.

The terminal was a mile further on. Apart from a couple of container lorries trundling through, the road continued empty and silent. Not till they approached the terminal gate did they begin to hear a clangour of unloading cargo, and the feral growls of manoeuvring vehicles. The concrete fence had now given way to linked galvanised stakes with viciously splayed points to discourage trespassers. Beyond the stakes stood row upon row of neatly parked lorries, so closely packed together there was barely space for a driver to open a cabin door. On the other side of the road were piled-up red containers, labelled HANJIN or MOL or HAMBURG SÜD, as big as prefabricated bungalows.

A freighter was waiting by the dockside. It was smaller than a channel ferry and its immaculate white flank was uninterrupted by windows. There were two orange lifeboats, each slung so high in the superstructure that Bryn wondered how near to foundering the ship had to be before they could be successfully wound down and floated off. Small blue and yellow flags fluttered from lines on both sides of the wheelhouse. A thread of smoke was drifting up from one of the ship's twin blue funnels.

Bryn left the negotiations to Agnete and she disappeared into a single storey building by the dock, taking their passports with her. When she returned, ten minutes later, she was accompanied by a cheerful, shirt-sleeved man who looked briefly at the VW, nodded and handed over two sheets of paper. They exchanged a few words, laughed, and shook hands.

It would be a couple of hours before the ship was ready. But Agnete had done it all before. She drove out of the terminal and down a rough road along the bank of the Thames, to a large public house standing alone in waste ground. The nearest other building was a centuries' old fort at the river's edge. She parked the car round the back of the pub and led the way inside.

It was an interior from Hogarth's and Dickens's England, scarcely reconstructed. Flagstone floors, blackened wood panelled walls. An oval bar stood at the centre of a satellite universe of dark drinking rooms, tiny booths, window bays, cubicles, alcoves. Tired-looking middle-aged men sat quietly together, with a scattering of women of a similar age, blonde and mascara'd. On one of the walls hung a jarringly anachronistic digital juke box, 'provided by Essex Leisure', and playing songs from the current charts.

Bryn bought two pints of bitter for a price startlingly lower than he'd paid earlier in the day. He found Agnete already settled in a corner. The dark walls either side of her were inscribed with quotations from Samuel Pepys, in cream paint and flowing manuscript.

'He used to visit Tilbury on Navy business,' he explained. 'At the fort…'

But she was listening to the juke box. One song finished; another succeeded it.

'Rap music,' he observed. 'Can you tell the difference?'

'Yes,' she said. 'And it's hip-hop.'

'Is it music though? Or some kind of rhythmic declamation?'

She turned deliberately towards him.

'It's nothing to do with age, Agnete,' he said pre-emptively.

'Well, you enjoy your Bayreuth, Bryn. I like Big Sean, The Roots and Jay-Z. As you English people say: End Of.'

'Lots of people your age go to opera.'

'To hear people shouting.'

'In a musical way.'

'Not like rap then, Bryn.'

He was enjoying himself. He had almost forgotten how much he loved a good argument.

'In that case there are two different kinds of music.'

'Really, Bryn?'

She sighed.

'There's the kind that, in a free world, anyone can choose to call music. No criteria need apply. And there's the second kind. The kind that new generations will be listening to a hundred years down the line. All the rest – that first kind – is, as someone else said, noise. Because like all noise it dies away eventually and for ever. Never to be heard again. Music, by contrast – like most art – is built to last. To be passed down.'

He was rolling. Agnete's irritation only fired him up further. The ice blue eyes were fixed on him, basilisk-like. It was more than sufficient reward.

'So this is about dead people, Bryn. Not different generations. It's got to be your blessed Wagner to qualify as music.'

'Certainly not. I rate the Beatles, Elvis, Buddy Holly – '

'Dead people.'

'Do you genuinely think that rap band will be listened to in a hundred years' time?'

'It's hip hop. But that's because it's music we want to listen to *now*. Why does everything have to be appeal to old people?'

'That's not what I said.'

'Why can't music be made by young people, for young people?'

'It always was.'

'Oh right. Mozart, Schubert. So what about all their other contemporaries whose work's been forgotten? Didn't they write music? How different are they from my bands?'

'They could be rediscovered.'

Agnete's tight-drawn face softened.

'You've lost this argument, haven't you?'

'Afraid so.'

'Never mind. Why don't you choose the next track yourself? Is Oasis old enough for you... '

A uniformed policeman had come in and was chatting across the bar with the landlord. Agnete watched him for a while, and took Bryn's hand and led him out through the back rooms to the VW parked at the rear. She veered off down a track that rejoined the road a hundred yards further down. In his side mirror, Bryn could see a second policeman waiting patiently in the main car park.

The ship was stern end to the dock. A large white truck was easing up the ramp into the lorry deck. Agnete tucked in directly behind it, carefully positioning the VW close enough to the ro-ro doors to prevent any other vehicle boxing it in.

A good-looking young sailor in a fluorescent jacket invited them to follow him to the upper decks. Almost as an afterthought, he asked for their 'papers' and Agnete handed him the two sheets Bryn had seen earlier. He noticed her name was printed at the top of one, the Hathrill alter ego on the other.

They climbed up two flights of iron steps and down a short corridor with numbered doors on either side. The young man opened the first of them and pressed the key solicitously into Agnete's hand.

'I hope you find it satisfactory,' he said.

It was a tiny but Ikea-efficient cabin for two people. In a space not much more roomy than an under-the-stairs cupboard, there were two beds (one hanging from the wall), a ceiling-high wardrobe and shelves, a shower/toilet/washbasin/everything else cubicle, and an armchair.

The young man was waiting at the door.

'I need your passports. Please?'

Agnete handed them over without demur. He glanced at the photographs, and dropped the documents indifferently into his jacket pocket.

'Stop worrying,' she said, when the man had gone.

'You said they wouldn't be interested in them.'

'He's not. He's only interested in us.'

She grinned at him.

'He was checking to see if I was your daughter. And if he had a chance.'

There seemed to be no other civilians on the ship. Nor, apart from the mess man, was there any sighting yet of the crew. The sole indication of their presence was a set of locked doors forbidding entry to 'crew quarters'.

Civilian access to the open air was through a fire door at the end of the dormitory corridor. Beyond it was an uncovered main deck packed tight with containers, as close as tiles on a kitchen floor. The working part of the vessel – living quarters, wheelhouse – was bunched together at the stern.

They found a small deck behind one of the lifeboats and watched the ship ease away from the dockside, past the piled slag heaps of metallic waste, and ranks of unshipped containers, towards the Thames.

Agnete slipped a hand into his.

'Relax,' she whispered. 'It'll be fun.'

'They've got our bloody passports.'

'It's not a problem.'

'How can you be so confident?'

'Because I know,' she said. 'It's all managed by the Border Agency in Croydon and they're not interested in Tilbury. They're resourced to cover the essentials – airports, Dover, the Eurotunnel.'

'How can you know all this?'

'Marcus told me,' she murmured diffidently. 'Five – MI5 – complain about them all the time.'

The ship was gliding, slower than walking pace, down a long brick-lined passageway so tight and narrow that there was barely a yard to spare on either side of the vessel.

Something else was nagging at him. An irritating and – no doubt – inappropriate moral scruple.

'I'm worried about the car,' he said at last.

'The what?'

'The hire car?'

She looked at him incredulously.

'We should tell the hire company where it is.'

'And give the game away?'

'In a couple of weeks' time, maybe.'

261

She turned away, as if trying to puzzle him out.

Seagulls hung in the air above, banked and wheeled away. Smoke from the funnels drifted into the darkening sky. The lock gates closed and the vessel began almost imperceptibly to rise to the level of the river beyond.

'Alright,' she said, and leaned gently into him. 'As soon as it's not an issue. We'll tell them in two weeks... I guess I'd forgotten you're nothing like Marcus.'

Giant yellow container carriers were gliding around in the arc lights alongside the lock, emitting shrill pulsing cries like robots from an apocalyptic future, bearing their bungalow-sized burdens away in their great jaws to more distant parts of the dock.

The riverside gates opened. The boat began to pick up speed into the river.

'We're not going to Denmark after all,' said Agnete.

'Hamburg?'

'Not even that. Göteborg.'

'What... *Gothenburg?*'

'It'll be fine. This is the boat I used to take to our family holidays in south Norway. It'll be a straight drive from there to Germany.'

'How long does it take to get across the North Sea?'

'Oh, Bryn.'

'How long?'

'Relax. It will be thirty-six hours. Together.'

Chapter 25

Og hør du, Agnete, hvad jeg vil sige dig:
og vil du nu være Allerk æresten min?

O ja saammaend, det vil jeg saa,
naar du t'ar mig med til Havsens Bund

Listen, Agnete, now listen to me
Will you be my sweetheart down in the sea?

O yes indeed, in truth it will be
When you take me down to the depths of the sea.

Old Danish Ballad

The evening deepened, and they were alone on the river. For an hour, the only other boat to pass them by was a small pleasure yacht, with half a dozen revellers enjoying a noisy private party. Schools of tied-up dinghies bobbed on their wake; a three-masted old-style schooner stood rock-like at anchor.

Beyond the river's edge was unrelieved industrial desert. Slag heaps and warehouses to starboard; power station chimneys, piled-up car bodies on the port side. Wide, flat wasteland and marshes; Canvey Island; chimneys, derricks, storage tanks, whole dominions of rust and crumbling concrete.

And, as the Thames widened towards the North Sea, a taste of the future. Wind turbines sprouting from hidden sandbanks, waving their skinny white arms like so many *corps de ballet*. Marker buoys diminishing into the distance. More wind farms. Scores upon scores of stranded, anorexic ballerinas. Open water. A lightship. And finally as the night descended, an other-worldly nothingness. The stars, the flat horizon of the black, featureless sea, and no sound but the deep bass chugging of the ship's engines.

A chill rose from the water and drove them indoors. They made their way back down the dormitory corridor to the other public area within the ship: the drivers' lounge.

This was a small space divided into two even smaller spaces. The first contained three round Ikea tables – each with a neat little black *broderie anglaise* doily at its centre – and some hard pine chairs. A stainless steel shelf ran along the inboard wall, with condiments, cutlery, a coffee machine, microwave. A serve-yourself dinner was set out on electric warmers. Stuffed eggs with shrimps and salad. Mixed whitefish stew and boiled potatoes, steaming and as yet untouched.

The other half of the room, tactfully separated from the eating area by a wood lattice screen, was the television parlour. Audible but muted sounds of humping: bass-baritone grunting and rhythmically precise squeaks, squeals and gasps. Bryn peered through the partition. A pile of unclassified DVDs – *A Night in China*, *A Night in Paris*, *Adult Affairs* – had been scattered on a coffee table, and an overweight man in an *Elvis Lives* t-shirt was sprawled fast asleep across the viewing sofa. Bryn took a helping of seafood and salad through and squeezed in alongside him. He flicked the remote channel control to an English television news station. The fat man slept on.

The airports situation seemed to be improving. After the initial chaos, many flights south and east from the UK had been reinstated. The airways above North America were still closed, however, as the volcanic ash cloud continued its relentless drift towards the Midwest.

There was a small item of local London news. Two men held in custody after the north London murder earlier in the day had been released without charge. They were expected to be deported to an unnamed Middle Eastern state.

The fat man woke up. He was restored to his blue movie.

Agnete had by now disappeared.

An apple cake had magically materialised on the steel shelf and Bryn sat at one of the tables, consuming a large slice. A second lorry driver wandered in and frowned perplexedly at the stuffed eggs and fish stew. He spooned out some boiled potatoes, added a chocolate bar from the fridge, and took his plate back to his cabin. Minutes later, the fat man followed him down the corridor.

Apart from brief sightings at mealtimes, they did not encounter the drivers again throughout the trip. Bryn assumed they spent most of their time asleep, building up reserves, like camels or oxen, for the long haul to come. He could see why their profession tended so much to the massive and obese.

Through the wide dining room windows, the squared-off stern of the ship gently rose and fell on the North Sea swell, weaving with the crosswind as the autopilot constantly adjusted the wheel. There was the faintest smudge of orange on the western horizon.

He had started to worry again about Agnete.

There was a steely resolve about her which he admired; but which had begun to alarm him. He could not suppress a slowly growing feeling that both of them now were fast tracked to disaster.

It had been a long and tiring day.

He shivered. Not with cold; the ship's quarters were as warm as a Swedish duvet. But because he could not see any outcome other than incessant flight, like Bonnie and Clyde, until catastrophe overtook them. Some professional with a more ruthless agenda than their own would inevitably catch up at the finish. He might hope – as he always hoped – that he could compromise his way out, temporise, do whatever was necessary. But that was not Agnete's way. He feared for her.

He went back to the cabin. She was deeply asleep. The rucksack had been placed beside her bunk and a hand lay across it as if guarding the contents against enemies. A category from which – for the time present – he did not suppose she entirely excluded him. He watched her for a while, head on the pillow, hair strewn across her face, and did not have the will – or the courage – to wake her up.

He pulled a scarf from the hold-all and returned to the tiny lifeboat deck. Round a corner, by the white-painted safety railing, was a weatherbeaten wooden bench. Not secured to the floor but free-standing like an old piece of garden furniture. A simultaneously surreal and comforting image.

He sat down and gazed out at the ship's wake. The churned water had a phosphorescent whiteness that he associated with southern oceans rather than the North Sea. Miles away on the port side, like tiny cut-out models, were the lights of other ships, creeping along the horizon.

He could not share Agnete's confidence that they had shaken off their pursuers. The likeliest scenario – it seemed to him – was that their presence on the freighter was now well known to the British; but no attempt would be made to intercept them on the high seas. Why should they bother? For thirty-six hours Agnete and he were effectively sealed up and packaged. En route to a safe delivery, with the Swedish immigration service as postman. And perhaps – after all that had passed – it would be a blessed relief. The fugitive role was not for him. He had had enough of running. He did not much care for the odds.

But what if she was right?

If... in spite of everything... they succeeded in passing through Gothenburg without challenge, what next?

She would surely want – even more so than before – to play through to a conclusion. He was convinced now that her end game was unachievable. That they could not, realistically, destroy the monster. That compromise – *his* compromise – was the way forward.

She was still asleep when he got back to the cabin. He let down the narrow overhead bunk and crept up the steel ladder, his stockinged feet flinching against the edges of rungs intended for men of hardier stock. Or who retired to bed with their boots on.

Agnete may have guessed what was in his mind. She rose silently and went early to breakfast and, by the time Bryn came down, had disappeared again.

He found her eventually on their private deck, leaning over the handrail, and gazing down the cliff-side of the ship at the onrushing sea. The rucksack, which he had begun to loathe, was zipped up and buckled on the wooden bench beside her. As he arrived she turned and caught him, and kissed him hard on the lips.

'Let's go with the flow, Bryn,' she whispered. 'Seize the day.'

'And tomorrow?'

'Tomorrow we will be in Sweden, driving down the E20 to Malmö.'

She kissed him again at length. This was going to be so difficult.

'We have to talk,' he said at last.

She contorted her face into a moue, shrugged her shoulders, and turned away to the North Sea.

'We can't, Agnete – not just the two of us – keep this going. You know what I mean. It won't be long before the wrong people catch up with us and everything you have hoped for will be lost. The best we can do is surrender ourselves, as early as possible, to the least dangerous.'

'Who would be?'

'Who would be our people. I know a man in British Intelligence called Burton.'

'Oh, I know you know a man called Burton. I expect his telephone number is there in your jacket.'

She was a virtuoso at throwing a man off his stride: she'd obviously been through his pockets. It would have been that morning in Ealing after she discovered he had done the same with her tote-bag. How ever could he out-stubborn her?

'The British are the least bad alternative.'

'Alternative?'

'To being killed by an Arab or an Israeli. Or an American. I really don't want you killed, Agnete.'

'Wooo…'

'None of these people are playing games.'

She turned back from the rail. For a fleeting moment he thought he might have persuaded her.

'I know you mean well, Bryn. I've been thinking too. And you're right that we probably don't have much time. We should divert to the Schacht Asse pit on our way to Dresden. And get rid of it. If you won't come, I'll do it on my own.'

He made the best arguments he could. That there was little chance of getting access to Schacht Asse – because, like any other dangerous site, it would be patrolled and protected. As for finding someone who could be persuaded to dispose of the package down a secure waste shaft, he described the idea as half-baked and impractical. A mad *fantasy*. Perhaps he was a little intemperate.

'It's the only option,' she said briefly. 'And if I think of a better one, I'll be sure to tell you.'

The conversation was clearly over.

The mess man passed by on the crew walkway. A couple of other men could be seen through the glass of the captain's bridge. Bryn looked up to the stubby ship's mast above, with its array of communication antennae and busy scanner, circling endlessly.

Agnete was facing the east, towards the Swedish coast. The sea-breeze had tossed her hair across her eyes, and her hands were stuffed, stubbornly, deep into her coat pockets.

She remained preoccupied through the rest of the day. The veil was only drawn to the side at dinner, when she chatted to the drivers and the mess man as if she had not a care in the world. For the rest of the time, she kept to herself. Bryn found her once in the corner of the lounge with an unread book on her lap and her eyes fixed on some unfocussed distant point. He did not disturb her.

He retired to the cabin alone and, for some contrary reason, slept exceptionally well. When he awoke shortly before dawn there was no sign of her. Her bunk was in disarray so she had obviously used it for some part of the night; but her absence was a worry, and after a period of sleeplessness, he crawled out, dressed and went off to find her.

She was in her old spot on the bench by the guard rail. She looked up as he arrived and flashed him a wan smile. There were tears in her eyes, though whether from the wind or from some other cause he could not tell. She made a space for him to tuck in alongside her.

'That's Arendal,' she said.

The ship was driving along at a higher speed than before. Its wake was thicker and more turbulent and white. A coastline could now be identified to the north: a skein of fairy lights in the darkness, sometimes intermittent, sometimes in knotted clusters. Every fifteen seconds or so, within a gap in the sequence, a much brighter light switched on and off. Arendal, he supposed.

'We're sailing through the Skaggerak. We left the North Sea a while ago and soon we'll be turning towards Göteborg. I holidayed on that coast as a child – every year – right where that lighthouse is. Until *mor* and *far* split up. It was my favourite place in the world.'

She drew a deep breath. His arm was around her shoulders and she leaned into him.

A yacht had appeared on the dark waters and was driving along on the wind parallel to them.

'Do you sail?'

'No,' he said.

'We sailed off this coast every summer. You have to know what you are doing. These are such difficult waters – all kinds of strange eddies, huge waves swelling up out of nowhere, even a maelstrom occasionally. It's because of the fresh water flowing in from the Baltic. And because the sea here is so deep.'

Her tone lightened and she laughed.

'You like poems, don't you, Professor Bryn?'

She inclined her head to the side as if trying to retrieve a memory and then sat upright and clapped her hands together. She was as pleased as a child at a school concert.

'*Below the thunder of the upper deep;*
Far, far beneath in the abysmal sea,
His ancient, dreamless, uninvaded sleep...'

'*... the Kraken sleepeth,*' he finished for her. 'And how on earth would you, a Dane, know Alfred Lord Tennyson?'

'Ah well. My father taught it me. Because this is the spot. Half a mile below the deck we're standing on. The Kraken's still sleeping there, according to the Norse legends. And one day he will awaken... shouldn't you be terrified?'

She stayed at the same level of febrile intensity for the rest of the journey. Perhaps she was less confident about their reception in Gothenburg than she would have him believe. For himself, he was – to say the least – ambivalent. He welcomed Gothenburg and he dreaded it. If they were intercepted, the nightmare burden would be off their hands at last. But the great adventure that had bound Agnete to him for a such a sweet, brief period would be over.

They had entered an avenue of winking fluorescent marker buoys – green to starboard, red to port – and the ship had slowed to a crawl. He left Agnete to her thoughts and went down to the lounge.

The passports – the lorry drivers' and their own – were scattered on the coffee table in front of the television set. His European Health Insurance Card, so authentically provided by Marcus in the Hathrill name, was still wedged into the photograph page exactly as he had left it. He doubted if his passport had even been opened. It was nothing much to go on. But he knew, as he looked at it, that Agnete was right.

They were not intercepted at Gothenburg.

No police boarded the freight ship. No dark-suited men were waiting as Agnete drove the VW off the ship and wound her way through the marshalling yards to the port control office. He lowered the nearside window to present their papers but the officer showed no interest and waved them through without a glance. They passed below a friendly banner across the exit ('*Välkomna till Göteborg*') and turned right into a highway signposted to Stockholm. He found himself, in spite of himself, caught up in her euphoria.

It was almost twilight. They skirted the city and took the motorway south towards Malmö. There was hoarfrost in the fields and banks of mist on the road.

They drove for three hours, for the most part on a fast dual carriageway with little accompaniment apart from an occasional lorry and a motor-cyclist who, like them, kept scrupulously within the one hundred and ten kilometres per hour speed limit. He found a Swedish music station on the car radio, mostly Grieg, Sibelius and Mozart. Pure music – without breaks for promotions or advertisements. Agnete was content to indulge him.

The landscape on both sides was low and flat. The rising sun had cleared the mists away and the sky had became bright and cloudless. There were long stretches when the road cut through overcrowding forest, as in California. They were smaller and lower trees though, with none of that fatiguing alternation of dense shade and brilliant sunlight. Sweden was an altogether softer country, with cool and muted colours, almost monochrome; not, he guessed, a land made for painters.

Shortly before Malmö, Agnete turned off down a slip road and followed the signs to a small industrial estate. While she went to buy supplies in the supermarket, he filled up the tank. Later, on the way back to the motorway, she pulled into a lay-by and leant over and gave him another of her more lingering kisses.

It was not the subtlest of preambles.

'I have a confession, Bryn. I think you will be cross.'

'Now why should I be cross?'

Sibelius' doleful 'Swan of Tuonela' was playing on the car radio. Agnete reached out to turn it off; and thought better of it. She waited until the last cello had faded to silence.

'I have been speaking to Burton,' she said.

As usual, it took him a while to process the information.

'Just now?'

'On the boat. They let me use the ship's telephone.'

'How did you know his number?'

His hand went reflexively to his jacket pocket but she was already passing the folded piece of paper back to him.

'I know Burton too, Bryn. My father knew him. I rang him because you were right. I could not tell you at the time because you were so certain of yourself. And so rude.'

'So I was.'

'You said I was stubborn and a few other things I should not forgive you for. But when I was by myself and able to think about it, it was obvious – even to me – that Schachte Asse would never have worked. So I've agreed with Burton that we'll rendezvous with him and hand it to him personally. That's what you wanted, isn't it?'

He was not sure any more. And there was something about Agnete's story that did not quite make sense.

'Why didn't Burton meet us off the boat?'

'I've no idea. Maybe he didn't want the Swedes involved. Maybe he needed time to make arrangements, get clearance, whatever civil servants do. After I rang him, I had to wait by the phone for half an hour until he called back. That's when he told me to rendezvous with him in Dresden.'

'Dresden? He knew we were going to Dresden?'

'Apparently.'

'How could he know that?'

'I'm afraid I told Anna-Grete. They traced the Volkswagen back to her. Sorry.'

He felt suddenly too tired to enquire further.

'We have to meet him in the church at the centre of the city. The *Frauenkirche*. Tomorrow at noon. He'll take us both into protection. He's promised there will be no questions and no consequences.'

'You've done well.'

'You're not cross?'

'You did the right thing.'

'Maybe…'

They drove on past Malmö to the Øresund Bridge and across it to Denmark, which they reached by midday. When they stopped to pay the crossing toll, there was – as before – no interest at all in their passports or papers.

They skirted Copenhagen and turned down the E47 highway towards Germany. It was not the obvious route. But it was the one Agnete knew from a dozen holidays and it took them south, through flat Danish pasture, woods, cornfields and wind machines, to the fast ferry service from Rødbyhavn.

A ferry was waiting to leave and they were the last to drive on. It was early afternoon now and quite warm. They went on deck and drank coffee with the smokers and the family trippers. Gulls floated beside them in the air, as stationary as balloons on strings, their metallic little eyes scanning the tables for scraps of food.

When the ferry reached the other side of the Baltic and the VW rolled off into Germany, it was still all precisely as Agnete had predicted. No checks, no police. Nor any following car, overhead helicopter, or any other evidence of interest. They drove on through Lübeck and turned south on the main A14 highway towards Jesendorf where, for the first time, she conceded weakness and surrendered the wheel to Bryn. And quickly fell asleep.

He continued through Mecklenburg and into Brandenburg and did not realise she had awoken until they were on the outskirts of western Berlin. When she spoke, it was as if her thoughts had been mingling with his.

'Should we trust Burton?'

'No further than we can throw him.'

Charlottenburg passed by on the right, followed shortly by the Kurfürstendamm.

'Why do you think he chose the Frauenkirche?'

'Somewhere easy to identify? Where our rendezvous would not be noticed amongst all the crowds?'

For five miles or more, she said nothing further. She watched him as he drove as if searching for an answer to her concerns in the expression on his face.

'And why not till tomorrow noon?' she said at last.

'You think there's something wrong.'

'I don't know what to think.'

'So when exactly did you call him?'

'From the boat? Yesterday. After you and I had had our big argument.'

'That would make more than forty-eight hours before we're supposed to meet him in the Frauenkirche. It is an awful long time to wait.'

'He's set us up, Bryn.'

'But why? Why should he do that? What does that mean?'

'*Min elskede* – he could surely have got someone out to Göteborg to meet us, or else somewhere on the road south. All that this delay achieves is to make everything riskier. How secure would my call from the boat have been?'

'Why should Burton want to take risks?'

'That's my point, Bryn. Precisely.'

He knew what was in her mind. But he wanted to hear her say it first.

She spoke slowly as if working through her thoughts.

'He has made sure someone else finds out about our meeting in Dresden. That's why he needed the delay. That's why he chose such an easily identifiable location. He's not just after the isotope, he's after the enemy. We are the bait, Bryn.'

'I think you've been working too long with Marcus.'

'No. He's set us up like tethered goats so that Six – and, I would guess, the BND – can catch the real wolf.'

Bryn didn't argue. As far as he was concerned, Agnete was now in charge of the package. She had kept it close by her since Tilbury and their mission had always been her commitment rather than his. He would support her and do whatever he could to protect her. Though he wished she could be, well, a little less dramatic.

Of course he had his own reservations about putting their fate in such uncertain hands. But the more he thought about it, the more he suspected that the explanation would – as it generally did – turn out to be a matter of convenience rather than connivance.

Sometimes the obvious explanation was the right one. Ordinary inefficiency. Bad organisation. Cock-up rather than conspiracy. But he kept these thoughts to himself.

'So you don't think we should meet him in the Frauenkirche?'

She didn't answer.

'Maybe we shouldn't go to Dresden at all?'

They crossed the A13 spaghetti junction with the Berliner Ring, and headed directly south into Saxony.

'In case I'm wrong… ' she said, 'we'll go to the Frauenkirche *early* in the morning, before anyone would expect us. Perhaps find somewhere where we can watch for a while. If there's anything at all suspicious, we'll leave.'

'I'd be happy with that.'

Agnete's godmother lived in one of the outer suburbs of the city. She was away, however, visiting relations in Leipzig. They learnt this from a neighbour, the very hospitable Frau Buchholz, who sat them down with coffee and cake while she and Agnete – whose German was as fluent as her English – shared news of family and mutual friends. Then, after an hour or so, a key was produced from a Dresden pottery vase and Agnete and Bryn crossed the road to a simple white-faced villa surrounded by pine trees and potted plants, opened the door and went inside.

Chapter 26

Like many Britons, Bryn approached Dresden with a sense of guilt. Until shortly after ten o'clock on the night of the 13th of February 1945, this was the most beautiful baroque city in Europe. For two days it was pulverised by British and American bombers. Twenty-five thousand people were killed. The old city was destroyed.

The centre of Dresden – the Frauenkirche and the ancient *Neumarkt* Square surrounding it – was still standing in ruins when the Communist regime collapsed in 1990, as a stark reminder to its citizens of who their real enemies were. After that, money poured in, some of it from Britain and America, most of it from Germans, and a new, fully restored Frauenkirche was reconsecrated in 2005.

Bryn and Agnete arrived well over an hour before their appointed time. They sat outside one of the cafés on the edge of the Neumarkt, under a canvas umbrella, watching and waiting. Tourists, most of them young people, many like Agnete with a rucksack on their back, wandered the square. A team of English morris dancers finished their idiosyncratic set and began to solicit contributions from the audience. Then, not long before noon, a large group of American pensioners rose like starlings from the tables, and Bryn and Agnete drifted with them to the entrance to the church.

It was like entering a candy store. The whole interior of the Frauenkirche was painted in the pastel colours of icing sugar, relieved by decorative features in white, silver and gold. Daylight streamed in through the windows. It was a child's dream of Paradise.

At the centre of it all was the altar: multi-tiered and pillared like a wedding cake, encrusted with statues of Christ and the four evangelists in contorted attitudes of baroque passion. White and gold putti and angels. Silver organ pipes. Gleaming gold leaf on painted marble. Tumbling bunches of grapes draped across pillars and spilling from marble vases. Everything, of course, entirely authentic: the way it was before later generations invented good taste.

A baroque chamber orchestra had started to tune up in front of the chancel for a lunchtime concert. The young conductor, in black polo neck and jeans, was flicking through his score. A male assistant, with elastic-banded pony tail, began to adjust some microphones. Some older people who were not perhaps tourists were lighting prayer lights at a low table nearby. A sign set a tariff of a single Euro for each devotion (*Friede sei mit Euch!*). It seemed to Bryn he could as well have been in Catholic Bavaria as Lutheran Saxony. So much historic conflict and bloodshed, and so little difference in the end.

He was contentedly reflecting on all this when Agnete's fingers tightened urgently round his arm. He followed her eye line upwards, past the altar and the Russian doll tiers of ascending galleries; to the sun-drenched *trompe l'oeil* dome two hundred feet above them. There was a small balcony running around it and for a moment a man's head bobbed into sight over the safety rail and peered down. His hand was cupped in front of his mouth as if he was speaking into a tiny microphone.

Bryn's first instinct was to assume it was Burton, or one of his minions. But something had alarmed Agnete and she pulled him away towards the main entrance. He moved as quickly as the press of tourists permitted but soon lost her. As he stopped to search the crowd, a blunt and painful object bit into his ribs and a voice two inches from his ear rasped:

'Steh' still.'

He knew at once it was the silenced barrel of a pistol. The sensation of hard metal. The confident, icy authority of the man at his ear. The gun propelled him, as instantly and obediently as a trained dog, through the multitude to a small door on the north side of the church and up a flight of stone steps within the walls, goading him relentlessly upwards. He caught a single, momentary glimpse of a face, and recognised the epicene features of Udell Strange's chauffeur. The man was fit, and as unaffected by the climb as Bryn was rapidly exhausted.

At the top was a low door which opened into a small stone chamber. Beyond a balcony rail, practically within touching distance, was the final dome of the church. A small group of men was waiting. Among them Udell Strange; and Marcus.

Agnete arrived behind him, driven up the steps by the pony-tailed technician whom Bryn had seen adjusting the microphones. Her face was a picture of fury. She had the rucksack still on her back.

Bryn was now close enough to the guard rail to see the tourist crowds below, so distant and tiny they scarcely moved. There was no sign of police, security; or Burton. If this was what he had intended, he had got his timing terribly wrong. His cock-up. Someone else's conspiracy.

'Have you brought it with you?'

Strange was addressing Bryn.

He said nothing. Perhaps if Agnete and he could tease it out a bit longer, help might arrive. About twenty feet away, discreetly recessed within the rococo curves of the cornice, was a miniature camera, watching out – he supposed – for would-be suicides. He fervently hoped someone was on monitor duty and eased himself into its line of sight. The chauffeur moved with him and laid his silenced pistol delicately against his temple.

'Is it here in Dresden?'

'Is what here?'

Why indeed should he know what Strange was talking about?

The chauffeur smiled coldly and made a tiny clicking noise with his tongue. Or it might have been the trigger mechanism of the pistol itself. The whole tableau seemed suspended in front of him. The two dark-suited retainers on either side of the closed door; Strange standing opposite him, rimless glasses glinting, not a hair of his immaculate steel-grey helmet out of place; the pony-tailed man holding Agnete; Marcus separated from the group with head inclined diffidently to the side as though detached from the proceedings and a little embarrassed by it all.

The silencer barrel bit into Bryn's flesh.

'*Isotopen er i min taske.*'

It was Agnete.

'In her bag,' translated Marcus, barely audibly.

Agnete compliantly opened the rucksack and lifted out the Christmas-wrapped parcel. She folded her arms around it as if reluctant to yield up her burden. With a happy smirk of recognition, Marcus started to walk towards her to accept it.

A number of things happened very quickly.

The pony-tailed man reeled back with a gasp of pain. Agnete took two strides to the balcony edge. She leaned back against the rail with the package held above her head, glanced downwards – and hurled it into the abyss. It took an eternity to reach the marble chancel floor. Agnete and Bryn alone watched the package fall. The others – Marcus, Strange, the suited men – all pressed themselves back against the stone walls, in an open-mouthed paroxysm of terror.

But when the package burst open there was no awful explosion.

No engulfing surge of vivid blue flame.

No great roar of sound.

And no sign at all of lead cladding or wooden boxing. Only burst paper and shattered glass and a light, viscous, brown liquid nonchalantly spreading towards the startled and unharmed musicians, twenty feet away beyond the communion rail.

The chauffeur was the first to react. He raised his pistol to fire at Agnete; and Bryn threw himself upon him. Though he had more weight, the chauffeur was fitter and stronger and knew far better than he where to inflict pain. Every last ounce of Bryn's strength and energy was committed to forcing the gun towards the floor, but it was a battle he already knew he could not win.

And then the door flew open and men streamed into the room. Shots were fired. A body fell heavily to the floor. Agnete cried out in alarm.

The chauffeur relaxed his hold on Bryn and the pistol slid from his fingers. Hands helped Bryn to his feet. The young man with the pony-tail was now holding a heavy automatic to the chauffeur's head whilst his one-time colleagues were lined face to the walls, and uniformed policemen were slipping white plastic restraints over their meekly offered wrists.

Udell Strange looked a broken man. He was handcuffed to a plainclothes policeman but was hardly able to stand. His eyes were fixed on the closed-circuit camera in the cornice, as if he had noticed it for the first time.

On the floor of the chamber, blood seeping from a wound in his chest, lay Marcus. Agnete had fallen to her knees beside him and was cradling his head in her arms.

A medic came panting up the steps. Adrenalin was administered. Marcus's shirt was stripped off and his right breast and shoulder bandaged. When it was all done, Agnete and the doctor together helped him to his feet. He took a few tentative steps and nodded weakly. He looked pale and shocked, but tranquil. Agnete gently cupped his face and kissed him. A policeman eased a handcuff around his unaffected wrist, and led him away down the stairs – almost apologetically – with Agnete following closely behind.

There had been no attempt to clear the church of tourists. A steady stream continued to flow through the doors, broadly oblivious to the drama. Even those who must have heard shots and seen policemen racing through loitered with at most mild concern. A small earthquake, apparently. No one killed. In the chancel, musicians were helping to sweep up the remains of the Christmas package. An audience was assembling for the day's concert.

And at a stroke, Bryn had ceased to be a player in the story. He joined a small crowd outside the church watching the characters come and go. Strange's minions were hurried away into a van. Marcus was taken to an ambulance parked up against the steps where he had a last conversation with Agnete, and a final tender embrace.

Strange himself appeared. As he descended the steps into the sunshine, uniformed policemen flanking him on either side, a cameraman jumped out ('Look this way, Mr Strange!') and snapped off a stream of photographs. Others quickly materialised beside him, snapping and shouting.

The adventure was over. There were a couple of things Bryn needed to do. Find a hotel for the night – there were plenty enough of those around the Neumarkt. The other probably was to look up the British consul in Dresden and see if he could regularise his position, begin the slow trek back to normality. Oh, and a third thing: say a good-bye to Agnete – should he get the chance.

The policeman in charge of the rescue squad had come rigidly to attention at the top of the church steps. A tall man in civilian clothes, with a Bismarck moustache that set off a distant lost chord in Bryn's memory, emerged and shook his hand. And suddenly Agnete was there, and all three were smiling and chatting together.

He was about to turn away and leave them to it, when she spotted him on the edge of the crowd and waved at him vigorously. The tall man looked across and gave him a friendly salute. He had no choice now but wait. She skipped across the cobbles and caught his arm, as brisk and vital as if nothing had ever happened.

'Marcus will be fine,' she said breathlessly. 'But we have to stay in Dresden until the formalities are completed. They're bound to want to interview you. You know you're a real hero, don't you?'

She smiled delightedly and led him away by the hand. Peremptory as ever.

'Oh come on, don't look so confused. We're going to have a coffee. And some cake.'

They sat in the open air, with Martin Luther's bronze statue between them and the great church. The American photographer who had shouted at Strange was sitting at the next table, a Blackberry to his ear. Bryn could hear fragments of his conversation and guessed he was talking to his editor, probably in the States. He was hyperactively excited.

'Yeah, yeah, yeah,' he kept saying. 'I tell you it's The Man. Oh yeah, pure as the driven snow; but *not* any more, buddy. He's here in Dresden and up to his ears. This'll stuff him and General Jim Scott and the whole friggin' F-O-R good 'n proper. These morons have been playing footsie with terrorists for Chrissake.'

As he spoke, a black limousine came round the church from the other side of the square. Udell Strange was in the back between two plainclothes policemen. A posse of photographers flocked around the car, like chickens after grain, frenetically snapping. Strange made no attempt to cover his face but sat bolt upright, a simulacrum of misery. In the front passenger seat was the man with the Bismarck moustache, wearing the contented smile of one who had just pulled off the coup of his career.

Bryn looked up at the building. Blackened elements from the original shell – bones from the past – had been embedded in the new sandstone as a reminder of the reality belied by that sweet interior. It soared above him in a perfect compound of power, economy and emotion like a great German symphony, and if possible more moving.

The English morris dancers were packing their bells and costumes into suitcases. Shorn of their eccentric gear they looked surprisingly normal – office workers even. A young man amongst them nodded at Bryn; he was beginning to feel as if everybody knew him. Two BMWs drew up beneath the Luther monument and the morris dancers climbed in. A balding figure in a neat three-piece suit came down the steps of the church and signalled to them to move on. It was David Burton.

He stood a few moments more at the foot of the steps, looked up at the sun, unfolded a panama hat and placed it elegantly upon his head. He raised a hand in regal acknowledgement and Agnete waved back at him. He strolled away across the square and disappeared into the lobby of the Hilton Dresden Hotel.

'Do you think he's disappointed?' said Bryn.

'I think he's relieved. It would have been a poisoned chalice. All kinds of problems.'

'You dropped it in the Skaggerak, didn't you?'

She laughed.

'It was such a charade. In the end I couldn't let any of them have it. I did it that morning before you came up and found me. Box, lead cladding, flask and all. We were passing over the Norwegian Trench, the Kraken's Lair, the deepest water in Europe, and – well, sometimes – the simplest solution is the best. It's burrowing its way through the glacial sands towards Australia, never to be heard of again. I kept the wrapping paper.'

'And the bottle? The one in the Frauenkirche?'

'You remember we stopped for petrol. There was a *systembolaget* – a sort of Swedish state off-licence – and I bought it while you were filling up. I looked for a similar shape to the flask. Such a waste. Five year old rum, lovely amber colour. I told Burton I disposed of the smithium somewhere between England and Sweden. That's six or seven hundred miles of North Sea to trawl. I don't think he'll bother.'

'Why didn't you tell me?'

'Because you're so unbearable when you're right. And because… '

A snatch of Lady Gaga erupted from her rucksack. It took them a time to realise that it was Agnete's iPhone, forgotten since Scotland. She delved into the bag and hooked it out. The caller on the display screen was Marcus.

While she was talking to him, her free hand descended on one of Bryn's and held it tightly. It was an odd sensation. The word *troilistic* crept disquietingly into his mind; no doubt there'd be a more normalising term in Danish. She seemed very happy. Marcus's injuries were superficial and he would not have to stay long in hospital. Bryn could hear his voice at the other end, energetic and cheerful and boastful.

She switched the phone off.

'He sends you his love and hopes you'll forgive him.'

'What's happening to him?'

'Oh he'll have to face the music. But he'll do a deal. Marcus always has a few cards up his sleeve. You know that.'

He did not respond. She looked at him curiously.

It was the moment.

'You love him, I suppose,' he said.

'Of course.'

She took her hand away. A breeze had picked up in the Neumarkt, tossing the tourist litter across the cobbles. A street cleaner with a motorised refuse buggy started to hoover up the drifts caught at the base of Martin Luther's statue.

'You have nothing to fear from Marcus.'

'Oh really.'

'You are an idiot.'

He could hear music in the distance. The little baroque orchestra in the Frauenkirche starting its concert at last. Playing the flute Badinerie from one of Bach's suites, with unusual energy.

'Do you not realise he's my father?'

Another person would have seen this coming from a mile away. Weeks ago. But not Bryn. To Bryn, it was a bolt from the blue.

'I thought your father – '

'*Min Far*? No. Unfortunately my darling Papa omitted to be present when I was conceived. I am the result of a brief and very happy fling that my mother had with your cousin. Thirty years ago when he was at the British Consulate in Geneva and

Papa was Danish ambassador in Bern. Papa always knew. People know how to look after secrets in the Diplomatic Service. And you are, Bryn, the first person for a very long time to share mine.'

It all took a while to digest.

'So we're cousins.'

'I think once removed.'

'Right.'

'Or possibly not.'

She sighed. Her hand had returned to his.

'I'm afraid Marcus isn't the only candidate, just the most willing. My mother is what you might call a free woman. She is on her fourth marriage now and my father on his third. They're still the best of friends, and good friends with all their previous partners. I don't suppose you find that easy to understand, but for me it's perfectly civilised and realistic.'

'Mamma mia.'

He couldn't help it.

She laughed.

'In any case, my mother and I are completely different. My limit is a single lover at a time. Are you happy now?'

'It's very complicated.'

'If you're English. Marcus was always an absent father. Years could pass without me seeing him. Not because my parents didn't want me to, but because that's the way he is. Someone who turns up unexpectedly. When it suits him. But in answer to your question: of course I love him, though obviously not as much as Papa, and in a different way. Who would not?'

Gradually, over successive cups of coffee and slices of *Erdbeerkuchen mit Sahne*, the story unrolled. How – early in the year, when she was at a loose end – Marcus had suddenly invited her to be his unpaid assistant. It had been an exciting ride. Being with Marcus was exciting. As a consequence, she'd been slow to suspect that something might be seriously wrong.

In the meantime, she had fallen in love with Bryn. She was not yet prepared to admit quite when this had happened, though he suspected he had passed an awful lot of time in unnecessary uncertainty.

She'd found herself painfully torn between him and her commitment to Marcus. The dilemma was still unresolved when she had come to him that evening in Ealing. It was all the more difficult because she did not know even whether she could trust him, whether indeed he might be working for another side. The folded paper with Burton's number for example. It was not until Scotland, when she realised he would be a dead man if she did not intervene, that she made her choice. Since then it had been the two of them.

They hung around in the square all day, eating, talking; embracing a lot. Late in the afternoon, a newspaper gusted across the square and wrapped itself round Bryn's leg. It was the outside double page of the morning's *Die Welt*. He picked it up: there was a photograph of an erupting volcano below the title banner, and a quantity of German text below. Agnete took it from him and translated.

Much had happened since they'd left London. Lassen Peak had – quite literally – blown its top. Like Mount St Helens thirty or forty years before, the summit had been entirely destroyed. The mountain had collapsed upon itself, sealing in for millennia the magna and everything that remained of its upper flanks. The earlier dust cloud was already dispersing over Alaska and Western Canada. On the east coast, the airways were beginning to return to normal.

On the inside front page, another picture caught their eye. Two men: a uniformed one in the foreground, waving; and beyond him in the shadows an older person, with rimless glasses and steel grey hair, turning away as if to avoid the photographer. It was easy enough to recognise General James Scott but Agnete had to help Bryn with the figure in the background.

'It's in the headline,' she said patiently. '*Die seltsame Königsmacher.*'

'Kingmaker I can work out,' he said. 'But what's the other word mean?'

A gust of wind ripped the loose page from his fingers and bore it off across the square. The street cleaner caught the cartwheeling paper on the end of his stick and dropped it into the maw of his machine.

'Here's my iPhone,' she said. 'Why don't you just look it up on Google?'